The Confluence

Gregory Josephs

Literary Wanderlust | Denver, Colorado

The Confluence is a work of fiction. Names, characters, places, and incidents are the products of the author's imagination and have been used fictitiously. Any resemblance to actual events, locales, or persons, living or dead, is entirely coincidental.

Published in the United States by Literary Wanderlust LLC, Denver, Colorado. www.LiteraryWanderlust.com

ISBN Print: 978-1-942856-50-4
ISBN eBook: 978-1-942856-61-0

Cover design: Pozu Mitsuma

Printed in the United States

Part One - Elliot

Chapter 1

August 13, 2019 - Tuesday

The ferocity of the first fat raindrops made it clear: Elliot had misjudged the storm. He flew around the curve in the path and into the too-wide exposure of the meadow, Lindsey hot on his heels, as a flash of light lit the sky. The thunder that followed punctuated the need to find shelter, fast. "Can you sprint?" he asked.

"For three miles?" she panted. "Forget about it. Let's get back to the woods."

"No," he pointed across the meadow. "Maybe we can wait this out at the old farmhouse."

"Isn't that place condemned?"

Elliot registered the concern in her voice, but couldn't spare the breath to address it. He glanced down at his ankles. Where moments before he'd been kicking up hot dust, splatters of warm mud reached upward, clinging to his calves with every stride. He lowered his head, pumped his arms, and pushed his legs harder.

The old farmhouse came into sharper focus—weathered clapboard siding that could no longer be called white, tall windows with cracked or missing panes, the wide porch with its decaying roof, the tired sign nailed across the front door with its red X against reflective white. It was two-hundred yards away, maybe less, when the sky opened and all was obscured behind a curtain of furious rain. They reached the low, young trees that had encroached on the field over the decades, and slowed. Behind him, Lindsey was laughing as they took the four rotten steps up to the porch two at a time.

She leaned—collapsed—against the wall of the house. "And you said we'd beat the rain."

He laughed as he folded his legs onto the floor of the porch. It was wet, and the wind sent sprays of rain into his face, but it didn't matter. He was already soaked. Judging by the quantity of water coming through the gaping holes in the roof, this could hardly be called shelter, but it was a million times better than the meadow.

"Yeah," he said. "It wasn't supposed to start for another hour. At least we got half our run in. Coach would be proud."

"Ha. I haven't thought about Coach since we graduated. He'd have yelled at us to keep going." She sat beside him and looked up. "I hope this thing doesn't come down on our heads."

"It's been here this long and hasn't fallen down, right? I wish we could go inside."

"That sounds like a terrible idea."

He shrugged, then stood. "Could be cool." To the

right of the front door, he peered in through the cloudy glass of a window. The room inside was dark, but he could see it had once been pretty. A living room. Water-stained floral paper peeled from warped plaster and an enormous brick fireplace devoured most of the exterior wall. He pushed the window frame and found it gave slightly. If he wanted to, he was sure he could force it.

Lindsey stood and shoved him. "Knock it off, Elliot. We're not going in there."

He wasn't sure he wanted to listen to her. There was a magnetism to this place, and he wondered how he'd never noticed before. The farm had been here, like this, his whole life—sold to the Town of Haverford as preservation land decades ago. He imagined it as it must have been—seven acres, family run, in continuous operation for over a century. Now it was just *this*—encroaching trees and receding meadow, pressed up against the banks of the Pentucket river, with this ruin of a farmhouse as the last holdout against nature's reclamation of the land.

Around them, the roaring, constant percussion of the downpour began to ebb. Then, as quickly as it had begun, the rain ceased altogether. The hot August sun broke through the thick clouds, and back in the meadow, they could hear the songs of the birds. The transformation was instantaneous, and as the sunlight kissed the lichen-eaten wood of the porch, steam began to rise into the air.

Lindsey put her hand on his shoulder. "Come on, Elliot. Time to go. We've got three miles left in soggy shoes. Let's get it over with."

He nodded but lingered a moment before following

her down through the young trees and back to the path. She started to run, and as he followed, he kept turning back for a last glimpse, then another—truly the last this time. He felt the place calling to him with the persuasive, comforting voice of an old friend he'd somehow forgotten. It pulled, and as his pulse quickened against the effort of his legs, he felt an inexplicable longing begin to bloom within him.

It was an old farmhouse—crumbling at that—but maybe also the most beautiful thing he'd ever seen.

He left Lindsey at her house and dragged his tired feet the remaining third of a mile back to his own. Though it was a Tuesday afternoon—and early at that—when he turned off Pentucket Road and into the short drive down to the New Colony Apartment Village, he saw both his mother's car and Tony's waiting outside their first-floor unit. The storm had lingered longer here, and the red brick of the tenements was dark with the remnants of the rain. The two-storied seventies architecture was plain and cheap—and dirty—but wet, it looked almost clean.

He sighed, wondering why his mother was home early, and whether she was going to lose this most recent job like she'd lost countless others. It was Tony's fault, he was sure. Tony, the flavor of the week who'd somehow managed to hang on. Tony, who'd moved in after two months and acted like he owned the place—owned Elliot and his mother too.

Still wet—it was too humid now for his clothes to have dried—he pulled his key from the little pouch in the front of his running shorts and opened the flimsy front door.

There they were—both on the sofa—his mother typing furiously at the little laptop Tony had bought her, and Tony with a cigarette hanging from his lips, leaning closely and watching over her shoulder. They stopped and looked at him as he closed the door.

"Why are you all wet?" His mother asked.

Elliot noticed the front blinds were closed. "There was a storm. Didn't you hear the thunder?"

"C'mon, Lari," Tony said as he tipped the ash from his cigarette into an empty juice glass on the beaten-up coffee table. "Let's finish this up."

Elliot bit down on his lip as he pulled off his soggy old running shoes. The place where the big toe of his right foot rubbed was wearing thin. He'd need a new pair soon if he was going to keep up his training. He was still a year away from transferring to a state school, and if he was going to walk onto the Cross-Country team as a junior, he couldn't afford to let his fitness lapse.

His mother smiled. "No, I guess I was so involved in this I didn't even notice. Tony and I are starting a business."

He fought the urge to roll his eyes. "Oh, what kind of business?"

"Baby hats. I'm going to knit them and sell them online. People go crazy for that kind of stuff. You should see these boards on Pinterest. We're just opening up the shop now, and we're going to make a mint."

"Have you actually knitted any?" Elliot asked.

"Well, not yet. But I'll start tonight. Once we're done with this part."

Tony laughed, and there was an edge of cruelty in the sound—like he didn't think she could do it, even as it was surely he who'd put the idea in her head. He dropped his cigarette into the juice glass and immediately reached for another from the pack on the coffee table.

Already fighting to keep from choking on the smoke in the room, Elliot cleared his throat. "I thought you were going to smoke outside from now on."

Tony narrowed his eyes, put the cigarette between his lips, and lit it. "Are you the one paying rent around here?" He puffed his chest and inhaled. "That's what I thought. Nothing to say. For a minute there I thought maybe the little fag boy had grown some balls."

"Mom—" Elliot began, hating the quiver in his voice—the way the lancing of Tony's tongue always left him babbling like a child. "Are you going to let him talk to me like that? Make him put it out. Make him apologize."

A shadow crossed his mother's face, and her eyebrows arched as she looked at Tony. "Oh, er—I don't know if you—"

"Shut up, Larissa," Tony said. "Are you going to baby him his whole life? If that little cocksucker doesn't like what I have to say, he can stand up to me like a man, and we'll settle it like men."

Elliot gaped at his mother, feeling hot blood burning in his cheeks. He continued to stare. Five seconds. Ten. "Unbelievable," he said, then stormed through, straight to the back of the apartment. He stepped into his room, slipped a pair of dry shoes over his wet socks, and grabbed his cell—a four-generations-old iPhone, with cracks on the screen that had been there as long as he'd owned it. Then he went out, through the kitchen and onto the patio.

There, his tired old mountain bike waited—the bike he'd gotten second hand when he was thirteen and was now far too small for his nearly twenty-year-old body. His fingers fumbled with the combination on the chain, but after a few tries, he got it undone and fished it out of the railing. He pushed the bike across the short strip of grass and onto the asphalt of the little street between his building and the next, climbed on and began to ride. He pedaled around his building and up the drive, back onto Pentucket Road.

Where to go? What to do?

Lindsey's? No.

He thought of the farmhouse, the field, the singing of the birds and the young trees. He pictured the once pretty room and thought he'd hide out there for a while. Calm down. Feel some peace. Though his legs were tired, he pressed the pedals and sped the bike south, away from town and Tony and his mother. With each revolution of the crank, he felt the distance growing and slowly started to relax.

The first mile fell away, then the next. To his left, past the other side of the road, the Pentucket churned—swollen from the afternoon storm. After months of running low—the whole dry summer—it rushed and gurgled and groaned like a neglected siren, lilting a warning to the breeze.

Finally, he turned the bike off the road and onto the muddy path that led through the preserve.

As he neared the old farmhouse, he slowed the bike and dismounted. The odd magnetism he'd felt earlier returned—stronger now than before—and he wondered how he'd spent his whole life barely noticing this place. How many times had he run this path, and never given the old farmhouse a thought? He ducked into the low trees, lifting the bike as he went, and felt his heart quicken. A sturdy sapling provided a safe place to lean the bike, so he left it and went on unencumbered.

Then it was there—looming in front of him—beautiful in all its decay. He fished his phone from his pocket, and with a swipe to the left from the lock screen, brought up the camera. He turned the phone sideways. Framed the shot. Bending down and tilting the phone further, he captured as much of the structure as possible. *Click*. He moved a little to the left and caught another angle. *Click*.

He started too quickly up the rotten steps of the porch and caught his foot on the second tread. As he fought to keep his balance, the phone fell from his hand and dropped neatly—perfectly—through a hole in the third tread, where the wood had long ago fallen away.

"Shit," he said, steadying himself. He kneeled on the second step and peered into the hole, hoping the phone had landed softly. There it was, blessedly face up, laying in a bed of detritus—decaying leaves, bits of wood, and a bleached potato chip bag that was probably as old as he was. He reached his arm downward, and as he closed his fingers over the phone, they grazed through the leaves and made contact with something else—something cold and hard. After pulling the phone out again, he wiped it on his shirt and flicked on the flashlight.

In the bright blue, artificial light, he was able to see. Where his phone had rested, something round and metal barely protruded from the matted leaves. He reached down, and, with a gentle wiggle, he loosened the thing and brought it up out of the hole.

As he regarded the tiny treasure—a coin of some kind—an electric shiver started in his fingers, rippled up his arm, through his chest and legs, and dissipated out through his toes. He rubbed the coin furiously between his thumb and forefinger, cleaning away the years of dirt and mud. Then he folded it in the fabric at the leg of his shorts and repeated the process. It still wasn't clean, but at least he could make out the face. Odd. Ancient, maybe—or perhaps just made to look that way. On the surface of the dark, heavy metal, there was a raised symbol that looked like a scythe.

Standing, he held the coin tightly and took the last two steps onto the porch. He leaned against the wall of the house and slid down until he was sitting, turning the coin over and over in his fingers as he descended.

It was probably a trinket—not old or important at all—but in his present frame of mind, it felt like something more. A lucky coin. A talisman. With eyelids pressed together, he closed his fist around the metal, and without knowing exactly what he was doing—or why—he started to wish.

He laughed quietly to himself. Why not? There was a lot to wish for. He wished his mother, who'd been slowly retreating from him for years, would realize Tony was worse than any of the others who came before and get rid of him for both their sakes. He wished she'd find someone worthy of her—of both of them—and experience the happiness she'd once known with his father. He wished for the next year to pass quickly, and for some scholarship money to come through—his ticket out of Haverford to a brighter future. And he wished for—clarity, he thought. Just a little clarity.

He opened his eyes and smiled. What could it hurt? While he was at it, maybe he ought to have wished for bigger things—a billion dollars, world peace.

Nah, best not to be greedy, right?

He stood, putting the coin in the little pocket inside the front of his shorts, and moved to the window beside the closed-off front door. He pressed the pane upward and it gave. One inch. Two. Then it was stuck. He pushed harder, feeling the strain in his forearms and shoulders, but the window wouldn't give. He could smell the stale, stagnant air of the pretty room beyond—wet wood and earthy mildew. There had to be another way in.

He skipped down the steps and surveyed his options. There were other windows around the side, he knew, without glass. But they were too high up. He moved off to the left, into the tall ferns and low brush, wondering if he could find something to stand on to gain entry. But then, from behind, a distinctly human sound—the aggressive clearing of a throat—froze his feet and lifted the fine hairs at the base of his neck.

Slowly, he turned away from the house and found himself staring into the angry face of a little girl. Beneath her nearly-black curls, the bluest eyes he'd ever seen pierced him straight through. Hands on her hips, she shook her head slowly. "What do you think you're doing?" she asked.

He sputtered. "I, uh—sorry, I—"

"Why are you standing in the middle of my nasturtiums?"

Chapter 2

Elliot looked down at his feet. Nasturtiums grew at the Haverford Community Farm, where he worked a couple of days a week—round, peppery leaves with orange and red flowers. The shareholders liked to harvest them for the weekly pick-your-own and add them to salads. But there were no nasturtiums here—only ferns, and wood poppy, some wild bluebells, and low shrubs he couldn't identify.

He looked at the girl again—really *looked* at her this time—and his eyes widened. She was short, with sun-kissed skin, somewhere between the ages of six and eight, he thought. Above her dirt-stained knees, she wore a denim dress in the style of overalls, with buckles at the shoulder straps. A white-and-red checkered hem framed the bottom, and the pockets sewn onto each hip. The dress was unlike anything he'd ever seen in a store, and he shivered—it was surely hand-made, and of another era.

He continued to stare at her with terrifying certainty. It wasn't just the antique clothing—something about the girl's skin was strange—a matte quality against the sunny day around them, as if she alone stood under a clouded sky. It was impossible, but—

This little girl was a ghost.

She was quaking now. "Get out of my flowers, you bully," she said with tears in her eyes.

Elliot stepped back, and as she continued to glare, he stepped again. "I, uh, I can't see them," he said. "Is this far enough?"

She rolled her eyes, and her quaking stopped. "Yes, dummy. What do you mean you can't see them? What are you doing here on my farm anyway?"

"Your...farm?"

"You'd better get out of here, Mister, or I'm going to call my Papa."

Elliot felt a twinge of panic. "Wait. Just wait." He needed to think, and fast. Wrapping his mind around *this* pint-sized specter was difficult enough.

Then he swallowed a sudden urge to laugh. Specters? He was losing it. This girl couldn't be a ghost.

"Okay," he said. "Where *are* your parents?"

The girl bristled. "I'm warning you, Mister. I'm not supposed to talk to strangers. You'd better get out of here, or Papa is going to be real mad."

Elliot crossed his arms. "Well, I think I'd like to talk to your Papa. Where is he?"

She looked suddenly uncertain. "He's in the wash house. He's going to be real mad if I have to get him. You get out of here." She was quaking again.

Seeing her fear, something broke in Elliot, and he

was overcome with the urge to comfort her, crazy or not. He stepped forward and reached out a hand, but she let out a high shriek and stepped back into the low saplings. Only, that wasn't exactly true. She stepped *through* the low saplings. As he looked at her, he froze. The trunk of a young maple now protruded straight through the top of her head.

The realization—she *was* a ghost after all—raised the fine hairs of his neck. Elliot considered whether he should flee, but the girl was still terrified, so instead, he raised his hands and sat slowly on the ground. "Am I sitting in the flowers?" he asked.

Cautiously, she shook her head no. "Please, will you leave?"

"Not just yet. My name is Elliot. What's yours?"

"S-Sofia."

He nodded and smiled. "Okay, Sofia. I have a question for you." He continued to marvel at the tree protruding through the top of her head. If he couldn't see what she saw, then perhaps she couldn't see what he did. "Can you look at your flowers, Sofia? Did I crush any of them, or are they the way they were before I got here?"

She cocked her head and crept forward, then around him, leaving a wide berth. When she circled back to the front her shoulders slumped. "No, they're all okay. But, you trampled them. I don't understand."

"Neither do I." He watched her for a moment, her face more distressed than ever until an idea occurred to him. "Maybe I'm your imaginary friend?"

Sofia's face smoothed into a smile. "You're dressed very funny for an imaginary friend." She looked past him back to the house—looked like she was listening. "This boy, Mama," she shouted. A few moments passed, and she continued. "Of course he's not there, Mama. He's my imaginary friend." She looked at Elliot. "Mama can't see you, so I guess you're right. You *are* my imaginary friend. Or maybe you're a ghost, but I don't think so."

Elliot laughed, even as he shivered. "Oh no? Why not? I *could* be a ghost."

"No. Ghosts are bad, and I'm protected from bad things."

He bit his lower lip, thinking maybe he should tell her, but held his tongue. "Oh? How are you protected?"

With a wide grin, she reached into one of the pockets of her dress. When she opened her closed hand, Elliot gasped. "It belonged to my Nonno," she said. Pale, cloudy light lit the coin—cleaner and brighter than how he'd found it, but the same coin, to be sure. He touched the little pocket in the front of his running shorts to be certain. Yes, still there.

The wave of sadness that descended upon him came even quicker than the summer storm an hour before. He stood, doing his best to keep smiling. "Um, it was very nice to meet you, Sofia, but I have to go now if that's alright."

She frowned but nodded. "Nice to meet you Elliot, my imaginary friend."

He hurried toward his bike, leaning against the sapling a few feet away, and the denial washed over him. This couldn't really be happening. Maybe when he'd forced the window of the farmhouse, he'd inhaled some kind of hallucinogenic mold. He turned one last time as he lifted his bike and headed back toward the path. Sofia was still there, watching him curiously. The moment he set his tires on the muddy path—beginning to dry now—he was away, feet pedaling furiously.

Say it was true—that there *had* once been a child named Sofia who lived on the farm. If she was real—if she was now the ghost he'd seen—then her little talisman couldn't have worked, and that was the saddest part. She believed, in her suspended state, that she was safe. But to be a ghost? To have died at such a young age? The irony was horrible.

But then, turning back onto Pentucket Road, the denial returned. The roar of the Pentucket—less swollen than before—the sweet, thick taste of the humid air, the hot sun on his back, the call of the birds, the swarm of gnats he rode through under the shadow of a tall oak—these things were real. They were incontrovertible. Ghostly children and lucky coins from an Italian grandfather—a *Nonno*? And yet, he could feel the coin in his pocket—feel its weight against his groin every time his legs turned the pedal cranks. This constant revolution of denial-acceptance-denial, spinning around in his mind as quickly as the bicycle cassette beneath his feet, was maddening. There was only one way to break it, and as he turned into the drive down to the New Colony Apartment Village, he knew what he had to do.

He'd find out if she'd ever lived. And if she had? He'd return to her.

Tony's car was missing from the front, and when Elliot stepped from the patio into the kitchen, he was relieved to find the apartment empty. There was a note on the little round dining table, and he glanced at it briefly:

Elliot,

Went to get yarn, etc. Be back later.

Dinner in the fridge if you get hungry.

Love,

Mom

Elliot looked at the clock on the stove. Not yet three in the afternoon. There was a craft store in downtown Haverford. Where the hell were they going to get yarn that they wouldn't be back for dinner? Connecticut? He didn't care. He took a shower, relieved to rid his skin of the sweat and salt and mud. Clean again, he retrieved the coin from his running shorts and set it on his nightstand. Then he crawled beneath the covers, despite the heat of the bedroom—no air conditioning—and was asleep before his head hit the pillow.

When he woke, it was after five-thirty, and he was drowning in enough sweat he thought he needed another shower. Tony and his mother were still gone, so he opened the refrigerator and pulled out the container of chicken salad he presumed his mother intended as *dinner*. He spread some between slices of bread and made a salad with what was left of the lettuce, cucumbers, and tomatoes he'd brought home after his morning at the community farm the previous Friday.

Then he sat at the little dining table with his phone, and between bites of chicken salad, typed furiously into the browser.

The information was sparse:

WRIGHT-CALISTI FARM RESERVATION: TOWN OF HAVERFORD, MA

Sold to the Town of Haverford under "generous and philanthropic terms" in 1962 by community real-estate titan George Calisti, the Wright-Calisti Farm Reservation is a 7-acre preserve at the heart of the Pentucket Natural Area. Consisting of new-growth forest and meadow, the farm connects trails from Lake Haverford to the confluence with the Merrimack River. The meadow is a sanctuary for several bird species...

Elliot scanned quickly and skipped ahead.

Founded in 1851 by Josiah Wright, the W-C Farm remained in continuous operation, under the same family until 1959. Following the marriage of Elizabeth Wright (1895-1958) to Italian immigrant Stefano Calisti (1893-1959) in 1918, the Calisti name was added to the farm. But Stefano Calisti brought more than his name to the W-C Farm. Throughout the last four decades of operation, Calisti's Italian influence introduced the people of Haverford to then-exotic European vegetables...

He scanned further.

A combination of family tragedy and the flood of August 1959 cut the season short, and the W-C Farm never recovered. While the loss of the farm was keenly felt by the community of Haverford, the Wright-Calisti

Farm Reservation still exists today as both a vibrant recreational resource and a reminder of Haverford's rich agricultural and industrial past. Although outbuildings, such as the wash house and greenhouses have long since been demolished, the two-story 1850s farmhouse still stands...

Elliot closed the browser on his phone. A family tragedy and a flood? His skin was suddenly clammy, and he chewed absently, no longer tasting the bread or chicken, the mayonnaise or celery. Cautiously, he reopened the browser on his phone and searched for *Sofia Calisti 1959*. The results were disappointing. Two full screens of Facebook and LinkedIn results spilled into a list of sites promising background checks. *Has Sofia Calisti been arrested? Check for free!* No good.

He wasn't going to find answers on the internet. He needed a more personal approach, which would be difficult, but possible. The Calistis were a prominent family in Haverford, and he'd known them intimately, once.

One in particular.

Cameron Calisti.

Of course he thought of Cam—who'd taken a job halfway through the season at the community farm. Cam, who he'd gone to school with for years and used to be his best friend. Cam, who he couldn't bear to talk to now—hadn't had a real conversation with in years—because Cam had changed in ways that made Elliot feel uncomfortable, and excited, and more than a little ashamed. The silence between them remained because their past was too painful, and Elliot had no one to blame but himself. But he'd see him tomorrow morning, and maybe if he could work up the courage—

Without realizing, he'd finished his dinner. After a quick rinse under the sink, he deposited his plate in the dishwasher and headed back to his room. He wanted to look at the pictures he'd taken and to text Lindsey. Most of all, he wanted answers, but those, he realized, would have to wait.

≈

When his mother and Tony came back in sometime after ten, loud and stumbling and drunk and jolly, he flicked off the light on his nightstand. Let them think he was asleep. After a minute there was a clumsy knock on his door and his mother's slurred voice. "Elliot?" He ignored her and pulled the covers over his head. It was time for bed anyways—he had to be at the community farm by seven the next morning. "Elliot, honey. Love you, El."

He squeezed his eyelids tightly together, ashamed of the dampness he felt at the corners. "Love you too, Mom," he said, quiet enough that she wouldn't hear.

≈

Three thousand miles away, Destin Duprée sat in her lavish apartment in San Francisco's Nob Hill and gazed out the bay window at the setting sun. She wondered, absently, if she'd miss this view. The bits of the bay she could see shimmered golden, and the sky was painted in bold strokes as high, lacy clouds blew in off the Pacific. She'd enjoyed San Francisco—in her mind, America's most Mediterranean city—but she'd longed to return to Europe. She began to curse her luck—to lament these years waiting and watching when all this time the coin had slumbered in Haverford. But then she laughed a little and took another sip of her bitter Negroni. Better to live in California than Massachusetts. Boston was fine but too small and cold for her taste.

She took in the last of the daylight before the long, lingering gloaming began to usher in the night. The years spent in California had been good—an unexpected reprieve from her duties—but that all changed now. The coin was awake. She could feel the pull—the unspoken mandate to reclaim what was stolen.

After another sip from the martini glass—she always preferred her liquor *up*—she retrieved her laptop from the floor and refreshed the page. Right on cue. Perhaps her influence these days was minimal, but sometimes minimal was enough.

TOWN OF HAVERFORD: OFFICE OF THE MAYOR - EXECUTIVE ASSISTANT - VACANCY TO BE FILLED IMMEDIATELY

She smiled as she clicked the link to apply, then attached the cover letter and resumé she'd prepared earlier in the day when she'd set everything in motion. In the end, she knew it was unnecessary. The job was hers. In another era she might not have gone to all the effort—might've just shown up—but times were different now. There were digital trails to everything. There were enquiring minds and, as she acknowledged, her influence wasn't as great as it had once been. Perhaps that was about to change, but right now, in this digital age, an inflated resumé was worth the effort.

After sending the application, she loaded the airline website and chose a flight early in the morning. Though she knew she wouldn't sleep, she was accustomed to a certain degree of luxury, so she selected a window seat in one of those nice new lay-flat pods they offered. It was egregiously expensive, but money didn't matter; she had more of it than she could possibly spend.

The Negroni was gone, so she went to the little bar cart and mixed herself another, delighting at the cold against her skin as she vigorously shook the metal shaker and watched its surface grow a frost from the humid air. She strained it into her glass and took up her former spot in the window. The sky was cobalt now, and as she took a sip of her fresh drink—nearly overflowing—she shivered with delight.

Where was Guillaume, she wondered—wondered if he even called himself that anymore. Would he be waiting for her when she landed—the old foe more of a friend than anyone she'd known in this life? And wasn't that ironic? Even through all the struggle, the world had always been her oyster. And yet, the thing she longed for above all else was the presence and familiarity of her old nemesis.

She laughed and drained her drink in a single, long, burning draw.

It was time to pack.

Chapter 3

August 14, 2019 - Wednesday

The blue jays woke him before his alarm, their incessant, accusatory chattering outside the window a far more effective disruption to sleep than the percussive chromatic scale his phone was set to play a few minutes later. Elliot sat up in bed and grimaced, wondering how many of his friends got up at 6:12 during the summer—wondering if he'd be able to go back to sleep, blocking out the sound of the birds if he didn't have to go to the farm.

Across town, he knew Cameron would be getting up now, too. The news came during Elliot's last shift—Cam would be joining for the rest of the summer. Home from college. The thought of him—of seeing him in less than an hour—sent a ripple of heat right through to Elliot's core, like hot coffee into an empty stomach. The excitement started to manifest, physically, and he quickly shifted his thoughts, unwilling to indulge the fantasy or suffer the aftertaste of shame that usually accompanied it.

Instead, he gently lifted Sofia's coin from his

nightstand and began to turn it in his fingers. Perhaps later he'd be able to scour the internet for clues to its provenance. He examined the raised scythe emblem and rubbed it gently with his thumb. But then his phone began to shriek, the digital xylophone screaming furiously up the scale. He canceled the alarm and headed for the shower.

Afterward, he slipped on a pair of cargo shorts and an old running shirt he didn't mind getting dirty, gathered his phone and wallet into his backpack, and headed for the kitchen. But before closing his bedroom door, he looked back at the nightstand and Sofia's coin. The sight of it induced a peculiar longing—the same magnetism he'd felt toward the old farmhouse—and he realized he couldn't stand to leave without it. Pulling the wallet from his backpack, he slipped the coin inside, put the wallet in his pocket, and felt better.

In the kitchen, he filled a water bottle and was ready to head for the patio when he heard his mother's bedroom door open. Puffy-eyed and half asleep—death warmed over, she might say—she stepped into the kitchen and stretched her lips into a tepid smile.

"Morning, El," she said.

In spite of himself, Elliot looked at his feet. "Good morning, Mom."

"You were in bed early." She hobbled toward the sink, pulled a glass from a cabinet and ran the water. "Everything alright?"

Like you care, he thought. "Yeah, had to get up for the farm this morning." He should leave it at that—knew he shouldn't say anything else—but the sight of her was too much. He could smell the booze evaporating out of her pores and see the anemic throbbing of the little vein at her temple. He knew the answer before he asked the question. "Are you going to work this morning? It's getting kind of late."

"Oh, Elliot. Why do you have to do that? I mean, I'm trying here. You know I'm trying, right?"

He looked at her—really *looked* for as long as he could before turning away. There was a time when he thought she was the most beautiful woman in the world, with her softly curling, long chestnut hair, and the fine, sculpted features of her face. High cheekbones. Shimmering gray-green eyes. Where was that woman now? She was still young—forty-two—but to see her like this? Her skin was so white. Sickly and translucent. The lines in her face were etched too deeply.

He deflated. "Sorry, Mom. I know you are. I, uh—I gotta go. See you later?"

She smiled, and for a moment that other version of his mother—the one from before—was back again, and he knew all was forgiven. She nodded. "See you later."

Turning, he went out onto the patio, unlocked his bike, and rode off into the bright August morning.

♒

A few minutes before seven, he propped his bike against the red brick of the wash house, and found Farmer Melissa inside, counting out twist ties for herbs. She smiled, and her infectious cheer warmed him more than the heat of the early morning sun. "Good morning, Elliot."

He smiled back. "Good morning." Melissa was impossibly cool—thirty years old, arms covered in whimsical tattoos, plugs in her ears and a piercing over her left eye. She had a master's degree in English Literature from Tufts and could talk about vermiculture with a passion and intimacy that left Elliot wondering if she was talking about worms or lovers. She was a warrior-hero on the front lines of modern agriculture, and Elliot thought she was maybe one of the most amazing people he'd ever met. "What can I get started?" he asked.

She gave him a handful of purple twist ties—*organically grown* printed proudly on their surface in white letters. "How about ten nice bunches of sage?"

"Okay." He grabbed a short black crate and a harvest knife and started out into the field.

He'd rounded the side of the wash house when he saw Cameron, strolling up with his too-relaxed swagger, and short dark hair, almost black, shining in the morning sun. He paused for a minute and gave Elliot a warm smile—the face-melting, teeth-sweating kind—and fished his delicate hand into the sporty messenger bag that hung from his slight shoulders. He pulled out a green baseball cap, smoothed the brim, and positioned it on his head. Boyish. Stunning. Devastatingly beautiful. Elliot felt himself start to blush as Cameron's smile broadened. "Elliot," he said, with a nod of his head, ice-blue eyes shimmering.

Suddenly, Elliot couldn't look away, though he desperately wanted to. Cameron's eyes were Sofia's eyes. And so odd—not the family resemblance so much as the color. How many Italians had blue eyes?

Cameron frowned. "Elliot? Are you alright? You look like you've seen a ghost."

Remembering himself, Elliot shook his head and

broke the trance. "Sorry. Still waking up."

"Okay." He shrugged, accepting the explanation as he walked past. "See you out there."

Face burning now, Elliot hurried off to the sage and buried himself in the savory aroma of the leaves. Idiot, he thought, as he began to gather the stems and cut.

≈

After the herbs, they moved on to lettuce, then summer squash and cucumbers, chard and collards. He wanted to talk to Cameron but was relieved when the opportunity continued to evade him. Cam was always in another row or in conversation with another farm hand. Melissa sent Elliot off to harvest the eggplant by himself—most of the crop had contracted downy mildew, so the yield was low enough for one person to handle.

But then it was mid-morning, and time for tomatoes. Melissa assigned Cameron and Elliot to the slicers, while she and a couple of others tackled the cherries and the first of the season's heirlooms. Armed with tall, white buckets, they headed into the field and picked a row, one on each side, facing each other.

It started with silence—plucking any fruits with a medium blush, pulling off the crowns, and setting them carefully, shoulders down into the buckets. Through the thick foliage of the plants, Elliot watched Cameron watching him back. The tension was palpable. Elliot reached for a tomato a few inches off the black plastic sheeting that lined the row and cursed as it let go of the vine and rolled to Cam's side.

"I guess I'll grab this one," Cam said.

"Um, yeah. Okay," Elliot replied, searching the

ground in an effort to look at anything but Cameron's eyes through the dense wall of leaves in front of him.

"Seven."

"Excuse me?"

"Seven words. I've been back here a couple of weeks already, and we haven't spoken *at all*. But today? We're up to seven words. Well—nine now. So far, you've said nine words to me this summer."

"You're counting my words?"

"Thirteen. Hey, we're getting somewhere."

Elliot scowled. "Okay, this is getting awkward. What do you want me to say, Cam? I mean, actually, I've been *wanting* to talk to you. I need to, but—"

"Fine. I'll start. How are you liking college?"

Elliot began to fold his arms in defiance, but quickly changing course, let them drop. Best not to be adversarial. Cam was trying to be friendly. He couldn't know Elliot was living in a private hell—that every day at the community college was a reminder: Elliot was stuck here. Elliot was stagnant. Elliot was withering on the vine, even as so many of his old high school peers were flourishing.

He exhaled long and slow. "It's—you know. I'm waiting it out at the community college for another year before I transfer to a state school. If I do one more year, I'll get a big cut in credit cost. And, with my family situation..."

"Right," Cam said. "Nothing wrong with that. You know, a lot of people—"

Elliot bristled. "Right. Yeah, I know." He paused, imploring himself to be nice. "College is—good? And how did you end up here at the farm? I wouldn't have thought this would be your thing."

"Yeah. It's good. I'm, um... Well, I think I'm going to study environmental science. I wasn't sure. That's kind of what I'm doing here this summer. My parents get a farm share, and they heard the farm was short-handed and thought it might be good for me to spend a little time working at a place directly impacted by environmental... and then I heard you were working here, and I thought—"

"You thought..."

Elliot pushed his arm deep into the greenery as Cameron did the same. Their hands closed around the same tomato. Fingers touched. Cameron laughed, soft and warm, and Elliot recoiled.

"I'm not a leper, you know," Cam said.

"Yeah, I know."

"And you don't have to be so uncomfortable all the time. It's totally natural. For god's sake, it's 2019 Elliot. It's okay that you—"

"I'm not gay!"

Cam flinched and raised his hands in the air—a gesture of surrender, a laying down of his arms. "Sorry. Just saying, if you were...it's alright."

Elliot sighed. "No, I'm sorry." He could still feel the place their fingers had touched—searing—and wanted to feel it again. It was easy for Cameron. His family owned half of Haverford. He hadn't needed a generous scholarship to get out of town—to escape to that fancy private college in Vermont. Hell, he didn't even *need* to get out of town. Cameron Calisti was free to be whomever he wanted to be, and Elliot had always envied him that. Cam didn't have to live with an alcoholic mother who was most often absent even when she was present. He didn't have to suffer Tony, who'd so quickly identified a truth Elliot couldn't yet embrace.

Cameron smiled and extended his hand through the tomato vines. "Truce?" he asked.

Elliot closed his fingers around the other boy's and felt the delicious thrill of their skin touching. He squeezed tighter and held his grip, knowing the gesture meant more than *truce*. It meant *sorry*, and *you're right*, and *I'm not ready for this yet*, and by the time he reluctantly let go, he knew that Cam understood all of it.

They continued in silence for a minute while Elliot chewed his thoughts. He hadn't had a real conversation with Cam since they were thirteen, but now maybe it would be easier. Now that Cameron had been given confirmation—that he'd been told without being told—maybe they could turn a corner. Maybe—if Elliot could keep his feelings at bay.

Halfway through the row, Elliot decided he couldn't wait any longer. "Look, can I ask you something?" Elliot demanded without waiting for a response. "Your family..." he stammered, "they owned the farm in the preservation land, right?"

"Yeah, why do you ask?"

"Do you know what happened there? I was running with my friend Lindsey yesterday—"

"I *know* Lindsey."

Elliot shook his head. Stupid. "Of course you know Lindsey. Sorry. Anyways, we got caught in a rainstorm and waited it out on the porch of the old farmhouse. I got a really strange feeling from being there, and then later I went back, and—"

"And?" Cameron had stopped plucking tomatoes.

Elliot shook his head. "It's stupid. Never mind."

"Oh no, you can't stop now. What, did you see a ghost or something?"

"I think I'm going crazy. There was a little girl there. She said her name was Sofia."

Cameron's expression darkened. "Okay, that's not funny. Who told you about Sofia?"

"She's *real*?" Elliot sighed, feeling the tension in his shoulders break like the air in the moments before a summer squall.

"Seriously. Who told you?"

The ice in Cameron's voice caught him off guard. "Really. No one. Cam, *am I* going crazy? I swear I *saw* her. I *talked* to her." He could see he was losing him. "And then there's this!" He reached into his pocket, pulled out his wallet, and handed over the coin. "I found it underneath the steps to the porch."

Cam took it cautiously, and his eyes widened. "No shit." The awe and wonderment that lit his face spoke volumes. Careful and reluctant, he handed it back, the skeptic-turned-believer. "I've heard about this. If it's what I think it is, my great grandfather brought it over from Italy—some crazy story I don't entirely remember. I mean, he was dead forty years before I was born, but wow. It was like, a family treasure, and then it disappeared. I think my grandfather is the only one alive who ever saw it."

"So, what happened?"

"It was terrible. My grandfather didn't have much to do with that farm. It was being run by his brother at the time, and Sofia was his daughter—that is, my grandfather's niece, right? The Pentucket flooded and washed the whole place out, and when the water finally went down they found my grandfather's brother and his wife, stabbed to death in the house."

Elliot shivered, despite the hot August sun. "And Sofia?"

Cam shook his head. "That's the saddest part of all of it. They never found her. No one knows if she was killed too...or if she drowned."

"Wow. And did they catch whoever killed her parents?"

"No. It was never solved. There *was* a suspect—some boarder that was renting a room at the house—but they never found him either. I don't know, my dad wasn't even born yet, so all of this is majorly second hand."

Elliot regarded the coin, still in his palm. "I feel like—I don't know. I feel like I should give this to you, but I also feel like I was supposed to find it. Does that make any sense? Like, I can't stand to be apart from it. Would you mind if I held onto it for a while until I figure all this out?"

Cam shrugged. "No one in my family has seen it for sixty years. Finders keepers, I guess. But, what do you mean *figure all this out*?"

"Either I saw her, or I'm losing my mind. But I know, crazy as it sounds, that I *did* see her. I think I need to find out what happened to her."

Cam whistled, then laughed. "Yeah, maybe you *are* going crazy. Good luck to you Elliot. You'll let me know if anything—"

"Yeah," he said, turning his attention back to the tomatoes.

When he returned home in the early afternoon, he found his mother on the couch with a pair of knitting needles and a skein of pink and purple yarn. The shades were turned, the apartment sweltering, and the television blaring—a too-thin woman on a daytime talk show lectured the audience about the importance of acting vapid on a first date, because, according to the book she'd written, intelligent women were a turn-off. A half-empty glass of white wine dripped sweat down its stem that pooled around the base—sure to leave another ring on the scarred finish of the coffee table.

"You should open some windows, Mom. It's an oven in here. And what are you watching? That woman is an idiot," he said.

She put down her knitting needles and looked at him for a moment, scrunching her brow until the skin of her forehead folded into canyons of confusion. "What time is it? You're back from the farm already?"

He sighed, not wanting to get into it because she was already sauced. She wasn't going to go back to her job—had maybe already lost it—and what could he do? For a brief moment, he was almost thankful for Tony, who had a decent, union-fortified income. Tony, who'd quickly tire of pulling all their weight and either leave or force her to find another job when this baby-hat business didn't work out.

"Yeah, it's after one, I think." He considered. "Are you going to be home for dinner?"

She turned her head to look at him, and her face dripped with exasperation, seeming to say: yeah, where else would I be? "Of course, Elliot."

“Alright. I’ll, um—I’ll make us something later. I’m going out now.”

She’d already turned back to the television, the wine, and the yarn, so without waiting for acknowledgment, he headed for his bike.

≈

He wasn’t sure what he expected when he reached the preserve. He leaned his bike against the same sapling that had cradled it the day before and walked slowly to the porch of the old farmhouse. Taking a seat on one of the decaying steps, he closed his eyes for a moment and opened them slowly, hoping Sofia would be standing in front of him. When she wasn’t, he was hardly surprised. There was still a chance it had all been a strange hallucination.

And if it wasn’t—he *knew* it wasn’t—how did it work anyways? Would his presence conjure her? He supposed he’d have to wait. His phone bleated, and he pulled it from his pocket to see a text from Lindsey:

"Wanna go for a run?"

He smiled. A run sounded good, but it wasn’t in the cards today. He wrote back:

"Tomorrow, maybe? I have lots to tell you. I’m ghost hunting, and I found this crazy coin at the old farmhouse."

At the bottom of the message thread, three bouncing dots told him she was typing. He waited, and a moment later her message came through:

"You better not have gone in there! You’re so weird."

He started to type his response, but then—

“Boo!”

He leaped to his feet and resisted the urge to scream as he looked down at Sofia, standing beside him. She was clutching her stomach with laughter and grinning broadly, pretty in a blue-and-white dress and muddy brown shoes. "I snuck up on you, Elliot. You should see your face."

Though his heart threatened to beat right out of his chest, he smiled with relief. "Sofia, you really *did* scare me. Where did you come from?"

She pointed out toward the field. "I was with Papa in the tomatoes. They're not doing so well. He says it's too wet. I saw you sitting on the steps and I told him I'd be back. What's that thing you've got?"

He looked at the phone in his hand and chuckled, finally slowing his breathing. "Well, it's kind of like—a telephone, and a camera, and a book, and a television all in one."

Confusion clouded her face for a moment, then she laughed. "You're funny! Did you come to play with me?"

"Sort of? Maybe?" He looked at the phone in his hand and had an idea. "Sofia, do you mind if I take your picture?"

"With your funny television camera telephone book?"

"Yes."

"Okay." She smiled widely, revealing a tiny chasm above her lower lip, where a baby-tooth once sat.

He raised the phone, flicked over to the camera from the lock screen, and sighed, closing it again. She wasn't there, at least according to the screen on the iPhone—just the low saplings and the meadow beyond, gently blurred by the August haze.

"What's wrong, Elliot?" she asked.

The question knocked the wind out of him, and he sat down hard on the steps of the porch. This joyous, playful, laughing girl had made him forget for a moment why he was here. And that punctuated the tragedy. Not only was she dead, but she was also unaccounted for, and how many decades had passed since anyone had bothered to try to find her?

How long had she been forgotten?

"Sofia," he said, voice quivering. His palms were wet, and he could feel the sweat beneath his arms. Cold. Crawling. "Do you know what happened to you?"

"What do you mean?"

"I mean—did someone—did you drown? Or, did someone—hurt you?"

Her face clouded. "Why are you asking me that, Elliot? I didn't drown. I'm right here. You're scaring me."

He exhaled. "Okay, Sofia. I'm not trying to scare you. I know it sounds strange, but just listen to me for a minute, okay? I'm your friend, right?" He pulled his wallet from his pocket, and removed the coin, holding it out so she could see. "Look, it's your coin, right?"

"How did you get that?" She plunged a tiny hand into the pocket on the side of her dress. He watched a flicker of relief light her expression for a moment as her fingers closed around her own coin. Then the confusion and fear returned. "Elliot, stop. I'm scared."

"You don't have to be scared. See, I found it yesterday. Here. Under the steps. I think—I don't know. I think you left it for me or—for someone—to find." He took a breath. Best to say what had to be said—not skirt around the issue any longer. "Sofia, I think you're a ghost, and I think, somehow, I'm supposed to set you free."

Her face twisted in tiny fury, and her eyes filled with tears. Stomping her foot, she crossed her arms over her chest. "I'm *not* a ghost! I'm alive, and you're not my friend Elliot. You're a bully who tramples flowers and says mean things to little girls. I don't want to play with you after all." She turned and started to run, passing like air through the saplings, and then bounded through the high grass of the meadow beyond.

Carefully, he put the coin back into his wallet and made his way to the bicycle.

He was sorry he'd upset her, but if he could do it—set her free—it would be worth it. Whatever was left of her—the energy that animated the little spectral version that remained—would thank him in the end. It was a tall order, solving a sixty-year-old mystery, but a steely resolve ran hot through his veins.

He climbed onto his bike, and as he pushed off onto the dusty path, he set his jaw and nodded to the oaks and maples, the alders and beech. He was six decades too late to save her, but Sofia Calisti was not forgotten.

He'd find justice for her still.

Chapter Four

August 15, 2019 - Thursday

Elliot finally found the attendant for the Reference Desk in a particularly dark corner of the periodicals section of the Haverford Free Library. The short woman, nearly as wide as she was tall, was struggling to push a bound annual of National Geographic onto a shelf barely within her reach. "Can I help you with that?" he asked.

She abandoned her struggle and turned to him with a broad smile. "Oh yes, thank you. I should've brought the step stool. I didn't realize this was so high up."

Elliot took the volume and placed it neatly onto the shelf. "I wonder if you could help me. Do you have any old newspaper accounts of the flood in 1959?"

The woman considered. "I should think so. Probably on microfiche. We were supposed to digitize all that back in '08, but then the recession hit and, well, you know. Projects got shelved. Do you know how to use the readers? We've got the old ones that are kind of like microscopes."

He nodded. "Yeah, I think I used one in middle school."

"Alright, give me a minute. That was, what—August? Wow, sixty years ago this month. What a terrible tragedy." She considered. "My mother used to tell me stories. Homes washed down for miles. Lucky for Haverford it was only the Pentucket corridor that got hit—the Merrimack swelled but never went over its banks. Kind of a morbid thing to be researching, huh?"

"Yeah, I uh...Got my syllabus early for the American history course I'm taking this fall at the community college. I'll need to write a paper on local history and figured I'd get a head start. Everyone else will probably write about the mills and factories, or the colonists buying the land from the Native Americans, so I thought I'd take a different approach."

She nodded her approval and bumbled away, returning a minute later with an enormous smile. "Looks like you're in luck. 1959 was one of the years we actually got scanned. Follow me." She led him to an ancient computer console and showed him how to work the system. "Now, it's not like Google—not yet. You can't search *flood* or anything, just dates. Start anywhere in August of '59 and you'll find it. I'm sure it was front-page."

He thanked her, and after she walked away, he started with today's date—the 15th—sixty years before. He clicked forward from day to day, for a little more than a week, until the screen lit up with an evening edition from Sunday, August 23.

The photograph on the front page was devastating. Taken from a window in one of the mill buildings at the confluence–the place the Pentucket emptied into the Merrimack–the photo showed an island of destruction churning through murky water. The roof of a house peeled off like the lid of an aluminum can bobbed alongside shattered tree limbs and a menagerie of incidental detritus. Though the image was grainy, Elliot imagined he could make out car tires, and mailboxes. One particular bump nosing up out of the dark water looked like the front end of a sedan.

WALL OF WATER WASHES OUT PENTUCKET CORRIDOR

Early last evening, the 22nd of August, at approximately 6:20 pm, a wall of water reaching a height of 20 feet in places, cascaded down the path of the Pentucket River, according to witnesses. Early reports from officials suggest debris blocking a bridge below Lake Haverford caused a damming effect, later resulting in the wave of terror when the said bridge gave way in the early evening.

It may be several days before the full scope of the destruction is known. At the time of printing, it is confirmed that at least 17 homes have been destroyed or irreparably damaged. In addition, at least four persons have been reported missing and are presumed drowned…

…While the Merrimack came close to overflowing its banks, water levels already high on account of this summer's record-breaking rainfall, downtown Haverford, the riverfront and mill districts were blessedly spared. The bulk of the debris has remained within the confluence, and rescuers continue to search the water for any sign of the missing…

Heartbreaking as the story was, most of this Elliot knew already. He clicked forward to the next day, and the headline caused him to catch his breath.

COUPLE FOUND MURDERED. YOUNG DAUGHTER STILL MISSING.

Late last evening, the bodies of Robert and Margaret Calisti, co-owners and operators of the Wright-Calisti Farm, were discovered in the farmhouse on their property, dead of apparent multiple stab wounds, according to police. The discovery was reported by one George Calisti, brother to the deceased and co-owner of the farm, who was forced to report the crime in person at the police station, as telephone service at the murder scene has been disrupted by Saturday's flood.

According to police, Mr. Calisti was hysterical with grief and has been admitted to the Haverford Regional Hospital. At this time, he is not believed to be a suspect.

Pressed for comment on the existence of other suspects in the nascent investigation, police directed the Haverford Herald to Detective Arthur Mulvaney, who will be heading the police inquiries.

"At this time, we have identified a suspect, but are not yet at liberty to discuss the details," Mulvaney said. "We understand both the violent nature of this crime, and the fact the deceased were much-loved members of our community, will draw great interest among the residents of Haverford. Unfortunately, the flood has had the effect of compromising the crime scene. While I have every faith justice will be served in this matter, I ask for patience as the department and myself work to solve this horrible crime."

In a further, tragic twist, the daughter of the deceased, one Sofia Calisti, aged 8, is unaccounted. Mulvaney expressed optimism that she may yet be found alive. "I believe it is significant that the daughter was not found with the parents," Mulvaney said. "There is every possibility she was able to escape the attacker and may yet be found alive. I can say with absolute certainty this crime occurred before Saturday's flood, and therefore have no reason to believe young Ms. Calisti was caught up in that other tragedy."

Mr. Mulvaney urges anyone with information as to the whereabouts of Sofia Calisti to contact the Haverford Police immediately. A photograph will be published if and when one can be obtained.

Elliot felt the urge to continue on—to keep following the thread of the story through the archives—but it was too much. He imagined Sofia fleeing from an attacker, terrified. Or had she succumbed, and somehow her body washed away, even as the corpses of her parents remained in the house? He closed the newspaper file and stood, slowly walking toward the edge of the periodicals section, yearning for the warmth and light of the hot August sun outside.

As he passed the Reference Desk, the attendant raised her face from the magazine she was perusing. "Did you find what you needed?"

"Um," he said. "Some of it. Is that—is it available anytime?"

She smiled. "Anytime we're open. Now you know where it is, feel free to use it as you need."

"Thanks," he said, then headed for the exit.

≈

Lindsey was waiting on the porch of her family's cozy two-story when Elliot walked up the garden path thirty minutes later. Rising gingerly out of her wicker chair, she greeted him with a warm smile. "So, which is it?" she asked.

"Huh?"

"Are you more Kristen Wiig or Melissa McCarthy?"

Elliot regarded her, confused. "What are you—"

"Ghostbusters, dummy!" She punched him lightly on the arm. "How's all your creepy paranormal investigation going? Or did you get heat stroke after our last run?"

"Har, har!" he replied, rolling his eyes as he started to sit.

"Oh no! On your feet. You're late already, and I have stuff to do after we're done."

"Fine," he said. "Ready?"

"Let's go." She started at a slow trot down past the garden gate. He followed, and when they turned right onto Pentucket Road, he began to match her stride—they were going for six miles today, no need to take it out too fast.

"I didn't have a heat stroke," he said.

"No? So, what did you see?"

"There's a little girl. Her name is Sofia Calisti, and she vanished sometime before the flood in 1959."

"As in *the* Calistis? Like, Calisti Hardware? Calisti Real Estate? Like...Cameron Calisti?"

"One and the same. I even talked to Cam about it yesterday at the farm. He confirmed she was real—like, that she lived. And she disappeared."

Lindsey stopped hard and placed her hands on her knees. "Sorry, what? *You had a conversation with Cam*?"

"Come on, Lindsey," he said, jogging in place. "It's

no big deal."

"I think it's a *huge* deal. You guys were so close when we were younger." She started to run again. "Does this mean—you guys should hang out. He could help you, you know—"

Elliot felt his face flush a deep red and knew he couldn't blame it on the as-yet minimal exertion from their run. "Help me what, exactly? Come out? Why is everyone always so concerned about my sexuality? Jesus Christ."

"Woah. Sensitive. I'm just saying—"

"Well, I wish you wouldn't."

"Fine. Lips are sealed, except—I was going to say I'm headed into the city on Sunday. Going to see Jared. Do you want to come?"

Elliot sucked in his breath and held it, despite the burning he was starting to feel in his lungs. Jared was Lindsey's older brother, getting ready to enter his senior year at Harvard. He was intelligent, attractive, confident, and—like Cameron—unabashedly open about his sexuality. Jared saw right through Elliot's facade. In fact, Elliot was fairly certain it was Jared who'd put the idea he was gay into Lindsey's head in the first place. He could imagine exactly how it would go: an afternoon at a little cafe in Cambridge, constantly avoiding Jared's all-knowing gaze, hours of trying to blend in with the walls, lest someone expose his well-guarded, but apparently easily-discerned secret.

And then, of course, there would be the *feelings* to deal with—the unwelcome sense of longing that would linger for hours, even days afterward. The phantom kiss of the sun long into the evening after a day spent on the beach. With Jared, it wasn't attraction in the traditional sense—not like he felt it with Cam. It was a realization there was another way to exist. A different way to be. An alien happiness. Nothing was more terrifying.

"I think I'm busy. Sorry."

"Shut up, Elliot. You're not busy. You're coming. In other news—more about this Sofia. How do you know she's real? How do *I* know she's real?"

"Great question. I don't know. I can't even convince *her* that she's a ghost."

"I'm still saying heat stroke."

Elliot shook his head, hard. "Enough talking for now. If we keep a pace where we can have a conversation, we won't finish until it's dark."

"Sheesh," Lindsey said. "Sorry." Then she leaned into her stride and pushed forward.

When he returned home after the run, Elliot's mother—on the sofa, wine and knitting needles in hand—informed him everyone would be around for dinner. Left up to her, that translated to cold-cuts between stale bread, so Elliot offered to cook. He went out and picked up three chicken breasts to grill, then prepared a salad of fresh tomatoes, cucumber, and onions—all from the community farm—and tossed it with salt and white wine vinegar from an old bottle starting to grow a skin. Later, once Tony got home, Elliot fired up the grill. He'd brought home some plump pattypans the day before, and he sliced and brushed them with oil to put on beside the chicken.

The meal came together, and they had a seat at the

little round dining table. Mostly they ate in silence—if you could count Tony as *silent*. Elliot cringed inwardly every time Tony took a bite—teeth gnashing behind a half-open mouth and inhaling sharply between swallows, as though the simple act of eating left him out of breath.

Halfway through dinner, his mother said, "You did good, kiddo. What is this vegetable you grilled?"

Elliot tried to ignore the slight slur at the edge of her words and take the compliment for what it was. "Pattypan," he said. "It's a summer squash."

"It's good! Tony, don't you think it's good?"

Winded. Ruddy-faced. Tony grunted.

His mother nodded her approval, then her eyes widened. "What's the date today?"

"The fifteenth," Elliot said. "Why do you ask?"

"Hoo! Time flies! Your birthday is—Monday?"

He fought from rolling his eyes. How many decent mothers needed to ask their own children to confirm their date of birth? "Yep. Twenty years old." There was ice in his voice, and he hated it.

She didn't seem to notice. "Well, we're going to have to *celebrate*. That's a big deal. No longer a teenager. Tony, isn't that a big deal?" Tony grunted and shoved an over-large slice of chicken into his greasy mouth. "What do you want? Anything. I mean, within reason, right? And what do you want to do?"

He sucked air through his teeth. "I don't know. We don't have to do anything."

"Elliot! Nonsense. I'll plan something. We'll do something really nice. But come on. What do you want? What do you need?"

To move out, he thought. To feel like an actual adult,

and not an overgrown adolescent. To be able to afford a four-year school. To be rid of the disgusting man sitting across the table, and to reclaim some semblance of the mother I once knew.

But then he registered the excitement on her face, and it reminded him of the woman she'd been before. There she was, if only for a moment: the mother he'd had when his father was alive. He smiled in spite of himself because she was still in there somewhere. "Well, I really need a new pair of running shoes."

Horrible Tony laughed and swallowed hard. "Oh, is that all?"

He set his face. "Yeah, that's all."

"What a goddamned waste. Maybe if you *worked* a little more and *ran* a little less, you could buy your own goddamned shoes rather than putting all that on your poor mom. When I was twenty—"

"I *do* work!"

"What, two mornings a week at your little hippy farm? Picking *arugula*? Fucking *pattypan*? More like *pansy-pants*." Amused by his own dim wit, Tony erupted in laughter so hard it ended in a coughing fit.

"Go ahead and laugh. I still see you shoving my fucking *pansy-pants* into your fat face."

Tony slammed his meaty fists down onto the dining table, rattling the plates and silverware with a seismic jolt. "Listen here you little *faggot*. You'd better watch your tongue and remember who's paying the bills around here."

To the bleating protests of his mother, Elliot shoved his chair back and stood up. "Elliot!" she cried. "Elliot, sit down please."

"No Mom. How can you sit there and let him talk to me like that? Who does he think he is? We were fine without him. We were *fine*. I'm out of here."

She turned to Tony, and for a brief moment, Elliot felt his heart swell with love as he regarded the rage coloring her normally too-white cheeks. "Tony! You apologize to him. You fix this."

Tony laughed, but when he spoke, his voice was dead calm and full of menace. "You'd do well to remember who's carrying the weight around here too, Lari. Now shut the fuck up and have another glass, why don't you?" Without looking at him, Tony continued. "Go ahead, boy. Run away like you always do."

Elliot shook his head slowly, not attempting to hide the hot tears that streaked down his cheeks. "No problem. I'm gone."

≈

The sun was dipping low as Elliot leaned his bike against the usual sapling, and commenced the slow, short walk to the old farmhouse. All around, the forest and meadow basked in the rich light of the golden hour—soft, warm, tender, hopeful—but he noticed none of it. He was a husk as empty and rotten as the farmhouse itself. As he sat clumsily on the second step of the porch, he realized there was no magnetism left to this place. Whatever he'd seen in it before had been an illusion—the naïve hope that something extraordinary might rise from the dusty detritus of circumstance. Its best days were behind it. So are mine, he thought.

He regretted it immediately—regretted the childish drama of the notion—but couldn't help the feeling. He knew he'd find a way out. He'd find the money and never look back. But in not looking back, he'd have to accept what he was leaving behind. He ached for his mother—for the woman she used to be—and wished so desperately he could save her. He wished Tony was dead—that somehow, he could've been the one walking down the side of the road that night instead of his father. It would be fitting. Tony, the enabler. Tony the drunk. Tony mowed down by an inebriated driver.

He thought of his father. Sweet. Kind. Strong. His father was killed by the recklessness of others. It was the car that had crushed his body, but alcohol in the driver's blood had been the murder weapon. How ironic that his mother—once so pure and pristine—had succumbed to the very substance that had ruined their lives.

But in the end, it wasn't Tony's fault. His mother was broken, and there would always be another Tony. There would always be—

"Are you sad because you're a mean boy?"

Startled out of his reverie, Elliot gasped to see Sofia sitting beside him. "You have to stop sneaking up on me!" He sighed. "Still, I'm very glad to see you."

She scowled. "I wasn't going to talk to you anymore, but you looked very sad like you wanted to apologize."

Elliot laughed. "Aw, Sofia. I *am* sorry."

"So, you won't say those mean things to me anymore?"

"Well, I'll try not to, but—" he took a deep breath. "Sofia, I'm not really your imaginary friend."

She crossed her arms. "Yes, you are. That's why no one can see you but me."

"Well, see, that's what I'm trying to figure out. Do

you know why I said the things I did?"

"That I was a ghost?"

"Yes."

"Because you're a mean boy?"

He laughed. "No. And I promise I'm not a mean boy. I'm a nice boy who wants to help you. See, what year is it, do you think?"

She rolled her eyes. "It's 1959. Everybody knows that, Elliot."

"Well, no. See, for me, it's not 1959 at all. For me, it's 2019. Sixty years later."

"So, you're from—the *future*?"

He laughed. "I guess. So, maybe you can imagine why I think a little girl from 1959 might be a ghost?"

She considered for a while, slowly nodding her head. "Okay, Elliot. But I'm still not a ghost."

"Well, I'd love to believe that, but how can I be sure?"

Leaping to her feet, she smiled, looking very certain of her answer. "Because I went to market with Mama today. It's Saturday and we always take vegetables to market on Saturday. And on the way home, we stopped in the cafe and Mama bought me a piece of blueberry pie. Ghosts don't go to market. Ghosts don't eat blueberry pie. Ghosts don't eat anything at all."

"That's true, but—" he stopped mid-sentence. Saturday? It was Thursday. Did that matter to a ghost? "Sofia, do you know what the date is?"

She nodded, slowly. "Saturday, August the fifteenth."

"And here it's—Thursday, August fifteenth. Sofia, when did you last see me?"

"Yesterday. You were mean, remember?"

He had an idea. It was crazy, but maybe—"Sofia,

does your Papa get the newspaper?"

"Yes."

"Okay, this is *very* important. Can you meet me here tomorrow at, say, three?"

"Yes."

"And can you look at the newspaper in the morning? Remember the headline. The first story on the very first page. Can you do that?"

"If I do, will you believe me? Will you believe I'm not a ghost?"

"If you do, I'm not sure what I'll believe anymore. But yes—*you*—I will believe."

Chapter Five

August 16, 2019 - Friday

When Elliot arrived at the farm the next morning, Cam was waiting for him. Leaning up against the side of the wash house, he tipped his hat forward and flashed his teeth. The smile was seductive, all knowing—the kind of smile Elliot could get lost in. "Good morning," Cam said.

Elliot supposed it was. He'd managed to get out of the house without encountering Tony or his mother—both sleeping off the booze. By the time he returned from seeing Sofia they'd gone out, and he wasn't sure what time they came back in.

His eyes traced Cam up and down, and he repressed the shame long enough to drink the image in. His face was sun-kissed—golden in the early light—and his slight shoulders ran down long arms to strong-but-delicate fingers—fingers he had touched and wanted to again.

A trim waist supported black shorts cut well above the knee—knees on slender but muscled legs, tapering down to delicate ankles. A statue. A god. Only when he noticed Cameron regarding him with similar intensity—still smiling, still knowing—did he shake his head and force his gaze to the other boy's eyes.

"Good morning," he said. "Why are you standing out here? Shouldn't you be counting ties or something?"

"Melissa isn't here yet." Cam extended his arm to indicate the empty expanse of wall beside him.

"Oh." Elliot took the cue, and leaned against the warm brick, leaving inches between their shoulders. It was too close. It wasn't close enough. In the periphery, he could see Cam's chest gently rising and falling as it filled with breath, then emptied again.

"Did you find anything else out? About Sofia?"

"No. Maybe. I don't know. She thinks she's alive and, crazy as it sounds—" Elliot didn't want to talk about Sofia right now. He wanted to enjoy the thrill of this moment—to appreciate the physical closeness and the tension that accompanied. He'd expected the shame and revulsion to surge forward at any moment, but something was different now. He had seen the hunger in Cameron's eyes—their searing intensity. He knew Cameron Calisti actually *felt* something for him—*wanted* something from him—and the knowledge that he could be so desired eclipsed everything else.

Cam turned his head. Still smiling. Still knowing. "This was the wrong time to ask, wasn't it?"

"Y-yes." Elliot closed his eyes and felt Cam's fingers graze gently over the top of his hand, and a current of pleasure electrified him from head to toe and back once more.

The sound of tires on the gravel drive leading to the wash house broke the moment—Melissa, surely—and Cam stepped away from the wall. "But you'll tell me later if we're alone?"

Exhaling long and deep, Elliot nodded. "Later."

Later came, finally, in the form of the tomato harvest. To Elliot, the distance between them early in the harvest had felt more than visceral. Meteorological. A constriction in his chest. Aching anticipation radiating through every muscle and bone against the barometric pressure of sudden, crushing attraction. But now, after hours of furtive glances separated by rows of greens and squash, beets and fennel, Elliot and Cameron were together again. Bent down, the thick foliage of the tomatoes offered cover—a blind to quell thirsting eyes and imaginations in the early throes of infatuation—and Elliot found he could concentrate for the first time all morning.

"So," Cam said. "The ghost of my—cousin? Dad's cousin? She thinks she's alive?"

"Yes. And I know it's crazy, but, what if I'm not seeing a ghost, but in fact seeing *the past*?"

"I guess it's no crazier than seeing a ghost. Well, maybe a little crazier."

"But I've got a plan—*we've* got a plan."

"Oh?" Cameron peeked over the tomatoes and smiled.

Elliot laughed. "Yes. It seems like—like time is moving in parallel. Yesterday for her was yesterday for me. It was four days ago that we met. For both of us. Get it?"

"Okay—"

"So, I saw her last night, and I said if she wanted to prove she was alive, she needed to memorize the headline from the Haverford Herald today, in 1959, that is. I'm going to meet her at three, and if she knows the headline—"

Cameron whistled. "Nope, you're right. This is all crazy. I have one question."

"Which is?"

He peeked over the tomatoes. "Can I come?"

There were a million reasons to say no. What if Cam couldn't see her? What if she failed to show up? What if the whole thing could be chalked up to hallucinogenic mold after all, and it was still working its way out of his system? He didn't know what this *thing* was—happening between them—but he was sure it would be over before it really even started if Cam found out he was *actually* seeing things that weren't there.

But Cam continued to peer at him over the tomatoes—continued to hold his lips in that irresistible, exhilarating smile—and Elliot knew he was powerless to say no. "Alright," he said. "I really hope she shows up."

⁂

They finished the harvest a little after one in the afternoon and rode their bikes into town. Cam's was a shiny new hybrid that cut across the asphalt like a speedboat over calm waters, and Elliot had to pedal with more effort than usual to keep up on his too-small mountain bike. They bought sandwiches in flimsy triangular packages from a convenience store and ate them under the shade of a massive oak outside the Haverford Free Library, then locked their bikes and went inside.

Against the heat of the outdoors and the thin sheen of sweat that glistened on their faces and arms, the air conditioning inside the library hit like an arctic blast. Shivering, Elliot led the way to the periodicals section on the second floor.

As they walked past the Reference Desk, the attendant raised her eyes and smiled. "Back for more research?"

"Yes," Elliot replied. "Just have to double-check one thing. Thanks."

"Well, you know where to find it."

They reached the ancient computer console, and Elliot prepared to sit but paused when he felt a hand on his shoulder.

"Stop," Cam said. "Let me do it."

"Okay—"

"Well, I figure that way you won't see it. Then if I don't see *her*, she can tell you what the headline says, and you can tell *me*, and then we'll both have our proof, right?"

It was a good idea. "Alright," Elliot said. "I won't look."

"Nope. Not good enough. You'd better wait outside."

"Ha! Don't you believe me?"

"No, that's the thing. It's all *about* believing you. Go on, I'll be out in a minute."

Smiling, but reluctant, Elliot turned away and felt their separation immediately. Acute. Devastating. He wandered through the periodicals, down the stairs, and back into the heat of the afternoon.

True to his word, Cameron emerged minutes later with a folded piece of paper in his hand. He tucked it neatly into the pocket of his shorts and nodded. "Alright, let's see what little Sofia has to say."

Elliot leaned his bike against the usual sapling and stepped away so Cameron could do the same. He lifted his shirt to wipe the sweat from his forehead and blushed through the heat already coloring his face as he felt Cam's eyes on his bare skin. He dropped the shirt back down, smoothed it, and sighed. "It's so humid today."

Cam looked through the saplings toward the meadow and sky beyond. Clouds were gathering in the distance—inky, churning, the color of a stormy sea. "Maybe after that rain, the heat will break. We're going to get caught in it, aren't we?"

Following his gaze, Elliot nodded. A thick haze hung above the meadow, and at the far edge, the tall trees shimmered and swayed—an optical illusion viewed through the lens of hot, heavy air. "Probably," he said. "It won't be the first time I waited out a storm here."

Cam started to walk through the low trees and tall weeds, pushing wood poppy and bluebells out of his way, sidestepping ferns and small, thick patches of grass. Elliot stayed back, watching, and as Cam drew closer to the old farmhouse, he slowed. Finally reaching it, he placed a hand gently on the wooden rail of the porch steps, stained green with lichen and the algae that bloomed within the ever-damp wood. Turning, his expression unreadable, he looked at everything and nothing.

Elliot followed, his voice barely above a whisper. "What are you thinking?"

Cameron shrugged. "You know, I've never been here?"

"Never?"

"No. My grandfather hated this place—probably still hates it, though who can say what he even remembers now, the dementia has gone on so long. My dad was born in the 70s, so this place was long gone by then. And I guess it was probably the memories. Knowing what happened here—I guess I can't blame them for never bringing me."

"It's almost too bad, right?" Elliot asked. "This place was in your family from its beginning. Too bad the way it ended has to obscure that legacy."

"Yeah. I mean, it doesn't have to. I'm here now, and maybe if—I don't know—if all this turns out to be real, I'll be able to see it differently." He sat down on the second step.

Elliot folded his legs down beside him. "I wish I could see it the way it was, you know? Like Sofia sees it."

"I should take you to see my Aunt Kathy. She's the only one apart from my grandfather who might remember it at all. She's his oldest—from his first marriage, before my grandmother—and she was pretty young then I think."

"That would be good. She'd have known Sofia?"

"I guess. Maybe? But if I do, don't call her Kathy. She hates that. Ever since she went into politics its Kathryn now. Even with family."

Elliot's eyes widened. "Politics? Wait—Kathryn? Is

your aunt Kathryn Locke?"

Cameron chuckled. "One and the same. Mayor of Haverford. Up for a second term this November."

"Wow, you guys really do own the town."

Cameron crossed his arms and scowled. "I hate when people say that."

Elliot shivered. The body language was too similar—too like Sofia's. "Sorry."

"No, it's alright. My grandfather worked hard, and he had a lot of kids. I mean, I know how lucky we are, I just—you know. It sucks sometimes when people assume things about you because of your name."

Elliot didn't know, but he nodded anyway. He pulled his phone from his pocket and checked the time. 2:58 pm. "Well, hopefully, any minute now—"

He stopped short when he saw her, smiling, skipping through the saplings as though they were made of air. And indeed, perhaps to her, they were. His body stiffened.

"Elliot?" Cam asked. "What is it?"

"Can you see her?"

Instinctively, Elliot reached over and grasped Cameron's hand. The other boy gave no resistance—opened his fingers and weaved them through. The delicious shock of their skin touching was as electric as ever to Elliot, but as Cam quietly gasped, any thoughts of their mutual attraction were forgotten. Elliot's heart swelled because he knew from the sound that all of it was true. Standing two feet in front of them now, Sofia placed her hands on her hips and cocked her head to the side. "Elliot, you brought another boy from the future?"

He nodded, slowly. "Sofia, this is my friend Cameron."

He looked at their hands, interlaced. Cam was gripping hard—too hard. "Cam, can you—let go for a minute?"

Slack-jawed, Cameron let go, and Sofia squealed with delight. "Elliot! He disappeared!"

Elliot looked at Cam. "Can you see her still?" When Cam shook his head no, too dumbfounded to speak, Elliot interlaced their fingers. "How about now?"

"Hey!" Sofia squealed. "That's a neat trick. I see him again."

Elliot laughed. "Yeah, some trick, huh? Well, um, Sofia, you're right on time. Did you—uh—did you see the newspaper?"

She nodded, squared her feet and lifted her chin. "Yes. The headline said *Local Crooner to Perform at Essex Fair.'* I don't know what a crooner is, though." She waited expectantly. Then, "Did I do good? Do you believe I'm not a ghost now?"

Elliot turned his gaze to Cameron, whose tanned face had gone ghostly white. With his free hand, Cam reached into the pocket of his shorts and removed the folded paper from the library. Still dumbstruck, he handed it to Elliot.

LOCAL CROONER TO PERFORM AT ESSEX FAIR IN SEPTEMBER

He leaped from the step up onto his feet, breaking the bond with Cameron, and cheered. "Sofia! Sofia, it's true. You *are* alive! Sofia, you—"

Cameron stood and slowly took his hand, reigniting the connection. "Elliot," he said. "She's alive but—in a few days..."

The flood. The murders. The image from the front

page of the paper in 1959. The reality came crashing down upon him, hard and fast—a roaring river, not of water, but of realization. In the distance, across the meadow, the first crack of thunder announced the impending storm in no uncertain terms.

He looked at Cameron. "We can save her. Cam, maybe that's what all this is about. Maybe we can save her."

Cam nodded, still overcome by disbelief. "Maybe we can. And her parents too."

Lip quivering, Sofia looked up at them in fear. "Elliot, you're scaring me. Save me from what?"

"Sofia, I believe you now. I trust you. This is *very* important. Can you trust me too?"

"Yes, but Elliot—"

"No, Sofia. Please. You have to listen to me very carefully—"

≈

Thirsting—hungry-eyed—Destin watched the waiter approach. "Will there be anything else at the moment?" he asked as he gently set the Negroni on the table.

She shook her head as she slid her thumb down to refresh the inbox on her phone. Things were taking too long. She reached for the glass and raised it to her lips as the inbox returned no new messages.

It was the coin's fault, surely. Her influence had been waning steadily—ever since her last stay in Massachusetts all those years ago—but this most recent drop in its potency was alarming. She'd had enough to cause the girl to quit her job without notice, meet the trucker in the bar, and head off with him on his long haul to Florida—enough to spark that *love at first sight* from three thousand miles away—but now, nothing? She'd never understood exactly how her abilities worked, but they'd never been as weak and unpredictable as this.

She sat back against the supple leather of the booth and looked around at the opulence of the hotel bar. What a shame to trade all of this—the vibrancy of Boston, despite its small size—for the downright rustic, provincial nature of Haverford. She shuddered.

Perhaps Guillaume had been right all those years ago. Perhaps she should leave it be. Perhaps it was out of their hands and always had been. A shame to consider that one's life work might've been a futile endeavor from the outset.

From out on the street, a low howl—a sound imperceptible to ordinary human ears—disagreed. Indeed. Best not to discount herself—her *purpose*—just yet.

She sipped the bitter Negroni and sighed inwardly. Tomorrow she'd go to Haverford and see what her influence could still accomplish. Closing her eyes, she prayed for a speedy outcome to the present situation—prayed to the same old deity that hadn't answered her in centuries. When she opened them, she expected to feel a sense of peace, but instead found an emptiness inside that was all too familiar.

She shrugged and took a deeper sip of her drink. No sense in fighting one's nature—one's purpose. Haverford tomorrow. She drained her glass, and as she waited to catch the eye of the waiter—*another please*—she was consumed by a single thought.

Where the hell was Guillaume?

Part Two - Sofia

Chapter Six

August 13, 1959 - Thursday

Silent behind the tall fronds of fragrant fennel, Sofia watched the cat. The cat watched the vole. Ears turned back, he pointed his tail and began to shift his legs, back end moving side to side with anticipation. The cat got low, lower, and then—*pounce*!

Sofia jumped up from the muddy path between the rows and squealed with delight. "You got him, Franklin! Good kitty." The cat turned, regarding her with eyes that quickly shifted from surprise to pride. With the prey still between his teeth—already limp with fear or paralysis—he sauntered away to enjoy his spoils.

She'd let him be, she decided. A shame. She'd enjoyed the hunt, and now she wondered what else there was to do on such a gray afternoon. Mama said she had too much energy to be in the house, and Papa was too busy washing the vegetables the farm hands were still bringing in from the fields, so she had to make do with the cat. But now—

Across the field, she heard the sound of tires on gravel and smiled as she saw Uncle George's pretty salmon-colored car pull up toward the house. When he'd first bought it last year—brought it around so Mama and Papa and Nonno could see—he'd said it was called a Galaxie, and that made sense. Long and sleek, with taillights that looked like rocket burners, Sofia imagined it was a spaceship disguised as a car.

Uncle George climbed out, slamming the door hard, before stomping up the steps to the house. Sofia watched as he went in, and then a moment or two later came out again. She could see—even from all the way across the field—that he was breathing hard. His belly was growing, and Sofia chuckled. Maybe if he spent a little more time farming, he'd be nice and thin like Papa—not so out of breath. She continued to watch, and George continued to stomp. Down the steps. Off to the left. He was going straight for Papa and the wash house.

Something about his gait—the urgency with which he trudged across the field—made her shiver against the warm, damp August air. Uncle George was usually grumpy—at least since Nonno died in the early spring—but today, he looked angry. She wondered if Papa was in trouble, and wished she was brave enough to protect him. But Uncle George wasn't a mean man or a violent one, so she probably shouldn't worry.

Still, if Papa was in trouble, surely there was something she could do to help. And she *could* be brave, she remembered. Reaching one hand into the pocket of her denim dress, she felt Nonno's lucky coin, cool against her fingers. It will protect me, she thought, and started to run across the field.

Her tiny feet were sticky with mud, and it was slow-going, but that was alright. As she got closer to the wash house—Uncle George was inside now, and she could hear him arguing with Papa—she thought of the cat. She slowed her feet, and instead began to slink on tiptoes like Franklin might do. Wiggling her jaw, she imagined herself as the cat. Ears back. Tail pointed.

She reached the wash house and pressed her body tight against the outer wall, a few feet from the door. *Wait. Wait. Then, when the time is right—*

The gravity of George's voice stayed her. There would be no *pounce*. Not today.

"...And I had to hear about it second hand? They're drowning in the fields, Robert," George bellowed from the other side of the wall. "Listen, I'm not saying you're not doing everything you can, but the time has come. You can leave all this behind. Move into town and get a nice, respectable job that won't put you in the ground like our father."

Papa spoke up. "One bad year isn't going to sink us, George. Our father worked this land for forty years, and the Wrights before him worked it for sixty. Do you think this is the first wet summer Haverford has seen in a century? Father would never have sold."

"Maybe not, but this was *his* dream, not mine. And if you don't mind my saying, I don't think it's yours either."

"Well, you never were much interested in getting your hands dirty, George. Even so, I can't figure how you think it's the right or honorable thing to sell our family home."

"Right? Honorable? Robert, we stand to make a *fortune*. Boston is bursting at the seams, and anyways, no one wants to live in the city anymore. Suburban life is no longer the future. It's the present. It's here. Listen, all these new developments get fancy names, and we could have a say in that. Call it *Calisti Acres*. Call it whatever the hell you please, but we have to sell."

"That's your opinion, brother, and you're entitled to it, but father left the larger share to me, and I'm of a mind to think it was to prevent this sort of thing from happening."

"Well, I'm of a mind to remind *you* that while that may be so, this farm is still my inheritance too. I'll be goddamned if I'm going to let you lose it all because of some goddamned soggy tomatoes."

There was silence for a moment, and then Papa spoke up. "I'll buy you out, then."

George laughed, and it wasn't a jolly, funny, happy sort of laugh. "You can barely afford the taxes."

"We'll make do. Margaret and I are thinking about taking on a boarder. Fifteen dollars a week."

"You're off your head. You'll never get it. And anyway, you talk about right and honorable, but you'd let out a room to any Tom, Dick, or Harry?"

"We'll see what I can and can't get," Papa said.

"We'll see, alright. I'm meeting with a developer and I'll be back with the plans. You'll see." His voice calmed. "I don't like to argue with you, Robert, but this isn't over yet. It's really for the best."

"If you don't want to argue, I suppose you'd better go then, George. Unless you're going to lend a hand. I've got a lot of work to do."

"By all means then. Don't let me stop you. I'll be going."

Realizing she'd stayed too long, Sofia looked around for a place to hide. Eavesdropping was rude—she knew it—and if Papa found out, he was bound to be cross. There was a raspberry bush at the corner of the washhouse, and she started to slink toward it, but then Uncle George rounded the corner, and it was too late.

"Hey!" he shouted at her. "What are you doing?"

Lip trembling, she turned her eyes up to her uncle's ruddy face. "Hi, Uncle George. I was pretending to be a cat."

He laughed—the same, mean laugh. "A cat, or a spy? Didn't your Papa tell you it's rude to listen in on conversations that are none of your beeswax?"

"Um—"

"Well, go on then. Scram!"

She didn't need to be told twice. Turning on her heel, Sofia sprinted—despite the mud—and didn't stop until she was safe amid the fennel. She kneeled down—bare knees in the dirt—and grasped the coin in her pocket. Protect me, oh please, protect me, she thought, imagining Uncle George as a ferocious dragon.

It was sort of a joke though, wasn't it? As she continued to imagine George—enormous, scaled, breathing fire—she fought the smile threatening at the edges of her mouth. She didn't know anything about selling a farm, and she sure didn't know what a *boarder* was, but of one thing she was absolutely certain: Uncle George was a grumpy man, and yes, mean sometimes, but he was family.

He'd never hurt her.

Across the field, she heard his car door slam, and then the soft grinding of gravel as he backed out of the drive. She waited—counted to fifty to be sure he was really gone—and then started the slow walk back toward the house.

When she got closer, she noticed a boy sitting on the floor of the porch. He stood slowly and walked toward the living room window, and Sofia marveled at his strange clothing—small, plastic-looking shorts damp with sweat, and a bright green-and-yellow shirt that clung to his body. But the clothing wasn't the only thing that was strange. Sofia turned her face to the sky, thick with clouds, and then back to the boy.

His sandy hair *glowed*—like he was bathing in sunlight.

The boy pushed hard at the window, and Sofia shook her head. What kind of robber was dummy enough to try stealing in the middle of the day—wearing bright green and yellow—while Mama was inside? He must've realized what a stupid idea it was because, after a couple of tries, he gave up and trotted down off the porch. Still facing the house, he started walking to the left, and then stopped, right in the middle of the patch of flowers she and Mama had planted in the spring.

Enough was enough. Suddenly furious at the fate of her flowers, Sofia marched forward and planted her hands on her hips. She cleared her throat and shook her head. "What do you think you're doing?"

The boy turned, startled, and she could see the fear in his gray-green eyes. He sputtered. "I, uh—sorry, I—"

"Why are you standing in the middle of my nasturtiums?" When he didn't move, she felt the rage building, and then a touch of fear. What was *she* doing? Uncle George surely wasn't dangerous, but this strange boy? Her little body began to quake. "Get out of my flowers, you bully."

≈

Forty miles to the south, Guillaume's chest heaved as his lungs flooded with the thick, stale air of his cramped office. As his shoulder blades pressed back against his chair—dug into the sharp edges of the wooden back—his hand began to tremble, etching ink from the pen he was holding across the page in front of him like a seismograph. His breath held of its own volition.

One second. Three. Ten.

Then, on the crest of a euphoric wave, it released, long and slow. He smiled as he shuddered, then leaned forward with a little laugh.

This was the moment he'd anticipated—even dreaded—for decades. It was forty-six years in the making, and here it was, at last.

The Chronicum coin was awake for the first time since that fateful night in 1913 on the pier in Palermo. The night he'd given it to Stefano Calisti.

He set the pen on top of the open notebook on his desk, then pushed against the chair, feeling its legs slide easily across the tracks they'd indented into the floor over so many years. He stood, stretched, and walked toward the tall, paned window that looked down onto Marlborough Street, and Boston's Back Bay beyond.

It took only a moment of gazing at the brick sidewalk three stories below to be able to focus his gifts. The connection with the Chronicum coin was clearer than it had been in decades—stronger now that it no longer slumbered—and as he listened to its unintelligible voice whispering to him across the miles, his vision clouded.

The young girl. Stefano Calisti's granddaughter. He could see her now—frightened and confused. And there was another figure, ethereal, a young man who somehow didn't belong. His presence was thin. Made of air, or—

Something about this was all wrong. He listened harder—beyond the watery voice of the coin—and heard the young girl's words, defiant now.

"—better get out of here, Mister, or I'm going to call my—"

The boy answered. "Where *are* your parents?"

The conversation faded in and out until Guillaume flinched as the girl shrieked. The boy raised his hands in the air and sat gently on the ground. "Am I sitting in your flowers? My name is Elliot."

"S-Sofia."

"Maybe I'm your imaginary friend."

"Of course he's not there, Mama. He's my imaginary friend." The girl—Sofia—reached into the pocket of her dress and pulled out the Chronicum, holding it so the boy could see. The boy's eyes widened, and suddenly he looked unwell.

Guillaume felt his stomach begin to twist. There was something about the boy's expression and a nearly imperceptible move of his arm toward his waist. That's when Guillaume noticed the slight weight at the top of the boy's odd-looking shorts. Impossible, and yet—

It appeared the boy—Elliot—possessed the Chronicum as well, tucked inside a waistband pocket. As Elliot turned cautiously and started away, Guillaume heard Sofia's voice one more time.

"Nice to meet you, Elliot...Come back soon."

With another shuddering gasp, Guillaume felt the vision dissolve and leaned forward with his hands on his knees.

Impossible, and yet—

He stood straight and looked around the stale office, covered in its perennial sheen of dust. For more than forty years, he'd waited, toiling away in this tiny room. His sanctuary during this long intermission.

With more than a little pang of regret, he acknowledged he had no choice now but to leave it. If he knew the coin had awakened, surely Destin did as well.

≈

Later in the evening, Sofia scrunched her shoulders as Papa tucked in the covers. Her eyes passed calmly over the blue wallpaper with the little white-and-yellow flowers that covered the wall, now set in the soft glow from the lamp beside her bed. Here in her room, high up on the second floor, everything was safe and good, and right. Franklin was already sprawled at her feet, and she could hear his tiny cat snores—little wisps of air, in and out.

Her eyes were heavy as Papa leaned over the bed and kissed her softly on the forehead. "I love you, my Sofia," he said and stood to go.

She turned her head and saw the glint of Nonno's coin on the table by the lamp. "Papa?" she asked. "What's a *boarder*?"

His face lit with surprise, and when he curved his lips into a conspiratorial smile, she knew he wasn't going to be cross with her after all. "I wonder—wherever did you hear a word like that?"

She giggled. "I was pretending to be a cat. Uncle George said I was spying, but I promise I wasn't."

"I believe you, my love." He paused. "A boarder. Hmm. A boarder is a person who pays money in exchange for a room and meals in a house. You know the farm is having a hard year, don't you?"

She nodded. "Yes. Because Nonno died?"

"Well, that didn't help, but no. Too much rain. Don't you worry about that though, *mia bella Sofia*." She smiled because she loved when Papa called her this—a little of Nonno's Italian with English, the way Nonno himself had done. Papa smiled too and then continued. "Your Mama and I are going to take on a boarder because the money will help a little. He'll sleep in Nonno and Nonna's old room downstairs, the one with its own door in and out."

"Do you know him already, Papa?"

He shook his head. "No, I've placed an advertisement to run in the newspaper tomorrow. I'm sure whoever it will be, he'll be a very nice man."

"Okay." She looked over at Nonno's coin. "Papa? Can you tell me the story of the night Nonno got the coin?"

He chuckled. "Again, tonight? I told you last night."

"I know, Papa, but I want to hear it."

Leaning over, he kissed her on the forehead once more. "I think I'm a little too tired tonight."

She tried on her best frown, but then Papa scrunched his face in a mean scowl, and she broke out into laughter. "Okay, Papa. Tomorrow?"

He kissed her one last time. "Alright, *mia bella*.

Tomorrow." He turned off the light and tiptoed out of the room, and she fell asleep before she could hear him reach the bottom of the stairs.

Chapter Seven

August 14, 1959 - Friday

Sofia woke to a slow, steady rain pattering softly against the window, and knew she'd be stuck inside all morning. The gray light from outside colored the wallpaper a deeper shade of blue, and she frowned.

It had been too long since she'd seen the sun.

She climbed out of bed and dressed in clean clothes. Nonno's lucky coin went into her pocket, and she plodded down the stairs to the kitchen where Mama was already kneading the dough for bread. "Good morning, Mama," she said.

"Good morning, Sofia. I'll make you some eggs in a minute."

"Okay. Mama, can you play with me this morning? It's too wet to go outside."

Mama cooed. "Sorry dear girl, I have too much to do. But tell you what, I'll telephone little Sue's mother and ask if she can come play if you'd like."

Sofia crossed her arms. She didn't like Sue very much—she cried all the time and hated to get dirty. Also, Sue only liked to play with dolls. By comparison, hunting with Franklin—or pretending Uncle George was a dragon—was far more fun.

Then, she thought of Elliot. "That's okay, Mama. I'll play with my imaginary friend."

Mama looked up from the dough and gave her a queer smile. "Are you sure, darling? I think you'd have a lot more fun with Sue."

"Oh yes, Mama. I'm sure."

≈

Sofia had hoped Elliot would join her for breakfast, but when he didn't, she decided he must be hiding. After she cleared her plate, she ran from room to room—to Mama's chagrin—opening closet doors and slamming them closed, looking under the beds and in the hallways. She crept down into the dark, damp root cellar, and still couldn't find him.

Impatient, but still kind, Mama suggested that maybe Elliot was running an errand and would show up later. She gave Sofia a stack of picture books, and some clean paper with crayons before heading back into the kitchen.

Four books and three drawings later—Uncle George in dragon form, Franklin with the vole, Elliot in his funny clothes and sunny hair—he still hadn't appeared, so Sofia tore through the house again. Mama was losing patience now, Sofia knew, so it was a relief when the rain abruptly stopped and a few weak rays of sunlight broke through the clouds. In spite of the mud, Mama ushered her outside, and Sofia was more than happy to go.

She continued to look for Elliot but soon gave it up when Franklin sprinted past her into the fields. The chase was on.

≈

The weather held—brightened even—and after lunch, Sofia joined Papa in the tomatoes. Uncle George was right; they were drowning. With leaves twisted and shriveled, the vines strained against the weight of the heavy, under-ripe fruit. She ran ahead down the soggy row, looking for any fruit with a blush, but they were few and far between.

Winded, she paused and let Papa catch up to her. She hated the frown on his face, so she took his hand and gripped it tight. "It'll be okay, Papa. The sun's out now. It'll be okay, won't it?"

He did his best to smile, but the frown lingered. "Of course, *mia bella*. Of course, it'll be okay."

Sofia squeezed Papa's hand harder still, then looked back toward the house and stiffened with excitement. "Elliot!" she said.

"What?" Papa asked.

"My imaginary friend. I'll be back." Then, without waiting for his response, she began to bound through the sticky mud of the row, out of the field, and toward the house.

≈

On a northbound train, four miles away from reaching the Haverford Station, Guillaume gazed out the window as the trees that lined the track—pines and maples, oaks and beech—blurred into a streaked, moving abstract in shades of green. He'd closed up his apartment in the Back Bay and headed to Boston's North Station with nothing but the clothes on his back and a small valise. He found it was best to travel light, and if he later deemed his stay in Haverford would be a long one, he could always send for his things or take a brief trip back to the city.

The seat beside him was empty, and he sighed, allowing his eyes to close, then open again as he heard the first whispers of the Chronicum dance across his inner ears. Though he risked falling in too deep and missing his stop, he let his vision glaze over and listened harder. The trees outside melted away and then, blurred, watery, he could see Sofia and Elliot.

"...Sofia...Do you mind if I take your picture?"

"...What's wrong, Elliot?"

"...Did you drown...Or did someone...hurt you?..."

The girl protested, and Guillaume watched in horrified fascination as the boy removed his own Chronicum from a billfold. The gesture induced panic in Sofia, who plunged her hand into the side of her dress—surely reaching for her own coin.

"...I'm *not* a ghost!... I don't want to play with you after all..." Then she turned and fled as Guillaume's vision dissolved back into reality.

The train was slowing now, with the trees falling away as the track climbed toward the bridge over the Merrimack. He exhaled, shivering despite the oppressive warmth inside the train car. The Chronicum couldn't be in two places at the same time. While it was true other coins had once existed—perhaps still did—he knew at his very center that the coins Elliot and Sofia held were one and the same. After all, he could never mistake *this* coin for another. No one on earth knew it more intimately than he did.

As his eyes caught their first glimpse of the Merrimack River ahead, a shimmer of a thought glanced across his mind. But if he was correct—

None of this was right. None of it.

≈

Sofia's legs burned as she tore down the row of tomatoes, shoes thick with mud. Catching a rock with her toe, she tumbled forward and landed hard—little hands squelching down into soft, wet earth. Feeling hot tears on her cheeks—yet more rain for the drowning field—she pushed herself up and continued on, more slowly at first.

But then she saw Papa.

Ignoring the mud and the tears, she bounded forward and wrapped her arms around him—buried her face in the rough cotton of his work shirt. The sobbing followed. Shrill. Fierce. Inconsolable.

Pulling her closer, Papa cooed. "Sofia. Sofia, what is wrong, beautiful girl?"

Breathing. Calming. Slowly, Papa's warm arms around her stayed the passion of her wails. "E-Elliot. My imaginary friend, he-he's not my friend at all, Papa. He asked me if I drowned. He said I was a g—I was a *ghost*. Papa, I'm not a ghost. I'm not."

At first, he laughed, soft and low. Then, dropping down to one knee—cutting the height between them—he placed his hands on her shoulders and looked very serious. "Sofia. Your imagination is *so* big. And it's beautiful. A true gift. I don't want you to ever lose sight of that, but you must learn to—you cannot give in to it. Do you understand?"

"Papa?"

"Dream, *mia bella*. Dream as big as you can. But don't forget the world around you, as you have a tendency to sometimes do."

"Papa! I'm not dreaming. This is real. He really said—"

Papa, seeming to sense her hysterics rising, shushed her—hard at first, and then softly, softer. "Now then," he said. "This Elliot. He's your *imaginary* friend, correct?"

"Yes."

"Then, there is your proof. Imagination lives in the mind. So does your Elliot. You are no ghost, *mia bella*, simply a beautiful girl—very much alive—who has let her imagination run away with her. Isn't that right?"

It was very hard to argue with Papa, especially when she wanted so badly to believe him. She nodded her head and turned her lips up—weak, but honest—into a smile. "Okay, Papa. You're right."

"Good." He pulled her close once more. "Now, how about you help me look for more ripe tomatoes."

≈

As the train from Boston announced its arrival on the platform with a long, belching whistle, the conductor pushed hard to open the door and bellowed, "Haverford!" Only, it sounded like "Havifud," and Guillaume smiled—despite the burgeoning sense of worry rumbling below his skin—as he rose from his seat. Even after the four decades he'd spent in Massachusetts, he never tired of the rich and varied accents spoken by some of the locals. It was the old English, but warmer. Rustic. American.

He'd lost track of how many languages he'd learned over the centuries—further, how many dialects he'd mastered. These particular varieties of English, however—unique not only state to state, but town by town throughout New England—eluded him. It seemed if one was not born into each accent's particular turning of the tongue, it was impossible to replicate them with any convincing accuracy.

Clutching the handle of his valise with one hand, he adjusted his fedora with the other, then nodded to the conductor as he stepped off into the bright August afternoon.

As he walked toward the edge of the platform—to the steps that led down to the street—he paused to take in the landscape. The station was located to the north of the Merrimack, carved into the top of the tall hill above the river's bank, and when he turned toward the rail bridge, the view of the wide, churning water below was breathtaking. Off a little to the left, on the other bank, he could see the place the locals called *the confluence*, where another smaller river—the Pentucket—opened and emptied on its short journey to the Atlantic a few miles to the east. All around, old mills towered—red brick blazing in the sun—proclaiming the glory of a city still radiant in its decline. Industry was moving on, and the giant water wheels that had powered many of these old brick palaces of manufacturing hadn't turned in years. Still, the scene was beautiful. Majestic.

He took the steps down onto Main Street and felt an

immediate familiarity with the place—with the quaint shops, the gas lights, the old apartments with their bay windows, stacked two and three stories on top. And why not? He'd seen this all before—seen it through his connection with the dormant Chronicum coin during the years Sofia's grandfather had carried it with him—though Guillaume had never dared to come here in person.

But now the coin was in play, and so were all the old rules that accompanied after its decades of slumber. He no longer had the luxury of staying away. This was what he was made for, and he couldn't ignore the Chronicum's call.

He knew Destin wouldn't be able to either. *It's only a matter of time*, he thought, then laughed at the irony. Few linguistic devices gave him more pleasure than a double entendre. *A matter of time.* If the horrible thought that occurred to him on the train was true—and he was almost certain it was—then this was *all* a matter of time.

He walked north—away from the water—about a block, and stepped into an empty cafe with a blue-and-white checkered floor that ran throughout. Along the left-hand wall, a lunch counter was hemmed with stationary stools, seats covered in bright red vinyl, while a collection of low tables dotted the rest of the floor. Guillaume selected one of these—where a former patron had left a newspaper—and took a seat.

From behind the lunch counter, a busty waitress in a blue apron—young, pretty—grabbed a half-full pot of coffee and started in his direction. "Would you like a cup?" she asked.

"Oh, yes. Very much. Thank you."

She set down a mug and filled it. "And a menu?"

"Please."

The waitress walked away, and Guillaume picked up the paper and thumbed through until he reached the classifieds. About halfway down the page, as he'd expected—foreseen in his consideration of probable futures when the coin first awoke—he found the listing:

ROOM FOR RENT - IMMEDIATE OCCUPANCY - $15/WK

Sunny bedroom with private entrance. Meals included.

3 miles south of Haverford.

Contact Robert Calisti.

There was a telephone number listed, and Guillaume considered. It would certainly be a risk, being *that* close, and under normal circumstances, he wouldn't have entertained the idea. But the Chronicum was in the possession of the little girl—and somehow, also the young man. The rules of the game had been clear for centuries—a policy of strict non-intervention on his side—but this Sofia? What could she possibly do against Destin's tactics—her *influence*, and—worse—her otherworldly hounds?

He could take the room while still allowing Sofia her independence, couldn't he? Perhaps even his presence would be enough to ward off Destin's inevitable advances. He closed his eyes then, channeling his gift to see all the possible outcomes—weigh them—but soon enough abandoned the endeavor. This was the cost of putting the coin into play. Every time it was used, a fraction of its power dissipated into the ether—becoming a little more the fabric of everything else.

But that meant Guillaume's abilities dissipated as well. In the end, that was the point—the desired outcome of this millennia-long struggle—but it made his job more difficult.

The waitress returned with a menu. As she placed it down in front of him, he considered further. The risk *was* great, and though he was blind to the possible consequences, he figured keeping the girl—and the coin—close, was the lesser of two evils. And considering the problem of the boy—that the only plausible explanation was Elliot existed in another time altogether—there really was no alternative but to plant himself as close to them as he could get. Turning his face to the waitress, he smiled. "I wonder, do you have a telephone I could use?"

In the evening, at bedtime, Sofia asked to hear the story of her Nonno's lucky coin. Papa sighed and sat on the foot of the bed, gently pushing Franklin out of his way. The cat gave Papa an annoyed look, then shifted and curled up at Sofia's side.

"Are you sure you want to hear this story again, *mia bella*? I could read you a book instead."

"No Papa, *this* story," she said.

"Alright." He sighed, tilting his head as though he struggled to remember. Sofia fought the urge to laugh, because, like herself, Papa knew the story by heart. A moment later he gave it up and smiled as he began. "It was a very long time ago on the island of Sicily. Your

Nonno had lived his whole life in the city of Palermo, but all of that was about to change. The very next morning, he would board a ship called the *Berlin*, and sail all the way to New York.

"He knew he would spend days and days in the belly of the ship, and he was sad to be leaving his homeland, so he decided to spend the whole night walking the city. Sometime after midnight, he approached the old stone pier, and then—"

"Go on, Papa," Sofia urged.

Papa smiled. "Why don't you tell *me* the next part?"

"Okay—And *then*, a horrible howl, like from a vicious dog, filled the air. And at the end of the pier, Nonno heard a man screaming. Nonno was scared, but he was also brave. He ran down to the water and onto the pier, and then he saw—"

"You tell it so well, *mia bella*." Papa chuckled. "Don't stop now."

"No Papa, you go on. This is the scary part."

"Alright. Nonno saw a big, hulking brute of a man stumbling toward a stack of wooden crates with a long dagger that *glittered* in the moonlight. And behind him, the air shimmered. There was more howling, and growling, and for an instant, the shimmer took form. It was—"

Sofia sat straight up. "The hound!" she said. "Big and black, and evil. It turned to Nonno and showed its mouth of full, sharp teeth. Nonno was scared. He wanted to turn and run away, but then he heard another cry of terror. The big black dog vanished, and past the brute, he could see a smaller man, crouched against the big crates."

"Hmm," Papa mused. "You said you couldn't tell the

scary part. I'm not sure this is the best bedtime story anymore." He winked.

"Papa—"

"But if you lay back down, I promise I'll finish."

"Okay." As Sofia listened, her eyes grew heavy, but she did not sleep. She loved this story—loved hearing how Nonno, once a brave young man named Stefano—had fought the brute and his hound. Just as the brute prepared to plunge the knife into the mysterious man pressed against the crates, Nonno picked up a heavy knotted rope that had been laying on the stone. He swung it, striking the brute hard enough to startle him and give his intended victim the chance to fight back.

In the face of Nonno's bravery—and his well-timed diversion—it didn't take much to scare off the brute and his beast.

But her favorite part came at the end—the part where the mysterious man gave Nonno the coin in thanks and told him that he would thrive in Massachusetts. That was the great mystery of it all—how the man had known where Stefano was bound. Papa finished, and she forced her eyes open.

"Papa?" she asked. "How did the man know?"

"Know where Nonno was heading?" he said.

"Yes."

"No one knows."

"I have an idea."

"Oh, you do?"

She nodded and began to sit up, but Papa put a hand on her shoulder, and she knew to stay laying down. "I don't think the man was really in any trouble. I think it was all a test for Nonno. I think the man was waiting to see if Nonno was good enough."

"Good enough?"

"To have the coin! The mysterious man couldn't just give it to anyone!"

Papa laughed, then kissed her on the forehead. "I think, like your Nonno, you have an incredible imagination. I love you, *mia bella.* Now, you'd better get to sleep if you're going to go into town with Mama tomorrow."

She looked at her father, concerned. "Papa, do you think Nonno's story is imaginary? Like Elliot?"

He kissed her one last time and smiled. Broad. Deep. Warm. "I don't know, Sofia. But it is a *very* good story." He stood then and turned out her light. Sofia listened as he crept down the stairs and let her mind drift slowly to sleep.

Chapter Eight

August 15, 1959 - Saturday

Guillaume hadn't realized how much he missed the smell of the country. But as he stood on the edge of Pentucket Road, looking up the short drive to the Calisti farmhouse, the intoxicating cocktail of scents swirling through the humid air left him wondering why he'd spent so many years in the city. Closing his eyes for a moment, he opened his mouth in an effort to taste the landscape. From down at the river, air scented with cool, clean water—running fast and high—caressed the tongue. Hints of damp wood and leafy decay—notes of mushroom—wafted in from the thick woods north of the farm. And from the verdant, sodden fields of the farm itself? Whiff of fennel. Taste of lavender. Notes of earth and herb.

Eyes open, he pulled up his shirt sleeve to look at his watch. Three minutes to noon; right on time. He turned and walked the length of the drive, up to the steps of the porch, and rapped his knuckles against the front door.

"Mister Khoury?" bellowed a voice from the other side. "Please, come in."

Removing his hat, Guillaume turned the knob and stepped into the hall. A door to the right led into a nice-sized living room with a fireplace against the exterior wall, and to the left, another door opened into the large kitchen. A man who looked to be of about Guillaume's age—physically—stood with his hands deep in the sink, scrubbing. "Robert Calisti?" he asked.

"Yes, yes," Robert said, still furiously scouring his hands. "Please, have a seat. My apologies while I finish up—I took longer in the fields this morning than I'd thought. And you're a few minutes early, I believe?"

Guillaume chuckled as he took a seat at the low, round kitchen table, checking his watch. One minute to noon. "I pride myself on my punctuality."

"Very good." Robert turned off the faucet and dried his hands. "Forgive my rudeness." He extended a hand, and Guillaume shook it before Robert took a seat opposite. "I didn't hear your car pull up."

"Oh, no." Guillaume shook his head. "I drive very little. I prefer the exercise that walking provides, whenever possible."

"You walked here all the way from Haverford?"

"It's not so far. A little more than three miles, I believe, and it was a pleasant morning. Not too hot."

Robert furrowed his brow but nodded. "I see. Well, I'm glad you could find the place alright. So, tell me. What is it that you do, Mister Khoury?"

"Oh, Guillaume, please."

"Guillaume. Very well."

"I do a little of this, and a little of that. Generally speaking, I am a writer—an historian. Matters of antiquity—mostly the Mediterranean."

"I see. And what brings you to Haverford, then?"

Guillaume laughed. "I'd have told you it was simply a chance to escape the city for a while, but now I believe it is to breathe the air of your beautiful farm. I confess I am enchanted. In the summer, the streets of Boston are hot. They smell of rotting food and sewage, and there is nothing to do but pray a sea breeze in the afternoon will blow it all out for a few hours. I need a refuge to work for a while, and Haverford seemed close enough to home, and yet? A world away."

Robert nodded. "Well, this is an active farm, so I don't know if it would be exactly the refuge you are seeking—"

"Nonsense. As I've said, I am enchanted. I don't count the occasional noise of a tractor as a distraction—not compared to the bustle of the city."

"Alright, well—you should also know my wife and I have a daughter. A good girl—very respectful—but she has been known to cause some noise from time to time. I only tell you this because, while the room is offered on a weekly basis, we would prefer a tenant with a longer-term interest. You understand?"

"Ah, yes. As I've said, a little noise is no distraction. If you'll have me, I think you'll find I'm quite an easy tenant. Would you mind if I see the room?"

"Not at all."

Robert rose from his chair, and Guillaume followed him back to the entryway. A staircase rose up to the second floor, but Robert led him back behind this, farther down the hall, where a door waited at the end. Robert turned the knob and revealed the room beyond. Large, with striped yellow wallpaper. A modest bed sat against one wall, and a small writing desk rested against the wall opposite. Directly across from the hall, a door flanked by two tall windows opened onto the back porch—a nice, private entrance.

"This was my father's room," Robert said. "To the right of the desk, through that door, there is a small bathroom with a tub. You'd be able to come and go as you pleased, and three meals a day are included with the rent."

"Very nice," Guillaume said. "I believe this will work fine for me."

"Then I'd ask for two weeks rent in advance, with the next week always to be paid the Sunday before."

"Not a problem." Guillaume reached into his trousers and removed a billfold. He retrieved three crisp ten-dollar bills and handed them over. "I'll need to get some affairs in order, but would it be alright if I moved in tomorrow?"

Robert took the money, visibly relieved. "Yes, tomorrow should be fine."

"Very good. I'll bid you adieu then, Mister Calisti."

"Robert, please." He held out his hand, and Guillaume shook it.

"Robert then."

"Could I offer to drive you back to town?"

Guillaume shook his head. "And waste this beautiful day? No thank you, Robert, though I appreciate the offer. I shall see you tomorrow."

"Tomorrow then."

Smiling, Guillaume nodded, then turned and walked down the hallway, out the front door, and into the August afternoon.

^^^

Sofia stuck her tongue out as far as it would go, and, lips open wide, licked the corners of her mouth, pretending to be a cat. Like sandpaper, her tongue moved—scoured across her skin—in search of any remnants of blueberry. She was Franklin after the kill, savoring every morsel. Lifting her hand, she licked at the wrist and brushed it across her forehead. It was important to clean after every meal, lest her next victim smell the scent of death—

"Sofia," Mama exclaimed. "Please, remember we're in a public place."

She scowled. "Mama, cats clean after every meal."

Mama laughed. "Well, that may be so. But you're a little girl—a *human* girl—and we clean with water and napkins." Mama retrieved one from the dispenser and handed it over. "Are you ready to go?"

Reluctantly, Sofia wiped the edges of her lips with the napkin, even though there was nothing left to clean away. "Okay," she said. It was still early—after seven—but her day selling at the market with Mama left her tired. The oversized slice of blueberry pie she'd eaten after her dinner sat heavy in her belly, and she knew she'd go to sleep early.

Mama removed a few bills from her purse, placed them under the check the waitress had brought and put the napkin dispenser on top. "Alright then, let's go."

On their way out the door, Sofia did her best to step

only on blue tiles, avoiding the white, and the waitress gave a warm wave as they went out the door. There was a short walk to the farm truck, and then Sofia climbed up inside. Mama switched on the engine, yanked at the stubborn gear shift, and they started down, past the rail station, and out onto the bridge over the Merrimack. Below, the water—so high this whole summer—glimmered gold and black in the late afternoon sun, and Sofia closed her eyes, thankful for the sunny day.

She must have fallen asleep before they finished crossing the river, because the next thing she knew, the grinding of gravel beneath the tires roused her; they were home. The miniature nap had revived her, so when she saw Franklin waiting at the edge of the field, she leaped from the truck and began the chase.

She followed Franklin for a few minutes while Mama and Papa unloaded the truck, but then the cat slipped away somewhere near the parsley, and she started back toward the house. As she drew nearer, she saw him waiting, and a little shiver ran the course of her spine.

Elliot. On the porch.

She drew closer still, and he didn't notice. How annoying. It was bad enough that her imaginary friend was mean and scary. It was worse that every time she found him on the porch he seemed like he was in outer space.

Stopping a few paces in front of him, she placed her hands on her hips and scowled. She waited, but he still didn't notice, and as she continued to look, her expression softened.

He looked very sad.

Finally, she'd waited long enough, and her annoyance

returned. “Are you sad because you’re a mean boy?” she asked.

Elliot gasped and sat up straight. “You have to stop sneaking up on me.” He sighed. “Still, I’m very glad to see you.”

≋

Three miles to the north, inside the cozy room he’d taken at the Hotel Haverford in advance of his move to Robert Calisti’s farm, Guillaume felt the already-familiar tingle of the Chronicum’s visions begin to play at the edges of his eyes. He moved to the wide window that looked out toward the Merrimack and sighed at the beauty of the day’s dying light. Then, resigning himself to the flood of sounds and images to come, gave himself over to the connection with the coin.

He could see them together: Sofia and Elliot, in front of the farmhouse. Even through the watery vision, the annoyance etched across the young girl’s face was palpable. Straining his ears, he listened for her words.

“It’s 1959. Everybody knows that.”

“For me, it’s 2019. Can you look at the newspaper in the morning? Remember the headline. I’m not sure what I’ll believe anymore. But—*you*—I will believe.”

“I’ll do it. I think I have to go now, though. I’m very tired.”

Guillaume blinked his eyes in rapid succession, clearing away visions of the Calisti farm and focusing on the river outside—crimson and black against the rapidly setting sun. He turned from the window and sat heavy in the hotel room’s thinly upholstered armchair. His suspicions—worst fears—were realized. The idea that first tiptoed across his consciousness on the train the day before was now confirmed as the reality.

Somehow, Elliot existed in the future—in a timeline running parallel. Though this was hardly the first time in two thousand years the Chronicum had behaved oddly, its abilities had never manifested quite like this.

It was deeply troubling. It spoke of predetermination. The boy's existence—his possession of the coin—required that certain events occur in a prescribed order.

And that ran counter to everything Guillaume understood about the coin. It existed as a weapon—a foil to fate. Its entire purpose had always been to strengthen man's self-determination. Over millennia it had allowed its keepers to see a *possible* future—to overcome otherwise insurmountable odds. But now? This time?

Of course, the nature of time was such that *the future* was always mutable. Nothing was set in stone until it happened, so in a sense, this boy's possession of the coin *couldn't* be predetermined. So, what was this then? A strong *suggestion* of how events should unfold? The whole thing spoke of fate and smelled like a betrayal.

He wondered if Destin had anything to do with this but quickly dismissed the idea. Like his own, her abilities were fading. She could still influence events in the very near future, but even in her prime—even when they were young and new—she wouldn't have been able to influence events sixty years before they occurred. And at this point, the Chronicum had diffused so much of its energy.

Perhaps this was the end—the coin's grand finale. Maybe the extraordinary power it took to connect the girl with the boy across six decades would be enough to tap it, once and for all. Perhaps soon they could rest—he *and* Destin—adversaries no more.

Standing, he moved back to the window and pulled the curtains closed. Really, there was no point in speculating. He'd lived too long and been surprised too often to put much merit in speculation. It was better to focus on certainties.

He was certain the coin was acting in a way it had never done before. He was certain it was important. He was *certain* he'd made the right decision in taking the room to be closer to Sofia. And finally, he was *certain* Destin would be here soon if she was not already.

Somewhere in the distance, a dog howled. Long. Low. Ethereal.

Yes, he'd be seeing her soon enough.

Chapter Nine

August 16, 1959 - Sunday

Of all the days of the week, Sofia liked Sundays best. It was the only day Papa didn't work, and she loved to watch him drink his coffee all morning, thumbing through the newspaper. Mama always seemed more relaxed too, even though she did as much on a Sunday as any other day. Still, she took her time in the morning, and it wasn't until after lunch that she usually headed to the kitchen to start work on the big Sunday dinner she always prepared.

But this Sunday was different. Papa had shared his news with her at bedtime: He'd found a boarder—a Mister Khoury—and he was coming to stay this morning. After that, she'd had a tough time falling to sleep. How would he be, she wondered? A valiant knight, come to slay Uncle George the Dragon? An evil troll who made bread from the bones of little girls? Papa said he was a writer, so depending on what *kind* of writer, he could be very boring or very interesting. Mostly, she worried about whether or not he'd be kind.

Eventually, she'd fallen into a light, fitful sleep. Paper thin. Transparent. She woke early—before Mama and Papa—and with Nonno's coin safe in her pocket, she installed herself at the living room window looking out at the drive. She waited there for a while—looking for any sign of the mysterious Mister Khoury—but as she was starting to grow bored of her vigil, Mama woke up and reminded her *a watched pot never boils.*

Mama enlisted her help in the kitchen, and Papa woke up as the coffee finished brewing. They sat together at the little round kitchen table and enjoyed a feast: pancakes, fried eggs, strips of thick, crispy bacon, and glasses of orange juice. Sofia helped clear the plates, and after, joined her father in the living room as he started to bury himself in the newspaper.

She laid down on her back at his feet—Sofia the Cat—and with one paw, batted the bottom edge of the paper. At first, Papa scowled, but then she opened her eyes. Wide. Innocent. She gave her best impression of a kitty's *mew*, and Papa laughed.

"Oh, *mia bella*," he said. "My little kitten." Then he set the paper down on the floor and reached out one hand to scratch her soft belly. The trap worked, and she closed her arms and legs around him like a snare.

Snap!

"Gotcha, Papa." She giggled. "Never touch a cat's belly. It's a good thing I don't have real claws."

"A *very* good thing." She released him, and Papa stood with a wink. "Time for more coffee before I read all about the sorry state of the world."

As he took his mug and walked off to the kitchen, Sofia remembered Elliot's request and spied the newspaper laying face up on the floor beside her. *The headline*, she thought, doing her best to commit it to memory.

"Sofia," Papa called from the kitchen. "Do you want to read the funny pages?"

Got it! "Alright Papa," she said.

Soon enough it was mid-morning, and Sofia was restless. Franklin was at the front door, asking to be let out, so she took the opportunity to go outside herself. Shoes on, she turned the knob and bounded into the gray light beyond, right on Franklin's heels.

She made it only as far as her nasturtiums before she saw him.

At the end of the drive, a short man in beige slacks and a white button shirt stood, looking at the farmhouse. Draped over one arm was a jacket of the same color as his trousers, and in his other hand, he held a battered-looking valise. The fedora that topped his head shaded his face, already dark—slightly darker than Nonno's used to get in the height of summer. This was the boarder, Mister Khoury. He shifted his gaze, and as his eyes found Sofia, she felt a chill ripple through the warm August air.

But then he smiled. Setting the valise on the gravel at his feet, he raised his hand in greeting. She raised hers in return, and slow, slowly, she walked forward. Chin lifted, shoulders back, she smiled, proud and confident. When, finally, she stood before him, she held her hand straight out.

Mister Khoury laughed as they shook. "Very official," he said. "You must be little Sofia."

She nodded, enchanted by the slight accent that hovered at the edge of his speech. It was like Nonno's had been, only—a little different. Not Italian, she decided. "It's very nice to meet you, Mister Khoury. Mama and Papa and I were expecting you."

He laughed. "And what a reception I've received. But please, you shall call me Guillaume."

"GEE—OHM? That's a funny name."

"It's French. Do you think it's difficult to say?"

She shook her head. "My Nonno's name was Stefano. If I can say, Stefano, I can say Guillaume."

"Ah," he said. "But can you *spell* it?"

Erupting in laughter, she shook her head. Just then, Franklin sprinted out of the field and started to weave himself through Guillaume's legs, rubbing his face against the man's trousers as he went. Sofia clapped with delight. "And this is Franklin. He doesn't like a lot of people, but he seems to like you."

Guillaume bent and scratched the cat directly on the top of his head. Franklin rolled his neck into the gesture and purred loudly for a moment before bounding off into the field. "Well," Guillaume said, "I am very honored." Retrieving his valise from the ground, he nodded. "I think I'll go see your Papa now, but I would be very happy if we could be friends, Miss Sofia."

"Yes. Friends. Very nice to meet you." She smiled once more, then raced off into the field in search of the cat.

⩰

Reluctantly, morning gave way to the afternoon, and the gray skies parted for a brief period of sun before threatening to close up again. Guillaume joined them for lunch—ham sandwiches with potato chips, and Mama's own sour pickles—but then retired to his room, saying he wanted to do a little writing. Sofia couldn't wait to get outside and make the most of the sunlight, so the moment she was finished eating, she put on her shoes and headed back to the fields.

She might have forgotten about Elliot completely, but then Papa found her near the squash. "Sweet girl," he said. "I'm heading into town to buy a few bottles of beer. You know Uncle George is coming for dinner tonight?"

She looked up from the earthworm she'd uprooted from the damp soil. "Yes, Papa."

"Would you like to come along?"

She considered a moment. "What time is it?"

"Just before three."

"No, I don't think so. Thank you for reminding me. I have to meet Elliot."

Papa laughed and kissed the top of her head. "Oh, *mia bella*. Alright, your Mama is in the kitchen now if you need anything. I'll see you soon?"

"Okay, Papa." She waited until he'd left her and covered the earthworm with soil. Then, repeating the headline she'd memorized in the morning, she started back to the house.

⩰

There was no sneaking up on Elliot this time. He was

sitting on the steps and saw her right away as she came skipping up toward the porch.

"Can you see her?" Elliot asked of no one in particular, causing Sofia to stop short. Confused, she watched as he reached his hand out to his side, weaving his fingers through the empty air. Then, the most remarkable thing happened. The light of the afternoon seemed to flicker for a moment, and suddenly there was another boy holding Elliot's hand.

The expression on both their faces was one of awe.

And this other boy? Sofia placed her hands on her hips and cocked her head to the side. There was something odd—too familiar—about him. He looked an awful lot like Uncle George, but younger. And his eyes were bright blue, like her own. "Elliot," she said. "You brought another boy from the future?"

He nodded, and she could see the relief in his body as he relaxed his shoulders. "Sofia, this is my friend Cameron." He paused. "Cam, can you—let go for a minute?"

The other boy—Cameron—vanished, and she squealed with delight. "Elliot. He disappeared."

"Can you see her still?" Elliot asked the air. When the air didn't answer, he made the motion of interlacing fingers, and Cameron reappeared beside him. "How about now?"

"Hey!" Sofia clapped. "That's a neat trick. I see him again."

Elliot laughed. "Yeah, some trick, huh? Well, um, Sofia, you're right on time. Did you—uh—did you see the newspaper?"

Squaring her feet, she lifted her chin and nodded.

"Yes. The headline said *local crooner to perform at Essex Fair*. I don't know what a crooner is, though." She waited as Elliot looked at Cameron, whose face drained of color. "Did I do good?" she asked. "Do you believe I'm not a ghost now?"

As she watched, Cameron removed a folded paper from the pocket of his shorts. He handed it to Elliot, who opened it slowly, then leaped to his feet. Cameron disappeared, and Elliot cheered. "Sofia! Sofia, it's true! You *are* alive! Sofia, you—"

Cameron appeared once more, fingers intertwined. "Elliot," he said. "She's alive but—in a few days..."

They exchanged a worried glance before Elliot spoke. "We can save her. Cam, maybe that's what all this about. Maybe we can save her."

"Maybe we can. And her parents too."

Sofia felt her lip begin to quiver as she looked up at the boys in fear. "Elliot, you're scaring me. Save me from what?"

"Sofia, I believe you now. I trust you. This is *very* important. Can you trust me too?"

"Yes, but Elliot—"

"No, Sofia. Please. You have to listen to me very carefully—"

Her tears came, fast and hot. "Elliot!" She was shaking.

"I promise. It can all be okay. I promise, but Sofia, bad things are going to happen."

Cameron interjected. "Elliot, I think maybe we're taking this too fast. I think maybe—"

"Cam, we don't have *time* to take it slow." He looked at Sofia and sat back down on the steps, taking Cameron down with him. Calmer, he continued. "I need you to be brave now, alright? Remember, I'm from the future. I've read in the newspaper and—things are going to happen very soon. Some of them you can prevent, and others you can't, but if you *listen* to me, everything can be alright."

She reached her hand into her pocket and felt Nonno's coin. Could she be brave? She nodded and set her chin. The tears stopped and she wiped her eyes. "Okay, I'm listening."

"First, there is going to be a flood. A very bad flood." Elliot shivered. "It'll wash out the whole farm, and you have to make sure you and your parents are *not* here when it happens. Do you understand?"

"Okay. A flood. When?"

She watched as Elliot appeared to do the math in his head. "The twenty-second. It's Sunday for you today?"

"Yes."

"So, that means Saturday. Six days from now."

"Okay," she said. "What other bad things are going to happen?"

He looked at Cameron, who shook his head. "Maybe it won't matter," Cam said. "If they can be away from the farm well before the flood happens—maybe we don't have to—"

Elliot nodded. "Yes. And maybe in case—maybe if we could find a way to *solve* it, we could also *prevent* it. Just in case, right?"

Sofia stomped her foot. "What aren't you telling me?"

"Nothing," Elliot stammered. "Something. Well, nothing you need to worry about right now. Just—find a way to go away on Saturday. Do you have family in another town? Relatives, you can visit?"

"No. Everybody lives in Haverford."

"Okay. We'll think of something. Just—tell your parents about the flood, alright?"

She felt the tears threatening at the edges of her eyes. "And what if they don't believe me?"

"Then you're going to have to find a way to make them believe."

"Elliot, I'm scared."

"So am I, Sofia. So am I."

Cameron pulled him to his feet. "We should go, Elliot. We have a lot to—figure out."

"Okay," Elliot said. Cameron let go of his hand and vanished. Elliot came closer and crouched down so that she was nearly his height. "Don't be scared, Sofia. I need you to be as brave as you can be."

"I'll try."

"I'm going to save you. I promise. I'll see you soon?"

"Okay." She wiped her eyes. "See you soon."

Frowning—sad—Elliot turned and walked back to his bicycle, and a few moments later, disappeared past the tall trees that flanked Pentucket Road.

Suddenly alone, Sofia felt the fist of panic tightening around her stomach. This was too much for an eight-year-old. Her tears started in earnest, spilling violently from the corners of her eyes, and alternating between whimpers and wails, she flew up the steps and in through the front door. Her vision was watery—half blind—but she stumbled her way into the kitchen. Mama was at the sink, an island of safety and comfort and warmth, and she set a course through the tempest of her grief. Mama, the lighthouse. Mama, the safe harbor.

She wrapped her tiny arms around her mother's legs

and slid to the floor in one last, final gasping sob.

"Sweet girl?" Mama said, placing a damp hand on top of her head. Warm. Safe. "What's wrong, Sofia?"

"E-Elliot! He s-said–"

Mama was kneeling down now. She put her hands on Sofia's shoulders and shook lightly. "Sofia. Sofia!" Then, softer, "Sofia. Your imaginary friend?"

"He's not imaginary. I thought he was, but he's real." Mama's fingers dug into soft flesh, and Sofia winced in pain. "Ow!"

Mama released her grip, but her body was stiff, and her face twisted. "That isn't something to joke about. If there is a stranger lurking around here–"

She shook her head. "No, he's not *here*–not really. He's in the future. He says there'll be a terrible flood on Saturday, and we have to get away because the whole farm is going to wash out. Mama, he thinks we're going to drown! He thinks–"

"Enough!" Mama stood, crossing her arms. "Sofia! Would you listen to yourself? You're absolutely hysterical. Now, take some deep breaths. Pull yourself together. There are no boys from the future. There is no flood. Once again, you've let your imagination run off with you."

She could feel heat coloring her face, and for a few brief moments, anger replaced her fear. She climbed to her feet and stomped hard. "I'm not pretending, Mama!"

Quiet. Cold. Mama's blue eyes held her in an icy grip. "Then I think you'd better go to your room until your Papa gets home."

Fine. She'd find another way. Mama was cross right now, but once Sofia could show her–prove it wasn't all in her imagination—Mama would apologize. She'd ask Elliot when she saw him—ask how he'd helped Cameron see. Mama continued to glare, hands on her hips, so Sofia turned and marched out of the kitchen, up the stairs, and into her room.

≈

Twenty minutes later, as she lay on her bed—half-dozing—she heard Papa come in through the front door. He met Mama in the kitchen, and through the thin walls, she could make out the tones of their voices as they began to argue. Mama sounded concerned. Upset. Papa was surprised, then cross. Snippets—phrases—wafted up through the floorboards.

"...Absolutely in outer space, Robert! She can't continue..."

"...Have to allow her to be a child..."

"...See a doctor? It isn't normal..."

"...And my father was entirely normal..."

"...Think I don't love her. I do, with my whole heart, but she..."

"...Maybe if there were other children around..."

"...Then *you* deal with her..."

The voices stopped abruptly, and she could hear Papa's feet climbing the stairs. Feigning sleep, she collapsed onto her belly and covered her face with her arm. The door opened and slowly, gently, Papa crossed the room. "Sofia?" he asked. When she didn't respond, he sat at the edge of the bed and placed one large, warm hand on her head. "*Mia bella,* I know you're not sleeping." Still, she didn't stir. "Alright then, maybe it *is* time for a nap. But you're not sleeping, and I know it, so maybe you'll listen to me while you pretend. Your Mama and I love you more than anything in this world, and she's sorry she's cross, but sometimes when you let your imagination get the better of you, she worries. And I worry too."

She rolled over and blinked away the tears forming at the edges of her eyes. "Papa, I promise I'm not pretending."

He shook his head but smiled. "There's my sweet girl. I promise—whatever you saw, or heard—whatever this *Elliot* said to you isn't real. There will be no flood. There is no danger. You are safe *mia bella*. Safe."

"Papa—"

He quieted her with a kiss to the forehead. "I'll hear no more about it right now. I do think a nap is a good idea. Uncle George is coming soon, and that means baby Kathryn will be here. You'll need to be rested so you can help take care of her."

"Why can't Auntie Dorothy take care of her?"

"Well, she *will*, but I might need your help. Uncle George wants to show your Mama and me some plans about selling the farm, and I agreed to listen. I thought maybe it would be nice if you could watch the baby while we talk."

She bristled. "Are you going to Papa? Are you going to sell?"

He kissed her and smiled. "No, *mia bella*."

"Then why are you going to listen to his plans?"

"Because sometimes, when you love somebody, you do things you don't always want to do."

She seized the moment, "So, since you love me, maybe we can go away on Saturday so we're safe from the flood? Even though you don't want to?"

Papa laughed. "Maybe. But it's only Sunday. Let's wait to see what else your *Elliot* may have to say between now and then. Yeah?" She nodded. "Now, get a little rest. I'll wake you when Uncle George gets here."

"Okay, Papa." He kissed her once more, then stood and walked out of her room, closing the door behind him.

Chapter Ten

August 17, 1959 - Monday

Guillaume pushed the wicker chair all the way to the wall of the house. It was far enough that when he took his seat, the slow, misting rain that danced down through the air missed him by inches and instead kissed the wood of the porch at his feet. He'd have preferred the view from the front of the house looking out on the fields, but the lush forest that stretched endlessly before him would do. He took a sip of the rich, black coffee Mrs. Calisti–Margaret–had given him, and sank into the chair.

Enjoy these moments, he thought, these last days of quiet. If what the boy told Sofia was true–if an imminent flood was the event that had roused the Chronicum from its slumber–he had only a few days to decide how to proceed. Normally, there'd have been no question. Non-intervention was the rule. But Sofia was only a child. The coin had never acted on behalf of a child before.

And the idea of a parallel timeline bothered him as well. Of course, the coin had the ability to shape fate—control an outcome. After all, it had been cast in part from the blade of that old, forgotten deity. But its *purpose* had been Her undoing—to put destiny back into the hands of humankind. The existence of this boy in the future—that Elliot lived in a time when Guillaume's present was his past—betrayed everything about how Guillaume understood the coin to operate. It was the very definition of predetermination, which the Chronicum's sole responsibility was to protect against.

Did that mean he was to fail—that Destin would finally triumph over him after more than two millennia? Was this strange aberration somehow her doing? He reminded himself that she'd never been powerful enough. It was impossible, and yet—

In the far distance, back toward town, he could hear Destin's hounds howling, though he knew they were audible to his ears alone.

He knew it meant she was here.

Closing his eyes, he exhaled. *Enjoy these moments.* He'd had over two-thousand years of *moments*, and it was sobering to realize that these could be among his last.

Guillaume opened his eyes to find Franklin the cat rubbing against him. He laughed and reached forward to scratch the cat's head as Sofia appeared around the corner of the porch.

"Good morning," he said.

"Franklin likes you," she responded.

"Yes, and I like Franklin." She looked sad, tired. "Are

you...well?"

She shrugged, then sat on the floor of the porch beside him, folding her legs beneath her. "I think you're a nice man Guillaume, so you should go stay somewhere else."

He laughed. "If I'm so nice, why do you want to be rid of me?"

"There's going to be a bad flood. You're not safe here. Mama and Papa don't believe me, but I know. You probably don't believe me either, but at least I told you."

"Now then, you should not assume what I do and do not believe."

Her face lit with excitement. "So, you *do* believe me?"

"I didn't say that, exactly. What if we say—I'm *open* to the idea."

She considered for a moment, then nodded. "Alright. Well, you should go then."

He crossed his arms and set his expression into what he hoped was a very serious frown. When she laughed, he knew he hadn't succeeded. "And what about you? Why haven't you packed your things to go?"

"I have to wait for Mama and Papa to believe me."

"Are you scared?"

She nodded. "Yes, but not as scared as I was before."

"And why is that?"

"My friend Elliot. Everyone thinks he's imaginary, but I know he's not. He's going to find a way to save me. Oh, and I have my Nonno's lucky coin. It will protect me too."

Guillaume considered—weighed the possible outcomes. Finally, he decided it was worth the risk. "Your Nonno had a lucky coin?" he asked.

"Yes." Reaching a hand into the pocket of her denim dress, Sofia leaped up and revealed the Chronicum in her open palm.

Last chance, he thought. But the coin was calling to him, and he knew he was powerless to resist. "Ooh. It's beautiful. Do you mind if I hold it?"

She shook her head and placed it squarely into his hand. It was too easy. She was too trusting. If he'd been Destin—

As the familiar weight of the coin and its scythe emblem pressed into his palm, a feeling of euphoria passed through him. Swift. Violent. The coin was vibrating—straining—and though he knew the vibrations were imperceptible to the girl, he could feel them rattling straight through to his toes. In all his years—all his interactions—the coin had never behaved this way. A sharp edge of worry began to encroach on the euphoric pleasure of the reunion, but the coin felt his thoughts and pushed them away.

He closed his eyes and listened—allowed it to communicate with him in its strange language of feelings and suggestions and ideas.

Safe, it seemed to say. *Good, necessary. Trust.* He saw Sofia's face, then Elliot's. He felt an overwhelming sense of love—a bond forming across sixty years. *Necessary.*

Guillaume formed his own thought—phrased it as a question. *Why*?

The coin responded with silence. He saw nothing, just black. He knew better than to ask why it worked the way it did, or how. He tried once more. *Is this the end*? His body tensed, and his heart filled with uncertainty.

Either the coin didn't know or wouldn't say.

His mind filled with the image of Sofia's face. *Protect.* But what? Sofia? The coin itself? The Chronicum remained silent, and the euphoria faded. He opened his eyes and found Sofia watching him, expectantly.

"Guillaume?" she asked.

He looked at the coin in his hand and wondered if it was better to stand up right now and run. She'd given it to him; it was his until he relinquished it. Destin would never be able to wrestle it away from him—he could protect it in a way Sofia never could. He could find another recipient—an adult—better equipped to handle the danger.

But, no. The coin's message had been clear. For better or worse, Sofia was to possess it: *Protect.* Slowly, reluctantly, Guillaume placed the coin back into Sofia's hand and said the necessary words. "It is yours."

She gave him a quizzical look. "Of course it's mine."

Overcome with a great sense of urgency, he placed his hand on her shoulder and filled his voice with gravity. "Listen to me now, Sofia. You're right, and this coin is *very* special. More than you know. There are people who may wish to take it from you, and you must guard it. Do you understand?"

Slowly, eyes wide, she placed the Chronicum back into her pocket. "How do you know that?"

"I've seen many things in my time, young lady."

Her shoulders slumped. "But it's supposed to protect *me*—that's what Nonno said when he gave it to me. How am I supposed to protect *it*? I'm just a little girl."

"And it *will* protect you. Listen, I'll tell you a secret. There's a trick."

"Okay—"

"No one can ever take it away from you. You must *give* it away, as you gave it to me. Understand?"

She nodded, then turned her lips up into a suspicious grin. "Guillaume, did you know my Nonno?"

In spite of himself, his eyebrows lifted in surprise. "And why would you ask me that?"

"Because I think you did. I think you gave him the lucky coin when he was still in Italy. That's how you know so much about it."

He laughed but swallowed hard. "And I think you have a beautiful imagination."

"Why does everyone say that?"

"Because it is the perfect thing to say when you cannot believe what you've heard." He winked, then touched her lovely, curly dark hair. "Now, you and I can speak more later. In the meantime, I'm afraid I have some things to think about. Why don't you and Franklin go off and play in the house where it's not so wet?"

Shrugging, shoulders slumping, she acquiesced. "Bye, for now, Guillaume."

"Bye for now."

⁂

By the early afternoon, Guillaume was restless. He'd moved from the porch to his little room, back and forth, over and over again. All the while, in the distance, the howling of the hounds taunted and teased. Ordinarily, he wouldn't have considered sparking a confrontation with Destin, but these circumstances were far from ordinary.

He could still feel the weight of the Chronicum in his

hand—the coin's almost violent vibrations. It seemed to be working harder than it had ever done—perhaps straining in its nearly-exhausted state to maintain the connection with the boy in the future. *Trust. Necessary. Need.* The more he considered, the more he remembered the futility of questioning the coin's motives—better to ask the earth why it turns or water why it's wet. The coin was still on his side—that much he knew—and his role was to do its bidding.

Perhaps if Destin knew—if she understood the gravity of the coin's atypical behavior—she might finally be convinced to give all this up.

A brief break in the rain offered his window of opportunity. He'd find her. Today.

Forgoing his jacket—the air was a thick blanket of August haze—he donned his hat, slipped out the front door, and turned north at the end of the drive to begin the long walk into Haverford. Beside him, a slight breeze off the Pentucket carried with it the sound of the normally-docile river's roar. Still, the breeze did little to cool him against the oppressive afternoon air, and by the time he reached town, his shirt hung heavy with dark rings of sweat at the chest, back, and underarms.

The ethereal, canine siren song was almost deafening now. He could tune it out—had learned to do so before—but he needed to hear it for as long as he could stand. The wailing was her beacon; the only sure way to find her. As he started onto the bridge over the Merrimack, he felt his knees begin to buckle. The vertigo was swift, amplified by the dizzying height of the bridge over the churning water below.

It was too much. He was falling.

Down on the pavement, he felt the warm, damp concrete through the thin fabric of his trousers. His eyes winced shut, and he knew he wouldn't be able to move again unless he could turn the sound off. The pressure between his ears pressed outwards against his skull with incredible violence. Volcanic. Tectonic. On and on the hounds howled.

He began to hum an old French *chanson*—to focus on the melody and the lyrics—and in response, the pressure started to ease. He continued, mumbling the words until he could fully open his eyes. Slowly, he pushed himself to his feet—still singing—and tested his balance. One foot in front of the other, he took a chance at whistling instead. The wailing of the canines began to ebb, and beneath the bridge, he could hear the rushing of the water. He cut the volume of his whistle and focused on the river. In the distance, the songs of birds drifted to his ears. On the far bank, mourning doves—disturbed from their half-slumber in a shade tree by a rambunctious squirrel—took flight across the river, lamenting the injustice with each beat of their wings. The high, staccato chirp of a cardinal pierced the air. Chickadees and finches sang merrily, and his ears greedily gulped up the sound.

Halfway across the bridge, he ceased whistling entirely. The shift was complete, and he wouldn't hear the wailing of Destin's hounds until he invited them in. It was a risk to operate blind—or deaf, really—but he had no choice. She was near—perhaps on the other side of the river. He'd rest a while in the cafe with the blue-and-white tiles, then turn his ears back to her beacon, if he could withstand it.

~~~

When he walked through the door, he was greeted by the same busty waitress as the day he arrived. She seated him at a table by the window and brought coffee and a menu. The coffee was rich and black, though not as expertly brewed as Margaret Calisti's had been that morning. Still, he sipped it gratefully and considered his next move. The ordeal on the bridge was sobering—another example of how his abilities were waning. Even a hundred years ago, he'd have been able to get within a few paces of Destin before the howls became unbearable. But now? She was near, but he had little way of knowing how near without subjecting himself to the torture and near-paralysis of the screaming hounds. And if the pain had been that immense all the way out on the bridge—he wondered if he could survive it this much closer.

His thoughts were interrupted when a pair of diners stepped loudly through the door. Two men. One tall, thin, uncertain. The other rotund, boisterous, overly confident. They took a seat at a table in a far corner of the mostly-empty cafe, and *rotund and boisterous* guffawed as the waitress brought coffee and menus.

Guillaume might have ignored them entirely, but something about the rotund man's laugh piqued his interest. He'd heard it before—last night, perhaps, as he took his dinner in his room. The walls of the Calisti farmhouse were thin, and Robert's brother had come to share the Sunday meal.

From behind the lunch counter, a radio played the local station. The handful of other diners chatted and chuckled and chewed. To an ordinary person, the conversation in the far corner of the cafe might've been
~~~

muddied beyond comprehension, but Guillaume was no ordinary person. He tuned his ears—still exhausted from the shrieking of the hounds—and listened.

"So, what are my options, Mister Calisti?"

"George, please. And if you wouldn't mind, I'd much prefer to call you Arthur, Mister Mulvaney. After all, if we're going to be doing business, I find a more personal connection to be the better approach."

"Sure. Fine. I suppose I'm curious what you've got to do with the financing."

"Well, the truth is, Arthur, I'm in the business of making my clients happy. Often times that means doing research to make sure things go smoothly, you understand. It's terrible, this business in Boston. Of course, Haverford could use a detective of your caliber, but I understand you took an awful cut in your pay to come here."

The thin man bristled. "I'm not sure what that's got to do with anything, Mister—uh, George."

Rotund and boisterous—George Calisti—guffawed. "Well, the financing, of course. I want very badly for you to be able to buy this house. It would be tough enough given the meager salary the department is paying you, but I understand you still have some—debts outstanding? Listen, I know it's none of my business, but if I was able to find out, you can bet the banks can too. The kind of thing we're talking about? Well, that could sink your chances of a loan."

"What exactly is this? I get the idea you might be threatening me, Mister Calisti."

"Please, Arthur. I asked you to call me George. In any case, no, I'd never threaten anyone, least of all an officer of the law. In fact, I'm really here to offer you a solution before it even becomes a problem. See, a lot of this business operates on favors and IOUs. I happen to know a banker who owes me one. I've filled him in on your little situation, and he's already agreed to finance you *and* take care of that debt back in Boston."

"And why would he—you—do that?"

"Like I said, I like things to run smooth. Also, consider it community service. Those aren't the kind of *debt collectors* I'd particularly like paying a visit to my little town."

"So, where's the catch?"

George raised his hands, innocent. "No catch."

"No favors? No IOUs?"

"Of course not. Now, should I ever be in need of a favor, and you be in a position to offer one? Well, that would be at your discretion. Mostly, I'd be honored if you'd refer me to your friends and neighbors, that's all. But listen, take this card—it's my guy. As an officer of the law, a detective, I'd expect you to do your due diligence. See what other banks have to offer, and then call my guy, and we'll get you that house..."

Guillaume felt a hand on his shoulder and looked up into the impatient face of the waitress. "Lost in outer space?" she asked. "Do you know what I can get you?"

He shook his head while across the cafe George Calisti stood up. "Uh, no," he said. "Nothing. Just the coffee."

The waitress shook her head and left a check. There was something about George—about the way he moved—that suggested his actions were not entirely his own.

It reeked of Destin.

After George went out the door, Guillaume pulled a few coins from his pocket and left them on the table. He counted to thirty, then stood and followed.

Outside, George was halfway up the street, walking fast beneath the gas lamps and lush maples. It had started to rain, and in the watery light, Guillaume thought he could make out a disturbance in the air behind George—a glimmer, a wavering—large and hulking and canine. He walked faster to keep pace as George—moving as though entranced—turned into an alleyway.

Guillaume stopped short, pressing himself tight against a damp brick wall near the alley entrance, and listened.

Destin's voice. Clear. Seductive. It was chilled Lillet on the tongue of the ear—cool, sweet, an autumn sunset on the French Riviera.

"No more dawdling, *mon amour*," she said. "Forget this—business of yours. Just until you've completed this business of mine. Don't you wish to please me?"

George, guttural and only half-awake, responded. "Yes. I wish to please you. But, when we're apart I—I forget."

Guillaume smiled to himself. Her influence was thin. Her abilities were waning as swiftly as his own. He listened harder, and she continued.

"Ge—orge" she lilted. "We've known each other for only a single day, and already you can forget me? Don't forget me. Please, I *need* you. Your father's coin. Don't do it for me, then. Do it for yourself. Give it to me, and I'll give you everything you've ever wanted. Every deal. Every sale. You'll *own* this town. Ge—orge. George. Don't disappoint me, please? Go. Now. Today."

From beyond the wall, Guillaume heard him whimper. This was one of Destin's powers—to inspire a desire to please that was so strong, to disappoint caused actual pain. But she was weak now. "I...can't today," George said, agony dripping from his voice. "Tomorrow."

"Fine," she said, the sultry tone in her voice replaced with ice. "Tomorrow. Now go."

Suddenly, George emerged from the alleyway and continued his lumbering march up the street. Guillaume knew the chance to act was upon him. Steeling himself—muscles tense with the anticipation of a fight—he took a deep breath and rounded the corner to the dark gap between the buildings.

Empty. Nothing. Just the fading stench of wet dog.

"Destin!" he called, as movement near the far end—the place the alley let out onto the next street—caught his eye.

Fluttering. A pigeon.

He couldn't imagine how she'd vanished so quickly. Their inevitable confrontation—their *reunion*—would have to wait for another day.

≈

After Papa switched out the light, Sofia waited until she heard his feet on the stairs before sitting up. In the dark, she reached out and patted her hand lightly across the surface of the nightstand until her fingers found the cold metal of Nonno's coin. Wrapping it tightly in her palm, she squeezed, enjoying the feeling of the rough edges pressing into her flesh.

Where are you, Elliot? She thought.

Despite the intermittent rain, she'd gone out at three,

expecting to see him. He didn't appear, so she went back inside, and tried again at four. She waited until Mama called her in for dinner, and when Mama asked what she'd been doing, she didn't say. Mama didn't want to hear about Elliot, and neither did Papa.

Truthfully, she didn't want to talk about him either—not until he reappeared, and she could find a way for Mama and Papa to see him too. But he hadn't come at all today, and now she was starting to worry.

What if he forgot about her? The flood, if it was real—if any of it was real, and not her *imagination running away with her again*—was supposed to happen in a few short days.

She'd ask Guillaume; he knew about these sorts of things. He liked to pretend—and maybe no one was supposed to know—but she was certain he was the mysterious man from Nonno's story. She saw it the moment he held the lucky coin; the expression on his face made her feel like it was alive, somehow, and that he and the coin were old friends. And maybe it was more than that, too. When Guillaume looked at the coin, it reminded her of Papa's face when he looked at her.

Keeping the coin safe in her hand, she laid down and closed her eyes. Dreams gathered at the edge of her consciousness like clouds on the horizon. Big. Building. Billowing. They encroached, and then covered.

She saw him. Elliot and—someone else she couldn't quite focus on. They were cowering in a corner, bodies shaking and tense with fear. The vision was awash with blur, and Elliot was the only point of clarity. She could see the tears on his cheeks—nearly taste their salt. A horrible, hulking shadow pressed closer to him and he tried to shrink away—small, smaller—but there was nowhere to go. Then, something else came into focus. A flash—a glint of light off metal. In a ham of a fist, a gun pointed and was eager to fire.

She heard his whimper, then the *crack* and recoil.

She screamed. "Elliot!"

Part Three - Elliot

Chapter Eleven

August 17, 2019 - Saturday

"You look fine," Cameron said. "Just relax–she's only my aunt."

Elliot scowled as he pulled at the collar of his polo, trying in vain to release the stubborn wrinkles that had formed from a year of being pushed into the bottom corner of a dresser drawer. Truthfully, it was more than the wrinkles. He felt stuffy wearing anything that deviated from his typical wardrobe of tees and running shirts. "She's not *just* your aunt, she's the mayor. And also, what if she thinks we're–"

Cam shoved him, playfully. The now-familiar electricity of their contact raised the fine hairs on his forearms and crashed through him–an ocean swell, breaking, racing all the way down to his toes. "Don't worry about that," Cam said, with a wink. "After all, we're not. Are we?"

Elliot wanted to melt into his sneakers. "Uh, no. Of course not. Let's get this over with."

"Okay." He shrugged, then pressed the bell.

A moment later, the wide front door opened, and a woman stood on the other side, dominating the threshold, despite being of only average height and girth. She greeted them with a warm smile, and the dappled light that passed through the leaves of the enormous maples in the yard danced across her short, curling silver hair. "Cameron!" she said. "I was so excited when you called." She folded him in a tight embrace, then turned her attention. "And you must be Elliot."

He shook her hand, wincing a little at the deceptive firmness of her grip. "A pleasure to meet you, Mayor Locke."

"Oh *please*. Call me Kathryn. And please, come in."

Once inside, Elliot felt swallowed by grandeur. From the street, the house had been impressive—the manicured lawn and vibrant flower beds, the long front porch, and the two-story white columns—but the opulence within caused him to catch his breath. The entry was grand, and overhead, a crystal chandelier refracted light down onto the gleaming parquet floor. Kathryn led them through—past a formal sitting room with antique furniture and expensive-looking paintings, beyond an elaborate dining room that could easily seat twelve, through the gourmet kitchen with its massive stainless steel hood over a stove on a center island, and onto a screened back porch filled with plush, padded garden furniture.

They took their seats at a round table where Kathryn had already put out a pitcher of iced tea and a tray piled high with finger sandwiches. Elliot sank into his chair—letting the cushion absorb the tension he'd been holding in his back and shoulders since they arrived—and gazed out at the lush backyard that sloped gently down to the forest beyond. There were more flower beds and a small vegetable patch. Toward the back of the property, he spied a cluster of peach trees, heavy with ripening fruit.

"Now," Kathryn said, pouring a glass of cold, dark tea, careful to keep the lemon slices that floated on top of the pitcher from escaping. "Cameron says you're interested in our family's history? That's an oddly personal thing to be researching, isn't it?"

Elliot swallowed hard. "Well, yes, I suppose. I got caught in a storm earlier this week while I was running, and I had to take shelter at your family's old farmhouse on the preservation land. I think you probably know I work with Cam at the community farm, so I have an interest in farming anyways, and I got to thinking—"

"I see. So, you wanted to know what it was like when the old farm was still in operation?"

"Partially. But then also, I found this—" He reached into his pocket, pulled out Sofia's coin, and opened his palm. "I showed it to Cam and he said it belonged to your grandfather, and then your cousin?"

Kathryn's eyes widened, and with great reverence, she lifted the coin from Elliot's hand. Turning it over and over between her fingers, she exhaled long and slowly. "How remarkable. My father is probably the only person alive to ever have seen this. Honestly, growing up he'd go on and on about it, and I almost doubted it was real." She fixed Elliot in her gaze. "Would you mind if I took this to him? His mind is mostly gone now—the dementia—but I'm sure if he saw this..."

He could feel the heat coloring his face, and wetness beneath his arms as his stomach twisted in panic. He'd made a grave mistake. What did he think was going to happen? He'd brought the mayor of Haverford a possibly invaluable family heirloom, and he hadn't even considered the idea she might like to keep it. Suddenly, the thought of parting with the coin was suffocating. He fought to form words—to tell her *no*; he wasn't sure he could breathe without it—but his tongue felt impossibly dry, and the words wouldn't come.

Beside him, Cameron cleared his throat. "Um, maybe another time Aunt Kathy—er—Kathryn. Elliot already arranged to show it to some experts in Boston who might be able to tell us a little about its history."

"Oh?" Kathryn half-smiled and handed the coin back. Her speed was glacial, and demeanor equally icy. "That's a fabulous idea. You'll bring it by once you've learned something, won't you?"

By the tone of her voice, Elliot understood it was a demand rather than a question. Still, relief washed over him, and he exhaled. "Oh, yes, of course." He didn't know why Cam had lied for him, but he'd be eternally grateful.

Kathryn took one of the finger sandwiches and chewed it thoughtfully. "As far as the old Wright-Calisti Farm, I'm afraid I can't tell you a whole lot. I was a baby when that horrible tragedy struck—maybe a year and a half old? After that, my father rarely went there. He had these grand plans of selling off the land and developing it, but after the flood, no one was interested in building there. Of course, it's maybe only once every couple of centuries the Pentucket swells up like that, but once a piece of land is labeled a floodplain, well, it's toxic. He sold it to the town a few years later."

"Sure," Elliot nodded. "And what about—I know it's sensitive—but what about your cousin, Sofia? I know your uncle and his wife were murdered, but Sofia—"

Kathryn bristled. "You're right, that *is* sensitive."

Cam interjected. "I think Elliot wants to know, because, you know—the coin."

"Right," Elliot said. "It's like—you find this relic, but it doesn't mean anything out of context. I guess it's had a powerful impact on me. I'm not trying to be morbid, Mayor—uh—Kathryn, but I feel this strange connection with her. Like, I need to know what happened. I promise it's good intentioned."

The mayor sank back into her chair. "So, you think you can solve a sixty-year-old disappearance?" She laughed.

"More like I'm trying to be a good historian. I want to gather all the facts and have a complete picture of this coin and the people who cherished it."

"Alright." She sighed. "I think it's an awful waste of your time, but I guess it can't hurt to tell you what I know. It's not much. See, that's something we didn't talk about. The murders were never solved—you probably know that. A friend of my father's headed the investigation—a detective Mulvaney, I think. Dad sold him a house not long after. Anyways, my Uncle Robert took on a boarder a few days before the flood, and the theory was always that the boarder committed the murders and was also responsible for Sofia's disappearance."

"Oh?" Elliot asked. "But they couldn't track him

down? Why did they think it was the boarder?"

"Well, he vanished the night of the flood. That was part of it. Then a day or two later, the detective found my uncle's truck two towns over. Dad always held out hope that Sofia had been kidnapped, because a body was never found, but, well, after the flood more than a few bodies were never recovered."

Cameron spoke up. "And this boarder, do you remember his name?"

"No. That was part of the problem. Dad met him once, but if they exchanged names, he didn't remember later. And Robert never drew up any kind of formal lease. There was no paperwork. Dad always said he was, I don't know, Middle Eastern? Or Mediterranean? Turkish, or Lebanese, or something?"

"What about this detective?" Elliot asked. "He isn't still alive, is he?"

She smiled, sad, and shook her head. "I couldn't say. He was younger than Dad, so maybe."

"Okay," Elliot said. "Thank you." It wasn't much to go on, but it was something. Perhaps if the detective was still alive—

"Now, why don't you boys relax a little and we'll talk about something else. Neither of you have even touched the sandwiches or the tea."

They lingered for another half hour, exchanging pleasantries and nibbling at the food Kathryn had provided. Then, apparently having had enough, Cam said they had somewhere to be, thanked her, and said they'd see their way out. Kathryn embraced him once more, gave Elliot another firm handshake, and wished them well.

Once they were outside, Elliot whistled. "That was—"

"Tough?" Cameron laughed. "She seemed a little put out at times, I'll agree."

"No, it's—I think she was disappointed I didn't give her the coin. I couldn't though. There was something—when she was holding it, I felt like I couldn't breathe."

"Well, there's no reason she should have it. Before today, she didn't even realize—" At the end of the path down to the street, a sleek black sedan pulled over and parked. "I wonder who *that* is."

A woman appeared around the front of the car. Tall and beautiful, with copper skin, she wore her black hair—a touch of silver—straight and long. Dark glasses shaded her eyes, but as she marched confidently up the path to the front door, Elliot could feel her holding him in her gaze. As she passed them, she brushed Elliot's arm and paused. "Pardon me," she said, lifting her glasses and turning her thin lips into a serpentine smile.

"Uh—" Elliot stuttered. "S-sorry."

She laughed lightly—only it wasn't light at all—and continued on her way. In her wake, she left an odor—faint, but despicable.

Wild. Animalistic.

Cameron looked at him, face twisted in alarm. "Want to get out of here?"

"Yes. Pronto."

≈

As Destin pressed the doorbell, she smiled at her own good fortune; a fortune, oddly enough, not of her own making. She'd been in town only an hour, and already she'd found the boy with the coin. Of course, it was an injustice she couldn't simply take it from him, but maybe this whole endeavor would be easier than she'd imagined. Not only had she found the coin, but Guillaume was still conspicuously absent. If he was in Haverford, surely she'd have sensed him already—maybe seen him. Guillaume could never leave well enough alone.

The door opened, and a silver-haired woman regarded her with eyebrows arched. "Oh, hello. May I help you?"

Destin smiled and extended a hand. "Madame Mayor? A pleasure to meet you. My name is Destin Duprée. I'm your new assistant."

The mayor cocked her head and folded her arms. "That's odd. I don't think we started interviews for that position yet."

She leaned forward and whispered, pouring all the sweet heat, passion, and desire she could muster into her voice. "It's *fate*, dear Mayor. It's *destiny*, and you shall serve it faithfully, will you not? You won't disappoint me by turning me away. I'm the one you've been waiting for."

First, confusion clouded the mayor's face, then the calm sleepy mask of surrender as Destin's voice pulled her into the trance. She blinked. "Of course. Destin! Yes. I've been waiting for you, won't you please come in?"

"Yes, thank you."

Once inside, Destin moved through the entryway as though she owned the place. Off to the right, she took a seat on a divan in the formal sitting room, and the mayor occupied a chair opposite. She looked around at the garish paintings on the walls and brushed her hand across the brightly colored, but unforgivably coarse, fabric of the furniture. Kathryn Locke—née Calisti—was her father's daughter; prone to excess, attracted to opulence, and utterly distasteful.

"So then," the mayor said, "strange they sent you out on a Saturday. I was devastated to lose my last assistant. She was with me all the way through my first term, and absolutely crucial as my reelection campaign ramps up. Of course, you're going to have to get up to speed about—"

Destin waved her hand dismissively and removed her glasses. "Who were the boys who just left?"

Kathryn blinked. "My nephew Cameron and his friend Elliot."

"I see. And why were they here?" Destin smiled as Kathryn's head dipped forward. She was under now—truly. This was always the most difficult part—the first contact. Ever since the coin started to diffuse its energy—the power stolen from her goddess—the human mind had grown steadily more resistant to her intrusions. Indeed, often it was the bigger interventions that were easier, such as the trick she'd pulled with the former assistant. Even from three thousand miles away, with enough concentration she could engineer a flat tire, tip a bartender's hand to pour heavy, spark an otherwise improbable romance with the suggestion of intimacy and a feeling of tension.

But none of that would get her the coin. That required the direct manipulation of hearts and minds. That required a devotion so inspired, it hurt. And now that she had her hooks into Kathryn Locke, she'd have to make sure they stayed there.

"Family history," Kathryn said. "They wanted to know about—my family's farm, and my cousin who disappeared, and my grandfather's lucky coin."

"The boy—Elliot. He had the coin with him?"

"Yes."

"Did you see it?"

"Yes." Kathryn blinked. "Sorry. What was it we were—"

Damn! Destin waved her hand, and Kathryn nodded. Her mind—her *will*—was fighting hard, and Destin had to acknowledge her own weakness. Normally she'd have sent Kathryn after the coin directly but with the bond between them this tenuous—

"Alright, listen to me Madame Mayor. This is important. It is imperative the coin be returned to you. As your—*assistant*—you will support my every effort to retrieve it, will you not?"

"Yes, but—why do I need it?"

She rolled her eyes, longing for the old days of dogged devotion among those she influenced. So many questions. So much reluctance. "Because if you—I—can retrieve it, I can guarantee you all that you desire. A second term as mayor? Yours without question." She thought for a moment, then upped the stakes. "And if you don't have it come election day?"

"Yes?"

"You will most certainly lose."

Kathryn shuddered. "That would be awful. Oh, awful."

"Yes," Destin lilted. "Terrible. You're going to wake in a moment, and when you do, you'll remember you chose me as your assistant the moment you saw my resumé. It will feel perfectly natural that I am here, and you'll go about your business as normal, except—"

"Yes?"

"You'll do everything I ask of you. Do you agree?"

"Yes." Kathryn blinked and looked around for a moment, disoriented. When her eyes landed on Destin's face, she smiled. "Ah, right. I was saying we'll need to get you up to speed on this campaign."

⩰

"Are you going to see her today?" Cameron asked, gazing absently down the drive to the New Colony Apartments.

It was late afternoon, and Elliot was exhausted. Perhaps it was the day spent out in the heat, or maybe the hours of finding anything to talk about except this *feeling* between them. Sure, after the meeting with the mayor they'd discussed their next moves—trying to find the detective, maybe even talking to the ancient George Calisti himself—but that was all surface stuff. Deeper down, beneath the skin, the pressure was building. Sooner or later, the geyser would have to erupt. Elliot wasn't ready, and he knew Cam knew it too.

But Cam was ready. Cameron—patient and kind. Cameron, who he'd hurt all those years ago—who'd always known, and forgiven, and waited.

Remembering himself—remembering the question—Elliot shook his head. "No, not today. I want to, but I don't think I can until I have something concrete to tell her."

"Well, what about the boarder?"

"No. We don't even know his name yet."

"Sofia might."

He shook his head. "You're right, but, the way we left it—I feel like we need more. Maybe if we can find the detective or talk to your grandfather. We have a little time."

"Right, so... speaking of... it's still early. Are you sure you don't want to do anything else?"

There were plenty of things he *wanted* to do, and not many of them had to do with Sofia at the moment. "I don't think so. I think I need to rest—decompress and process, you know?"

"What about tomorrow?"

"Yeah," he nodded. "That sounds—oh shit!"

"What?"

"I forgot I have to go into Boston with Lindsey. We're visiting her brother in Cambridge. Maybe tomorrow night?"

"Yeah," Cam said. "Alright. I should—go then?"

Elliot smiled. Weak. Sad. "Yeah, I guess."

Cameron put a hand lightly onto his shoulder and leaned close enough for Elliot to feel his breath against his face. He stayed there—waiting—for what felt like hours but couldn't have been more than seconds. Elliot froze, paralyzed, and knew the terror and desire were etched in equal measure across his face. Finally, Cameron turned his lips into that same annihilating smile and laughed. "Tomorrow," he said, turning, walking away.

Elliot watched him go, struggling to catch his breath. Beneath his skin, the pressure was building—almost painful now. Well played, Cam, he thought. Well played.

⩰

When Elliot stepped through the apartment door, Tony was waiting. "Need a cold shower?" he asked over the blaring of the television.

"Excuse me?"

Tony laughed and flicked the ashes of his cigarette into a mason jar. Leaning back into the couch, he put his feet up on the coffee table. "You're always harping on your Mom to open the damned blinds. Good thing she listened for once; hell of a show up there on the street. That your boyfriend? Hoo-eee! Hot!"

"Fuck you," Elliot said under his breath. Looking at the ground, he started to move through the living room.

Tony was up on his feet—lightning fast, blocking his path. He raised his arm, closing his meaty hand into a tight pink fist with puddles of white at the knuckles. "The fuck did you say to me?"

Chin jutting, anger rising, Elliot lifted his gaze to Tony's ugly, ruddy, twisted face. "Fuck you, Tony," he said. Louder this time. Then, involuntarily bracing, his eyes closed, and he waited for the blow. In the dark behind his lids, he anticipated the crushing and crumpling—imagined the shattering of a clavicle or the hollow gourd sound of a fist to the top of the skull. He waited and waited—an eternity in two seconds, three, four.

He reopened his eyes, and Tony was still there. The fist opened to a flat hand—large, a saucer. It came down swiftly and clapped him hard on the shoulder, then again, and again, and suddenly Tony's face twisted once more, but this time—

A smile. Self-satisfied. He laughed. "There it is, at

last. The little faggot finally grows some balls. I'm almost proud of you, Elliot." He stepped back. "I don't give two shits what you do with your life, but if you're not going to own it, this world'll chew you up and spit you out." He took a deep drag off his cigarette and blew the smoke—slow, billowing—out into the thick living room air. With a jerk of his head, he indicated dismissal. "Now get outta here, I'm busy."

He didn't need to be told twice. Without a word, he scurried past, into the relative safety of his bedroom. Collapsing on the bed, he exhaled and pressed his eyes firmly closed. *I'm almost proud of you, Elliot.* He hated it, but he was almost proud of himself, too. Rolling to the edge of his bed, he yanked open the drawer of his nightstand and pulled out the framed picture he kept there—face down, shut away, safe from the prying eyes of Tony, and the debilitating sadness of his mother.

Laying on his back, he held the picture at arm's length. A happy scene—two loving parents and their twelve-year-old son, standing in a sunny field. He looked at it as long as he could—staring, willing that reality back to life—until his vision clouded with tears and his eyes burned to blink them away. He'd give anything to go back to that day—back to a time before alcohol and the drunken hit and run, to when Cameron Calisti was still his best friend because their dads were best friends too. Back then, there was no tension between them—no years of silence and avoidance and shame. He was still a child—knew who he was with an unshakeable certainty.

If you're not going to own it, this world'll chew you up and spit you out. And who was he now, two days from his twentieth birthday? Fatherless. Motherless for all intents and purposes. Confused, angry. In love? Still ashamed. In the glass that shielded the picture, he regarded his own reflection.

I'm Elliot, and I'm going to own it. I'm Elliot and I'm—

He let his arms collapse against his chest, bringing the picture down with them and extinguishing the moment.

He wasn't ready to finish the thought.

Chapter Twelve

August 18, 2019 - Sunday

Elliot vaulted off the seat of his bicycle as the train's first whistle announced its imminent arrival. Quickly, fumbling, he shoved the front wheel into the rack, wove the chain through and locked it. He took the steps up to the platform three at a time and scanned the small crowd waiting at the top. Eyes darting left, right, left, he searched until he found her—Lindsey looking toward the track—shoulders heavy with disappointment.

The engine was pulling into the station now, slowing, six silver cars in tow. He placed a hand on her upper arm, and she whirled in surprise. "Elliot! You asshole!"

"Sorry," he laughed. "I know I'm almost late."

"What the *hell*? You said you were leaving forty-five minutes ago."

"I was." He felt in the pocket of his shorts for the cool, rough metal. Sure enough, Sofia's coin was still there;

he'd made it nearly to town before realizing he'd left it. "I did, but I forgot something and had to turn back."

"What did you forget?" The train had stopped now, and the doors slid open. She started marching forward, stepping higher and harder than usual to punctuate her anger.

He followed her onto the train, to a pair of empty seats and slid in. Pulling the coin from his pocket, he opened his palm. "Sofia's lucky coin."

Lindsey scowled, crossing her arms, but as she looked down at the coin her expression softened. Curious, she took it to examine closer. "It looks really old. What is that on the face? A sickle?"

"A scythe." The train whistle bellowed, and with a mighty jolt, the locomotive started forward.

"What's the difference?"

Elliot laughed. "Well, they both have curved blades, but a sickle is hand-held. Smaller. A scythe—that's grim-reaper stuff. It's like the size of a rake. With a sickle, the blade is usually rounder, also. See how this one has a gentle curve, and—"

She waved him off and returned the coin. "Yeah, yeah, farm boy. It's cool."

He considered as he tucked the coin back into his pocket, content to feel its weight against his leg. He turned his eyes to her face and read the incredulity. He wanted to tell her all of it—that Sofia was real, and *alive* in some parallel timeline, that Cameron knew and had seen her. He wanted to tell her that Sofia was in danger, and at the last minute he'd almost missed the train—on purpose—because he had so much to do, and spending the day with Jared in Cambridge was a distraction he didn't need right now; a little girl's life was on the line.

Instead, he looked out the window as the train crossed the bridge over the Merrimack—watched the glittering of the mid-morning sun off the black mirror of the water below.

"So," Lindsey said, "Do you know anything about it? Where it's from?"

"No. I haven't had time to even start looking. I mean, I did an image search for scythe coins, but no luck."

"You can show it to Jared."

"Sure, but—why?"

She shrugged, and for the first time since he'd found her on the platform, she gave him a genuine smile. "He knows stuff. He's really annoying like that."

⁂

The trip into Boston's North Station took about forty minutes. They transferred to the rickety Green Line trolleys and gritted their teeth, bracing against the screeching and twisting and *shrieking* of the train through narrow tunnels. At Park Street Station they switched to the Red Line, and Elliot was relieved to be on a proper train. They glided out from beneath the earth, over the beautiful Longfellow Bridge—its ornate salt-and-pepper-shaker towers standing guard above the Charles River—and plunged back beneath the surface on the other side.

When they reached Harvard Station a few minutes later, Jared was waiting for them above-ground in the square. Handsome and clean-cut, preppy and confident, he pulled Lindsey in close and kissed her forehead. Then he smiled, bright—a mouthful of too-white teeth—and pulled Elliot in as well. "Hey, guys, nice to see you. Trip in okay?"

"Yes," Lindsey said. "Except Elliot here almost missed the train."

"That would've been a shame," he said, giving Elliot a little shove. "Glad you made it."

"Yeah," Elliot said. He was uncomfortable. Jared was almost too beautiful to look at. It wasn't a matter of attraction—he wasn't interested in *that*—it was his *awareness* of Jared's beauty that troubled him. There was a pleasure in tracing the lines of his face, enjoying the curves of his broad shoulders, appreciating the form of a man—his alluring geometry—and in the end, he supposed it *was* a kind of attraction. But less to Jared the person; more to what Jared *was*.

To what Cameron was.

To what *he*—

"Man of many words." Jared clapped him on the shoulder. "Are you guys hungry? It's almost lunchtime."

≈

Jared took them to a tiny pizza place tucked into a narrow street—almost an alley—off the square. They had two large rectangular slices each, with bottles of sparkling water mixed with sweetened orange juice, and all the while Lindsey and Jared recounted their various summer adventures. Jared was working full-time in one of the libraries during the summer break and hadn't been home to Haverford since Memorial Day.

Elliot kept quiet. Listening. Eating.

The food lost its flavor, and Elliot lost his focus on the conversation. As Lindsey and her brother continued on, he found himself transfixed by the movement of Jared's lips—delicate pink lines dancing open and closed, then expanding suddenly outward into joyous, luminescent smiles.

He could imagine himself drowning in all that light.

And wasn't that exactly what he'd feared in coming here? An attraction to Cameron was easy enough to explain away when he wanted to. They'd been friends. They had a history. He could deny the greater implications of his *feelings* when it came to Cam. But Jared stirred something primal within him—a problem that couldn't be dismissed as a consequence of familiarity.

Then Jared's face turned, and their eyes locked together. There it was—the look that said *I know your secret, you can stop fighting*. "Have you—taken a vow of silence since I last saw you?" Jared asked.

Elliot swallowed, hard. "No. Sorry, just letting you two catch up."

"Well, we're caught up." He laughed. "So how about you? What've you been up to?"

Oh, the usual, Elliot thought. Just trying to repress everything you're pulling out of me right now, which is funny because there's this thing happening between me and Cam, and thanks to you I can't stop thinking about—

Lindsey cut in. "Ghost hunting." While he was relieved for the interruption of his thoughts, Elliot took aim beneath the table and kicked his foot out. "Ouch!" she cried when he hit his mark. "What was that for?"

"I'm not *ghost hunting*," he said.

Jared whistled. "Wow, sore subject?"

Elliot shook his head. Deflated. "No, it's—" he glared at Lindsey. "It all sounds crazy. At first, I thought I was losing it. I'm pretty sure I'm not, but it wouldn't surprise me if everyone else thought I was nuts."

Rolling her eyes and rubbing her shin, Lindsey sighed. "You know the Calistis?"

"Yes," Jared said.

"Elliot found this weird old coin at their farmhouse in the Pentucket Natural Area. Ever since then, he swears he's been seeing the ghost of this Calisti girl who disappeared in the fifties."

"You're right," Jared laughed. "That does sound nuts."

Elliot turned his palms toward the ceiling. "That's why I didn't bring it up." Under the table, Lindsey kicked him back. "Ouch!"

"Well," she said. "Show him!"

Sighing long and slowly—deflating further—he reached his hand into his pocket for Sofia's coin and laid it on the table.

Jared whistled. "Wow. Looks old. Is that a scythe?"

"I told you he knows stuff," Lindsey laughed.

"Yeah," Elliot said. "I haven't really had a chance to research its provenance, but I'd love to find out *how* old."

"Yeah," Jared replied. "Definitely. This is going to sound strange but—I feel like I've seen this before. Do you mind if I take a picture?"

Energized for the first time since they arrived, Elliot sprung up in his chair, spine erect and eyes sharp. Alert. Questioning. "Really? Yeah, of course. You mean in a book or something, right? This particular coin was lost for sixty years, so—"

Jared laughed. "Yeah, yeah. In a book or something.

That's the advantage of being a literature major. Lots of books." He pulled his iPhone from his pocket, held it over the coin, and snapped a shot. "If I can figure out where I saw this, I'll let you know." As he prepared to put the phone back, a *ding* announced a new message. His eyes flitted across the screen, and he smiled. "Ah, you guys about done? There's someone who is dying to meet you both."

"Oh?" Lindsey trilled, causing Elliot to shudder at the shrill excitement in her voice.

Jared winked. "His name is Ernesto, and he's *fabulous*."

≈

After finishing their drinks and the remnants of their slices, they tidied the table and left. Jared led them through narrow streets with brick sidewalks, and they tried their best not to trip on the ruptured edges—all the miniature mountain ranges of red, pushed up by the swollen roots of mature old trees. Finally, he stopped at a weather-beaten brownstone building and led them up the stoop. Inside, they took two flights of stairs, he fumbled with his keys and opened a door into the sweltering third-floor heat of his little apartment.

"That stupid AC is broken," a lightly-accented voice lilted from within.

"Sorry, we'd better get another one," Jared called back, ushering his guests into the short hallway.

From the living room beyond, a man appeared—Jared's age, shorter, Latino, with flawless bronzed skin and black hair, long on one side, shaved on the other. He smiled wide and danced a little on his toes. "Oh!" he said. “I’m so excited to meet you. Lindsey and—Elliot?”

Elliot swallowed hard in an effort to slow the blush blooming across his cheeks. The man—gliding forward now on the balls of his feet—flouted qualities Elliot could never imagine finding in himself. Proud. Confident. Fearlessly flamboyant and unabashedly unashamed.

“Guys,” Jared said. “This is Ernesto.”

“Wow,” Lindsey said, giving Ernesto a gentle embrace. “It’s so nice to meet you. I didn’t even realize Jared was seeing anyone.”

Ernesto laughed. “It all happened very fast; didn’t it, darling?”

With a clumsy hand, Elliot wiped at the sweat beading at his forehead. It’s hot in here, he assured himself. That’s all it is. Get it together. But even as the thoughts breezed across his consciousness, seeking to comfort, he saw their lies. The gulf between his life and Jared’s—and Ernesto’s—revealed its true, vast expanse. Their unmistakable auras of freedom and joy ought to have been lightening. They should have lifted Elliot up. Showed him what was possible. Instead, they surrounded and suffocated like a thick, toxic fog. Elliot felt a weakness in his knees and fought to take full breaths in the sweltering, stagnant air.

I can never have this, he thought. I can’t have it, because I won’t let myself—

Jared laughed in turn. “Yeah, it’s been about a month, but—we’re thinking about having Ernesto move in here when his lease is up in a few weeks.”

“Wow, do Mom and Dad know?”

“Not yet.” He looked at Ernesto. “We thought we’d get you on our side first.”

Ernesto looked at Elliot. “And what about you, honey? No hug from you?”

Elliot sputtered. “I, uh—” but then it was too late, and Ernesto was pulling him in close. He smelled like lavender and vanilla, and sweet, clean sweat. The nearness—the skin against his skin—was almost more than he could take. He thought of Cameron—wished they could be this close. And couldn’t they? Shouldn’t they?

I can’t have this. And yet? A tiny voice he’d buried so deep—one he hadn’t allowed himself to listen to since after his father died—cried out from the depths. All he had to do was say it. Out loud. To himself. Damn the consequences. Would there even *be* consequences?

After all, despite the repression, guilt, and unfounded shame, this was the truth: Elliot, Jared, Ernesto, Cam. They were the same. Whether Elliot could say it or not didn’t alter the facts. He was gay, and—

Ernesto released him and pouted, cocking his head a little to the side. “You got some demons in you, honey?”

The expression on his face was absurd, and the question rhetorical. Elliot laughed. “Yeah, I—” Lindsey looked at him expectantly. So did Jared. Collectively they drew in their breath and held it—two seconds, three, four—until finally, Elliot continued. “Yeah, I’ve got some demons. Don’t we all?”

Ernesto made a little *pu-pu* sound with the air between his lips and flicked his wrist in dismissal. “Honey, I exorcised *those* demons years ago! But we all do it in our own time.”

Elliot drew his shoulders in a little and swallowed hard. He was tired of people seeing through him. Tired of all the struggling and ignoring and repressing. Maybe if his father hadn't died—if he hadn't spent the last six years picking up the broken pieces of his mother and gluing them back together to break all over again—he would've been able to focus a little more on himself. Maybe he could've addressed these feelings—this identity—like Cameron had. Like Jared, and Ernesto. But it hadn't worked out that way. Maybe the circumstances were an excuse, but whatever the reasons, the reality persisted.

The tiny voice inside was roaring now. *Say it*! *Just say it*!

When he spoke, his voice was coarse and dry. "I'm—getting there," he said. The voice inside retreated, sated by its small victory.

In silence, Lindsey folded him in her arms and held him there. Tight. Safe. They wouldn't speak of it anymore today.

Elliot kept quiet for the remainder of the visit, and during most of the train ride home. They arrived back in Haverford a little after five, and as they prepared to part ways at the station, Lindsey placed a hand on his shoulder.

"I'm proud of you, Elliot."

He blinked. Smiled. He didn't need to ask why. "Thanks for being my friend, Lindsey."

"Forever and for always."

Fifteen minutes later, as Elliot coasted down the short drive to the New Colony Apartment Village, a flash of black in the parking lot caught his eye. A sleek, shiny sedan—the same he and Cameron had seen outside the mayor's house the day before—waited a few spots to the left of his front door. He shivered a little, despite the heat of the afternoon and the elevation of his pulse from the pedaling. A phantom sensory memory of the strange and beautiful woman brushing against him on the walk gripped him, and he had to focus to maintain his balance. Rounding the backside of his building, he came to a stop, climbed carefully off the bike, and locked it on the patio.

The moment he stepped through the kitchen door, he knew something was wrong; the house was dead-silent. No squabbling between Tony and his mother. No blaring of the television. He walked forward on the balls of his feet and made it to the short hallway before he called out. "Mom? Tony?"

His mother's voice answered back, from the living room. "Elliot? Can you come in here please?"

Gooseflesh. Something about the tone of his mother's voice—the fear, or maybe anger—gave him pause. He crept further, inching slowly, and as he came to the end of the hall, he saw them. Tony, arms crossed and scowling, sat on the couch with his mother. She was worried. Red-faced. And standing by the door—

"Elliot," the mysterious woman said. "I don't believe we've formally had the pleasure." She smiled, serpentine, and her voice was sweet—too sweet—colored lightly with an edge of French around the vowels. "My name is Destin Duprée, and—"

His mother cut in, struggling to keep the words steady. Half sauced. Astounded. "She says you—s-stole something? Elliot. Is this true?"

"What? No! I'd never—what does she say I stole?"

Destin slowly lowered her eyelids, then opened them, smiling all the while. "I believe you are in possession of a treasured family heirloom that belongs to my employer. That coin has been in Mayor Locke's family for over a century. I'm going to need you to give it to me."

Elliot could feel his throat constricting, and through an extraordinary force of will, he resisted the urge to plunge his hand into his pocket to feel the cold, rough metal concealed there. "I—didn't steal anything. I found that coin after it had been missing for *sixty years*."

"That may be so, but your refusal to return it to the mayor is tantamount to theft. Now, while we waited for you, I told your parents that the mayor has no desire to involve the police, but if you won't willingly turn it over—"

"I don't have it," he lied.

Destin raised her eyebrows, and her smile broadened. "No?"

"I took it with me to Boston today. I—I dropped it somewhere."

"Is that so? I think you're lying." She turned to Tony, who simmered, opening and closing his fists on the edge of the couch. "Sir, would you allow me to search his bedroom? I know this is a—delicate situation, and I'm simply looking for a swift and amicable resolution."

Shifting his jaw back and forth, Tony squeezed his hands so tightly against themselves his knuckles turned white. Suddenly, brusquely, he stood and stepped menacingly forward. "I think you'd better get out of here, lady."

"Pardon?" she asked, recoiling.

"The kid says he doesn't have it."

"But clearly he is lying."

"And clearly, you don't understand mutherfuckin' English! I said you'd better get out of here. Now, I sat here and listened to your story about some special old coin like I gave a goddamn, but now he's home and he says he doesn't have it. And I'll be damned if I'm gonna let you tear through my goddamned house. You want a search? Call the police. Have them get a warrant. No one'll issue one though, because he didn't steal anything."

From across the room, Elliot could see the fire in her eyes. She seemed to consider—to size Tony up, as though she could possibly raise a hand to him and survive it. The moment stretched, vibrating with tension. Tight. Tighter.

Finally, she spoke. "There'll be no need for all of that. Elliot?"

He stuttered. "Y-yes?"

"I trust in the end you'll decide to do the right thing. Mayor Locke will be waiting." Then she turned and went out the front door.

The apartment remained silent until after they heard the engine of Destin's car turn up the drive toward Pentucket Road. Elliot gazed at Tony, who lumbered back down onto the couch. He couldn't believe Tony stood up for him—couldn't believe the horrible oaf of a man defended him like that. Surely there was a catch. A twist. Slowly, he lowered his hands into his pockets—both hands in an effort to not give anything away—and felt the cold, rough metal right where he expected it to be.

He exhaled and closed his eyes. "Thank you."

Tony grunted and lit a cigarette. "Don't say I never did anything for you. I don't know what you got yourself into. Why the hell did you go see the mayor?"

"I—"

Tony waved him off. "Never mind, the less I know, the better. Now, tell us both the truth. Do you have this—whatever the hell? This coin?"

He bit his lip. In light of Tony's unexpected heroism, he wanted to be honest, but something held him back. It was too good. Too easy. There was always an agenda with Tony, so he shook his head. "No. I really did lose it."

"You're a goddamned idiot, then. It was probably worth a lot of money."

His mother sighed and reached a shaky hand forward to lift her wine glass off the coffee table. After a long sip, she turned her eyes to Elliot. "I didn't really think you could've stolen, El. Are you going to be around for dinner?"

At first, he shrugged, but then remembered Cameron. "I'm not sure. Um, don't wait for me. I have some things to do."

"Okay," she said, putting down her glass and picking up her knitting needles. "But tomorrow, right? Your birthday?"

He smiled at the excitement in her voice. There she was—a tiny bit of his mother's former light shining through the cracked and beaten exterior of the woman she'd become. "Yeah," he said. "Definitely tomorrow."

⩯

Later, when he texted, Cam responded within a minute,

and they agreed to meet at a little Greek take-out. They ordered gyros and marinated olives to-go and found a quiet patch of grass in the park near the library where they could eat, legs folded beneath them. The sun was dipping low, and in the golden light of the golden hour, Elliot watched Cameron chewing slowly. He was beautiful, and they were together, and for the first time all day, he would have been absolutely happy, except—

This visit was about business before pleasure. He thought of the mysterious Destin—waiting for him in his own home—and the worry must have clouded his face because Cameron wrinkled his brow. "Elliot, what's eating you?" he asked.

He closed his eyes a moment and reached his hand into his pocket, closing his fingers around Sofia's coin. He prepared—anticipated the constriction in his throat—and pulled it out. "I want you to hold onto this for a while," he said, handing it over. "Please, take it."

"Elliot, are you—"

"Please?"

Cameron took the coin, and Elliot thought he could feel a quick, sharp pain. A slicing. A severing. And then, that was it. Nothing.

Cam put the coin in his own pocket and smiled, sad. "What's going on?"

"That woman from your aunt's house yesterday? She was waiting for me when I got home. She was in my *house*. She told my mom and her boyfriend that I stole it. Apparently, she's working for your aunt, and threatened to get the police involved."

Cameron laughed, but the lines etched into his normally smooth face betrayed his worry. "So, you're giving it to *me*?"

"Just for now. I mean, I don't want you to get into trouble, but I figure it's *your* family, right? If your aunt really wants it, at least if it's with a Calisti..."

"Right," he scrunched his forehead as though he was chewing his thoughts. "Well, I think you're the one that's supposed to have it. This is the connection to her—to Sofia—isn't it?"

"I think so."

Cameron nodded. "Alright. I'll keep it, for now—to take the heat off for a little while. Why do you think this—Destin wants it? My aunt can't need it that badly. She thinks it's a trinket."

"No." Elliot shook his head. "I don't think so either. There's something about that woman, like she's—I don't know. There's something more to this. I get the feeling she knows what the coin is. Like, where it's from. What it can do."

"And what *can* it do?"

"I don't know. Save a little girl's life? Save her parents? All I know is—she can't have it."

"No."

They sat in silence for a while, eating, enjoying the sun and the nearness to one another. Elliot knew they ought to discuss their next steps but focusing was difficult—locking eyes on a point on the horizon from the center of a vortex. He thought about Jared and Ernesto—their freedom, and the easy way they moved about their lives and their skin.

Cameron laid his hand on top of Elliot's. Electricity coursed through him, as swift and fierce and sharp as it had ever been. "What are you thinking about?" he asked.

"I'm thinking about—well—*us*, I guess. Did you know I'm turning twenty tomorrow?"

"No." His eyes widened—deep blue sapphires catching the light, holding it. "I mean, yes, maybe. I should've remembered from when we were younger."

"From when we were still friends?" Elliot asked. He could feel himself slumping as the weight of their past—all the impossible tons of it—sat down on his shoulders.

"We're friends now, aren't we?"

Elliot closed his eyes and nodded, feeling a coolness on his cheeks as a few rogue tears escaped and the August breeze endeavored to kiss them away. He supposed Cameron was right, they *were* friends now. Maybe more than friends. But with every kindness Cameron showed him, the memory of what he'd done in their dawning adolescence was painted in bolder colors.

"Yes," he replied. "But I don't know what I did to deserve it. After the way I acted when we were younger, I—"

Cam lifted his hand and placed two fingers against Elliot's lips. "You don't have to bring it up."

"Yes, I do, Cam. I treated you like—I know it must've hurt you. I know—"

"That was a different time. I think even then I knew you didn't really mean it. There was so much happening. Your dad had died, and, you know—I'd asked a lot of you."

"That's not an excuse."

Cameron crossed his arms. "So, are you going to dwell on it? Are you apologizing? Is that what this is?"

He exhaled—forced every bit of air from his lungs until he felt empty. Clean. He breathed in, only the good—the sweet air of a summer evening, filled with all its light and warmth. "Yes. That's the least I can do."

"Alright then, let's not talk about it anymore." Unfolding his legs, he stood up.

"Wait," Elliot said, scrambling to his feet. "Where are you going? Did I upset you?"

Cameron's smile was thin, but Elliot was sure a touch of warmth lingered there. "A little. It's alright. Don't worry."

He reached out and took Cam's hands in his own. "Cameron, I—"

"Shh," he said, leaning forward. Quick—lighter even than the breeze, and faster than the heartbeat of a hummingbird—he touched his lips to Elliot's forehead and withdrew them again.

Elliot gazed at him in confusion, overwhelmed—trapped in the eddy of longing and repression. "Cam," he whispered.

"It's alright, Elliot. I waited for you for seven years. I can wait a little longer." He stepped away. "I'll reach out tomorrow, okay?"

Elliot couldn't speak—only nodded—and watched as Cameron walked slowly away.

Chapter Thirteen

August 19, 2019 - Monday

Elliot expected to wake on the morning of his twentieth birthday entirely new—at least that's what he'd intended to tell Cam the night before. In practical terms, he had another year wading around in the brackish water between adolescence and adulthood—another year at the community college, another summer waiting for the transfer to a four-year school. Perhaps if his father had lived, things would be different. There might have been enough money right out of high school. He might have left Haverford behind already, never looking back.

But of course, that wasn't the reality.

And the age—twenty—*felt* like it should mean something. He'd wanted to tell Cam that once the day turned over, all his childish repression and misgivings and fears would blow away. No longer a teenager. He'd be adult. Confident. He'd be able to say it.

Everyone else could say it—*did* say it when he wasn't around.

I'm Elliot, and I'm gay. I'm a lot of other things too, but I'm gay. I'm in love with Cameron Calisti, and probably always have been, and I don't care who knows.

But when he opened his eyes a little after seven-thirty, he wasn't so sure. Strangely chilled, he pulled the blankets tighter—layered and tucked and twisted—until he formed a cocoon. Out the window, through a crack in the blinds, he could see a dense gray fog had moved in overnight. The August heat was harsh but fleeting.

Autumn was on the way.

He laid there a few minutes, not feeling *different* or *new* at all. And there was something else: yesterday had been a waste. For Sofia, the flood was only three days away, and he'd done little to figure out who was going to murder her parents or solve her disappearance. And he hadn't been to see her since Friday. Did she wonder where he was? Did she worry?

Every muscle fiber in his body felt heavy. Drained. But the thought of Sofia pushed him to a sitting position. The detective was his next lead, so he searched his memory for the name. Mulvaney—Adam. No. Arthur. He'd seen it in the newspaper archives, and Mayor Locke had mentioned him. He reached for his iPhone and typed the name into the search bar in the browser.

Has Arthur Mulvaney been arrested? Search public records for FREE!

Arthur Mulvaney on Facebook (See 10 matching profiles)

Obituary of Cora Mulvaney - Williams Funeral Home, Haverford, MA

On a hunch, he tapped the third search result and was redirected to a gaudy website that looked like it hadn't been updated since the late '90s, despite the obituary bearing a date of April 2010. Quickly, he scanned:

Mrs. Cora Ellen Mulvaney (née Smith) passed away Sunday evening after a valiant fight with cancer. She is survived by her husband Arthur, two children, Thomas and Nancy, and seven grandchildren...

...service will be held at St. Joseph's Catholic Church at 11 am Wednesday, with a reception and celebration of life at the Mulvaney residence (17 White Birch Road, Haverford) beginning at 4 pm. Flowers may be sent to the Williams Funeral Home...

The obituary was nine years old, and there was no guarantee the detective was still alive or still lived in his home. Elliot supposed he'd be in his late eighties, but there was always a chance. Hopeful and energized, he climbed out of bed and headed to the shower.

He was dressed and ready by eight-thirty but stopped in the kitchen long enough to toast a couple of slices of wheat bread. The toast popped, and he was retrieving the butter from the fridge when his mother stumbled into the room.

"Morning El," she said, voice hoarse and eyes

bloodshot, radiating red outward from the irises. "Happy birthday."

"Good morning," he said, noting the way she winced at the sound of his knife scraping across the bread. "And thanks."

"Where are you off to so early? No farm today, right?"

"I have some errands."

She crossed her arms, disappointed. "I hoped maybe you'd let me make you breakfast. I've got a long day of knitting ahead, but I thought it's the least I could do."

"That's sweet of you, but I'll be alright with this toast."

"And you won't be out all day, will you? We're going to celebrate tonight, right?"

"Yeah."

She smiled, warm and bright. The fog outside was lifting, and Elliot wondered if maybe the fog was lifting from her as well. She was hungover, sure, but he was touched by the smile and touched by her effort. "Wish me luck?" she asked.

He took a bite of toast. "For what?"

"I'm putting my first batch of hats on the store today."

"Oh?" He raised his eyebrows. "Good luck."

She walked forward, feet heavy, and wrapped her frail arms around him. She pulled tight, and he felt himself relax into her. "I love you, kiddo, don't you forget that." Dry lips pressed against his temple, and he could smell the wine evaporating from her pores, but he didn't mind. She held on longer, pulled a little tighter, and finally stepped away. "See you later?"

He nodded. "Love you, Mom," and watched as she

slinked back to the dark of her bedroom.

In four large bites, he finished his toast and headed out into the gray morning.

⩯

The house on White Birch Road was quaint and pretty, despite an air of neglect that hung about the property. Set back into the wide lot, the house, with its blue siding, was nearly engulfed by the untamed climbing roses that weaved and stretched across its surface like something out of a fairy tale. The weedy lawn was in desperate need of a cut, and the picket fence that ran the perimeter could've used a coat of paint. Still, a sedan parked in the drive—nearly as old as Elliot himself—gave him hope the detective still lived on the premises. He leaned his bike up against the fence and walked the short, weedy path to the front door.

He didn't have to wait long after pressing the bell. From inside, he could hear the sounds of entry; a deadbolt clicked, a chain slid back, and then the door opened. A young woman in blue scrubs regarded him, curious. "May I help you?" she asked.

"Um, yes. Does Arthur Mulvaney still live here?"

The young woman looked behind her into the dark of the house, then fixed her gaze on Elliot's face. "What is this regarding?"

"Sorry, I'm—I knew it was a long shot, but I wanted to ask him about a case he worked in the late fifties. Is he—alright?"

She gave a thin smile. "He's sick. He doesn't get many visitors, and I don't know if—"

"Would you mind asking him? I promise I won't take

long. Or maybe if he's willing to see me, I could come back later. It's a little bit urgent, though, so if you would ask him, I'd really appreciate it."

She sighed. "I'm not sure how a case from the fifties could be urgent, but–alright. I'll ask him." She closed the door.

Elliot tapped his foot. He was eager. Impatient. He reached up and pulled down a white rose, close to his face, breathing in its potent perfume. One of the finer thorns pierced the skin of his finger, and he wondered if he'd fall into an enchanted sleep for a couple hundred years. Releasing the flower, he tucked his finger into his mouth and sucked at the first small bead of blood.

The door opened, and the young woman gave him another thin smile. "He says he'll see you, but please be careful. He's very weak. Follow me." She led him into the house and to the left, through to a dark living room with thick, matted carpet underfoot. In a corner, near a window partially obscured by the roses outside, an old man sat in a recliner with an oxygen tank adjacent and tubes running up to each nostril. A small television across the room hummed with a morning news magazine. "Arthur," she said with more volume than Elliot was expecting, "this is–what did you say your name was?"

"Elliot. Sorry, I didn't say."

"This is Elliot." She disappeared into an adjacent dining room and returned with a chair. Placing it directly in front of the ancient detective, she indicated Elliot should sit. "Are you sure you're up to answering some questions?"

Voice coarse and cracking, the old man chuckled. "Oh, yes. Thank you, Jackie." He looked at Elliot, eyes pressed to slits beneath folds of weathered, spotted skin. “She’s my nurse. One of the good’uns.” Jackie nodded and wandered away. “Not too many visitors these days. What can I do for you, Elliot?”

He swallowed. “Well, thank you for—”

“What’s that?” Arthur boomed. “You’ll have to speak up. I’m a little hard of hearing. Eighty-eight years old, you know.”

Louder, Elliot tried again. “I said, thank you for seeing me. I wanted to ask you about a case.”

“There were a lot of them. Mostly little stuff. Forgettable. I’ll tell you what I know if I remember. Which one?”

“Sofia Calisti.”

Arthur coughed, and his face clouded with fear. Softly, he asked, “Now why the hell do you want to know about that?”

“I’m trying to find out—I know it was never solved, but you had your theories, didn’t you?”

Gripping the arms of the recliner, Arthur began to rake his withered old fingers up and down the fabric. His eyes darted around the room, and Elliot could see his breathing was labored. “There are things you don’t go digging up. Why do you want to know about her?”

Elliot sighed, closing his eyes. How much should he say? What would the old detective believe? Why was the idea of discussing the case so disturbing to him? He decided honesty was the best approach, minus the supernatural elements.

“I found something that belonged to her, and now I *need* to know what happened. Please, if there’s anything you can tell me—anything that didn’t go into the papers...

The boarder, did he do it? The parents? What was his name?"

Arthur deflated, sinking deep into his chair. "What is it you think you found?"

"A coin. An old coin."

He began to cough—loud, ferocious—shaking every inch of his frail frame. From the other room, Jackie rushed in and kneeled in front of him. "Arthur!" she said. "Arthur, breathe. Calm down. Breathe." As the coughing fit slowed, she turned her gaze to Elliot and glared. "I told you to be careful. You'd better go. You'd better—"

Arthur reached out a hand and placed it gently on her shoulder. Clearing his throat, he used his other hand to wipe at the tears leaking from the corners of his eyes. "No, Jackie. It's alright. Let him stay a moment." He fixed his eyes on Elliot. "I don't know what that coin is—what it's good for—but if I were you, I'd take it out on a boat and drop it in the ocean."

"Sir—" Elliot began.

Arthur waved him away, and when he spoke, his voice cracked. "Greatest regret of my life, that case. The boarder's name—French or something. Guillaume Khoury. But don't waste your time. He's a ghost. You won't find anything. No birth certificate, death certificate. No census data. Nothing."

"Okay, but—did he do it?" Elliot asked. The old man shook his head, and now his tears were falling full-force. "But you know who did?" The old man nodded. "But you—won't say?"

He coughed. "You could never prove it, and even if you could, I wouldn't want you to. Like I said, there are things you don't go digging up."

"But *why*? Please, I have to know. What if I told you I could—I could save her!"

Jackie scoffed. "That's enough. Time to go."

Arthur cleared his throat. "If you think you could save her, then you know—you *know*—what you're dealing with. He wasn't even human."

"Guillaume?"

"No. Not Guillaume. The—I can't—if I ever tell, I—" he looked at Jackie, then at Elliot. "Jackie's right. I think you'd better go. Leave it alone, kid."

Elliot swallowed hard but nodded. Jackie got to her feet and didn't have to ask. "Thank you," he said and hurried to the door.

⁂

On his way home, Elliot stopped at the library and headed directly to the periodicals section. The attendant gave him a little nod—old friends now—and didn't question him as he headed for the ancient computer console with the newspaper archives. He navigated to the days following the flood and scanned the articles for any more information about the investigation into the Calisti murders.

Of course, there was nothing. Arthur had told him as much. No mention of the mysterious Guillaume Khoury. No other suspects.

He left the library utterly disheartened; the leads were drying. He took a seat beneath the tall oak where he and Cameron had lunch on Friday and put his face in his hands. Time was running out. And maybe it had been foolish of him to think he could make a difference—change the past.

The conversation with Arthur disturbed him—to think a man could still be terrified about something that happened sixty years earlier. And what did he mean *he wasn't even human*? Who? The killer, clearly, but—

He thought of Destin. There was something about *her* that was other than human. Something off. And the smell. He'd only got the smallest whiff, but it was clear and pungent. Something animal. Perhaps he really was in over his head. *There are things you don't go digging up.*

One thing was clear now: the coin was at the center of it. He'd suspected as much all along, since the first moment he couldn't bear to be apart from it. But Destin's lust for it—she said it was for Kathryn, but Elliot knew better—was further evidence. And hadn't Arthur all but confirmed it? He hadn't even flinched when Elliot suggested he might be able to *save* Sofia.

Which all pointed to—

This was something he was meant to do. The urge to stay there beneath the tree and feel sorry for himself was strong—all but paralyzing—but he pictured Sofia, missing for sixty years, probably dead. It was enough to get him to his feet. There was one more lead he could follow. He'd need Cameron to arrange it, of course, but any further clarity could come from only one source.

George Calisti.

As he walked toward the rack where he'd parked his bike, he pulled out his phone and sent the text.

"Hey, found the detective this morning. Can we go see your grandfather?"

He waited a full minute before pushing the phone back into his pocket, disappointed not to receive an immediate response. He wasn't sure why, but the silence felt like a betrayal. He pushed the thought from his mind. Cam said he'd be in touch today—he was probably busy at the moment. Elliot climbed on his bike, pushed off, and headed home.

≈

Slow and reluctant, the morning gave way to the afternoon. He left his mother alone in the living room to her knitting and daytime television, downing cup after cup of coffee and manically refreshing the browser on her laptop in hopes of seeing her first sale. Of course, he was excited for her, but only cautiously optimistic about her chances for success.

They had lunch together—egg salad on toast—and she asked if he'd sit with her, but he declined, saying he needed a nap. Truthfully, he was feeling frustrated. Cam still hadn't responded, and his spirits were sinking at the prospect of another wasted day—another day closer to the flood with no real progress.

Lying on his bed, he opened the browser on his phone and searched in vain for any trace of a Guillaume Khoury that might've been alive in the fifties and sixties. Ultimately defeated, he dropped the phone and closed his eyes for what seemed like only a minute.

His mother woke him when Tony got home.

"El?" she said through a crack in the door.

Groggy, he wiped the crust from the corners of his eyes and sat up. "What time is it?"

"A little after five-thirty. Want pizza?"

He shook his head in an effort to firmly ground himself back in the realm of consciousness. "Yeah, sure."

"Alright, I'll order. Coming out, now?"

"Yeah, okay."

After his mother closed the door, he stood and stretched, feeling more depressed than ever. What before had felt like a potentially wasted day was now confirmed as such. He grabbed his phone, and his shoulders slumped when he saw Cam still hadn't responded to his text.

In the living room, they were waiting. Tony sat in his normal corner of the couch, cigarette hanging from his lips, and when Elliot walked into the room, he tilted his head back and exhaled long and slow. The smoke curled upward—twisting, dissipating—poisoning the air. He smiled, and there was an edge of malice in his beady brown eyes. "Happy goddamned birthday," he said. "Twenty. Sounds like a good age to start paying rent, huh?" He guffawed.

His mother had traded the coffee for wine, but both the glass on the coffee table and the bottle beside her were full, so Elliot suspected she was still sober. She turned to Tony and tapped him lightly on the shoulder. "Now, now." Looking at Elliot, she smiled and extended her hand toward a box wrapped in light blue paper sitting on the edge of the table. "Pizza is on the way. Want to open your gift?"

It looked like a shoe box, and despite Tony's jab, he smiled. "Okay." He sat nimbly on the carpeted floor and took the box into his lap, slightly baffled by its lightness. "Thank you."

"Of course," his mother said.

Carefully, he unwrapped the paper. Sure enough, a shoe box. He thought of his old, tired running shoes, and dipped his eyes closed for a moment, thankful. He lifted the lid, and—

Inside, covered loosely with a piece of white tissue paper was a pair of navy-blue crepe running shorts. He felt the corners of his mouth pushing downward, and breathed in sharply, forcing a too-wide smile. Blinking rapidly to relax his face and banish the disappointment, he pulled the shorts from the box and looked at his mother. He swallowed once, twice, and as cheerfully as he could manage, said "Thank you! Oh, they're perfect."

She frowned a little and took a sip of her wine. "Really? I was worried you'd be disappointed. I know you had your heart set on some new shoes, and—"

His face was falling, and he wasn't sure he could hide it any longer. "No, Mom. Really. These are great."

"But I'm going to get them for you—the shoes. I promise. You know, it's—with starting this business, money is a little tight. But within the next few weeks, I promise."

He pressed his eyes closed, ashamed of the touch of wetness he felt at the corners. "Really Mom, don't worry about it."

From the edge of the couch, Tony guffawed. "Really, Lari. Really. He wouldn't want to sound ungrateful, now would he? Maybe if he hadn't lost that damned coin that lady was after, he could've sold it for a lifetime's supply of running shoes."

"Tony—" his mother began.

"Naw, really. Isn't that so, Elliot? Or maybe you *do* still have it and won't say. Sound about right?"

He blinked. "Where is this coming from? I thought you were on my side for once."

“Oh, I’m on your side alright. But I don’t think you’re being completely honest with me, boy.”

“Tony!” his mother said.

Elliot’s mouth was dry. He searched in vain for words to defend himself but stopped when he heard a *ding* in his pocket. He removed his phone and stared wide-eyed at the message on the screen.

"She’s here."

⩬

Destin exhaled, closing her long, delicate fingers into fists, then opening them again. She’d needed to walk the bartender through the ingredients, but in the end, he’d mixed a passable Negroni, and the first thrilling waves of warmth from the liquor were now heating her ancient veins. She turned her lips up into her brightest smile—cruel, patronizing—and breathed in.

“The part I don’t understand is why the two of you thought I wouldn’t find out,” she said. “I suspect you know a little of what the Chronicum is capable of.”

Across the wide entryway, the boy—Cameron—pressed himself against the banister of the stairs. “I don’t know what you’re talking about.” She watched as he glanced down at the phone in his hand—nervous and expectant. The terror radiated from him; she could smell it—a beautiful perfume with notes of tension and flight and white-hot fear pouring from his pores.

“I think you’d better put that back in your pocket,” she said. She raised her hands, innocent. “Believe me, I wish you no harm, but since it’s just you and I, I hope we can be honest with one another.”

The boy didn’t move, instead set his jaw and puffed

his chest a little with false bravado. She'd seen it before—a brief moment of *fight* before the overwhelming urge to *flight*. "My parents will be home from work any minute. And two swipes of my finger and I can have the police on their way."

She laughed. "So dramatic! As I said, I hope we can be honest with one another. It would be an awful shame if an animal were to run across the road in front of your parents' cars—something little and insignificant. A squirrel. A rabbit. How horrible if they were to swerve to avoid it and go right off the road. I could do it, you know."

The terror returned to the boy's face, and she smiled as she watched his lips quiver. "What *are* you?" he asked.

"Nothing, really. I'm a servant. A priestess charged to reclaim what was stolen from my goddess. Really, young Mister Calisti, you have no idea how wonderful it feels to say it out loud. This honesty thing is incredible. Now it's your turn. Admit that you have my coin and give it to me. Once you do, I'll be gone from here forever."

She watched as he considered. "I don't believe you. I don't believe in goddesses or priestesses or magic coins."

"Then why don't you give it to me?"

He set his jaw. "Why don't you take it from me?" She ground her teeth and winced a little as he smiled back at her. "You can't, can you?"

She closed her eyes a moment, longing once again for the days when men feared the gods. He couldn't know her threats were empty—that the bond she'd forged with the mayor was already waning, and she wasn't sure she presently had the power to influence even a rodent from any kind of distance.

Luckily, fate—not of her own making—had smiled on her in the little bar. Perhaps the old goddess was still looking out for her after all. The man—Tony—had stopped in on his way home from work. He'd seen her and taken up the adjacent stool, reeking of smoke and machismo and rage. She knew how to seize an opportunity when one arose, and all it had taken was a suggestion of the coin's monetary value. She'd cursed herself for not thinking of it yesterday. He'd turned to her, wide-eyed, and then she'd whispered in his ear—got him on the hook—and her hounds moved in. The bond was weak—weaker even than the one with the mayor—but at the time it was only a backup plan.

If it came down to using Tony, the strength of the bond wouldn't matter. He'd go after the coin for his own greedy purposes. And fair was fair. She'd pay him. No price was too great for perhaps the one thing on earth that was truly invaluable.

She watched Cameron and considered. The boy was right, of course. She couldn't take it from him. The rules of *Le Jeu*—put in place millennia ago—demanded the coin be *given*. And perhaps her little visit here was enough for him to *give* it back to Elliot. And once Elliot had it again—

The phone in the boy's hand began to ring. "Elliot?" she asked, already knowing the answer. "Last chance."

Cameron looked at the phone. "Go to hell," he said.

She nodded. "As you wish. But, you should know, if I don't get it soon, you'll know no end to the suffering I'll unleash."

He blinked, dumbfounded, and she walked out the door before he had a chance to respond.

Part Four – Elliot and Sofia

Chapter Fourteen

August 19, 1959 - Wednesday

A sharp, tiny prick above her heart brought Sofia out of sleep. She could feel the scream building in her throat but relaxed as she saw Franklin's orange face and yellow eyes staring down at her. The cat continued to knead his paws into the fabric of her pajamas below the shoulder, and she gently placed her hands against his chest to push him off.

"Ow, Franklin," she said. "That hurts."

The cat blinked twice and continued his little ritual into the blankets beside her. She sat up straight in bed, and ran her hand along his spine, blinking away the terror of her dreams.

She'd dreamed of Elliot again.

Two nights ago, when she'd had the first dream, Papa rushed in and held her while she cried. She tried her best to explain—to tell him that Elliot was in danger—and eventually, Mama came into the room as well. They sat with her until she calmed, and after they thought she was asleep, they started to talk in hushed voices.

Mama thought she needed to see a doctor—a psychologist—which sounded very scary. Papa wasn't so convinced, and he said they'd talk about it more in the morning. She didn't know what a psychologist was, but she was certain she didn't want to find out, so last night when she'd woken from another nightmare, she'd cried as softly as she could into her pillow, gripping Nonno's coin tight in her tiny fist.

She scratched Franklin lightly on the head, thankful he'd woken her. She'd been having the dream—Elliot the only point of clarity in a blurred, watery world. She could still see him cowering next to the other figure, and the glint of light off the metal of the gun. But before the worst part—the deafening shot—

"You're a good kitty," she said. Franklin rolled a little to his side, thankful for the praise, and began to purr.

≈

After breakfast, Sofia found Guillaume sitting on the porch behind his bedroom with a book and a cup of coffee. The sun was out, and it lit the leaves of the forest beyond like a million tiny green lanterns. She sat gingerly on the planks of the floor and looked up at him. Patient. Curious.

Smiling, he closed his book and adjusted his glasses. "Good morning, young Ms. Calisti," he said. "Is there something I can do for you?"

"What's a psychologist?"

The skin above his forehead wrinkled into a maze of

funny little hills, and she had to fight hard not to giggle. "Where did you hear *that* word?" he asked.

"Mama thinks I need to go see one."

He made a sound—*puh*—a little puff of air from between pursed lips, and shook his head. "A psychologist studies the mind, often to help a person overcome a problem. Why does your Mama think you need to see one?"

"Elliot." She shrugged. "Do I have a problem, Guillaume?"

He laughed, and it was warm and bright. His face relaxed, and then she started to laugh also. "No, dear girl. I don't think so. What is it about Elliot? They don't believe in him?"

"No." She exhaled, and despite the reassurance of Guillaume's words, she felt the sadness and fear of the last few days clouding over her. "I'm worried. Something bad is going to happen to him, and I haven't seen him since Sunday."

"Hmm. That's *very* curious. Why do you think something bad is going to happen?"

"I dream about it. He's scared and all crouched down. And there's someone with a gun, and then it goes off, and then—"

She felt her body start to shake and blinked fast to keep from crying. Guillaume put his hand on her shoulder and said "Shh. That's alright. That's alright." She started to calm and wiped at her eyes. "And you've had this dream more than one time?"

"Yes. I have to see him. I have to tell him! And he said he'd come back—because of the flood. He said—"

"Shh. Don't get too excited."

"Guillaume, can you help me find him?"

His lips dipped down into a frown, and Sofia crumpled forward, knowing the answer before he said it. "No, dear girl. I'm afraid I can't."

"But you believe he's real? You believe me?"

"Of course I do."

Suddenly, she felt her fear and worry blowing away. A hot wind, red with anger, swept over her mind and ushered in a defiant rage. She pushed her lips out and planted her hands on her hips. "Then why can't you help me?"

"I would if I could. It doesn't work that way, though." He stopped for a moment, rubbing at his temple. "Do you have your Nonno's coin with you?"

Of their own accord, her eyes rolled. "I always keep it with me."

"Good. That's good. I'll tell you a secret you probably already know. Are you ready?"

"Yes."

"Your Nonno's coin is the key to Elliot. It's the reason you see him at all. And you know something else? I think it *wants* you to see him."

She shrugged. Deflated. All the rage went out of her and she felt empty. Hollow. "But it doesn't want me to see him now?"

"I don't know. I can't know. It has never worked this way before. But I'll tell you one thing I know for certain. Maybe it is best if you don't talk about Elliot anymore, except to me. You don't need to see a psychologist, Sofia, but your Mama and Papa are concerned about you. They love you very much, and they don't understand. Now, why don't you go play? The sun is out today. And maybe, if you're lucky, you'll see him."

"You think I'll see him again?"

He winked. "I am almost certain of it."

Guillaume watched Sofia disappear around the side of the veranda, then stood and walked back into his bedroom. With the door closed, he drew the curtains and sat at the edge of the bed. For the first time in the Chronicum's history, it seemed this ongoing battle was to be waged on two fronts—the present and sixty years in the future.

Elliot's absence these last few days was troubling to Sofia, but it was terrifying to Guillaume. Of course, it stood to reason he'd have the opportunity to defend the coin in that distant time, as he did at present, but it was the not knowing—the inability to do anything about what was currently occurring in 2019—that had him in turmoil. Predetermination, as much as he loathed the concept, suggested he'd be able to fend off Destin now—*needed to* more than ever—otherwise, the coin would never come into Elliot's possession in the first place. But what if she'd gotten her hands on it in the future? It made a horrible sort of sense. With the Chronicum, even in her weakened state, she'd be more powerful than she'd ever been.

And it wasn't just the coin's ability to shape fate that was troubling—it had been minted from the blades of *two* deities. It was the contribution of the god *he'd* sworn to serve that was truly horrifying.

With the Chronicum, Destin might be able to shape fate in *time*. If she got her hands on it in 2019, it was possible that all this aberrant behavior was her doing after all.

But what he'd told Sofia was true. He didn't know. He *couldn't* know. His only glimpses of Elliot had come when he and Sofia were directly interacting. The whereabouts of the boy were as elusive to him as the location of a single dolphin in all the wide ocean.

There was nothing to be done about it now, he realized. If necessary, he'd spend the next sixty years plotting and planning and researching. He'd find a way to defeat her in the future as well, as he'd done for centuries. But at present, there were more pressing matters. The flood Elliot predicted was only days away.

And then there was the problem of George Calisti. George, who he'd expected yesterday, but never came. George, who even now was under the influence of one of Destin's hell-hounds—who told Destin he'd come when he met her in the alley.

He closed his eyes and tuned his ears—listening and searching.

Miles to the north, he could hear them, howling in anguish. From this distance, the canine cacophony was a dull roar—tolerable. He moved to the desk, retrieved his journal, and began to record his thoughts.

≈

He heard *it* before he heard *him.*

Guillaume was at his desk after lunch, when the howling intensified. A single, deep, baritone voice—vicious and hungry—separated itself from the pack. As it drew nearer, Guillaume felt the paralysis setting in and quickly hummed to turn it off.

Through the thin walls and the echo of the corridor beyond, he heard Robert and Margaret in the kitchen. Their voices were muffled, but he could make out most of the conversation.

"...not the time, Margaret. She could come back in at any moment..."

"...can't ignore this, Robert! I'm really worried..."

"...hasn't even mentioned it again. She's just an imaginative girl. You know how my father..."

"...already called for the appointment. How will it look if I cancel?..."

"...be damned with the appearance! Anyways, do you think we could afford it?..."

"...wouldn't be the worst idea. If we sold, we could live in town. There'd be other children..."

"...my father's dream! My family's legacy! *Our* family's..."

Outside, the sound of tires on gravel eclipsed the rest of the conversation. A car door slammed, and then George's voice boomed.

"...Father's old coin. No, it doesn't matter. I need it for a little while..."

"...to Sofia. What could you possibly need it for?..."

"...utterly irresponsible, as usual! You know she'll lose it! It's a family heirloom..."

"...will break her heart! Do you think you could be responsible for that?..."

"...ask her myself then! Where is she?..."

The front door slammed, and Margaret's voice cut in.

"...let him go, Robert..."

Guillaume sat up straight, rubbing his arms against

a new, thin sheen of sweat. Non-intervention was the rule—always had been. He could battle with Destin—interact with her directly—and defend himself if need be, but never once in all his years had he interceded directly on the coin-holders behalf.

But never before had the coin-holder been a child.

He stood, shaking, and looked at the door out onto the porch. To interfere now could mean undermining everything the Chronicum stood for—free will, self-determination, a world where man decided his own fate.

He closed his eyes—pressed his lids so tightly he could feel the blood forced out and away—and pleaded for guidance.

Skipping through the fields, Sofia stopped beside the lacinato kale and brushed her hand along the deep-green, velvety surface of a leaf. It was long and thin. A feather—a sword. Reaching down, she pinched near the base and freed it, waving it wildly overhead and skipping on. Behind her, at the house, she heard a commotion and turned to see plump Uncle George lumbering down the steps.

She laughed as he started in her direction, stomping, red-faced and angry. Uncle George the Dragon! She wasn't afraid. Tipping one hip forward, she brandished her leaf blade and waited. Winded, he reached her row, and turned down, with his scaled, taloned feet leaving dinosaur-like tracks behind him in the soft dirt. She watched—grinned—as little tufts of smoke escaped his nostrils and he bared his sharp dragon teeth.

Behind him, the air shimmered and moved, as

though disturbed by an invisible, hulking mass of a beast. He was closer now, paces away.

"Stop there, dragon!" she shouted. "Come any closer and I'll *slay* you!"

The dragon laughed, heartily, only the laugh wasn't a laugh. It sounded more like a howl. And there was something about Uncle George's smile. It wasn't dragon-like at all anymore. It was canine. Wolfish.

She looked at the sword in her hand, only the sword wasn't a sword. It was a leaf. The first little wave of fear washed over her from head to toe as Uncle George leered, and she began to shiver and shake.

"Don't be frightened, Sofia," he said with a gravel-filled voice. "I came to ask you if I could borrow Nonno's old lucky coin." His smile was wide, with too many teeth.

She thought of Elliot, and then of Guillaume. She had to give it away, he'd said; no one could take it from her, and as long as she had it, she was safe. Still gripping the kale leaf between white knuckles, she reached her other hand into the pocket of her denim dress and felt the rough, cold metal.

Behind Uncle George, the shimmering mass of air took form for a moment, and she bit down on her tongue to keep from shrieking. It looked like a horrible dog—a massive hound with matted hair, black and evil. The eyes—cold and enormous and yellow—locked onto her own, and the beast snarled down its long snout.

It was exactly as Nonno described it in his story. And it was terrifying.

She whimpered, and it was gone. Then back. Then gone.

Squeezing hard, she felt the coin press into her

flesh, giving her enough courage to speak. "N-no, Uncle George! You can't have it!"

He leaned forward, and the humor went out of his voice. "Listen here, you're going to give it over, or else!"

"Nonno gave it to me. It's mine, and it'll protect me. Now, you get out of here you mean old dog!"

George laughed, and the horrible canine sound went right through her. Before she knew it, her legs gave out, and she was down on her knees in the damp earth of the row. He leaned closer still, and pulled a pocket knife from his trousers, flicking the blade out into the bright light of the afternoon with a single deft movement of his thumb. His breath was hot and sour and terrible as it blew against her face in deep, heavy waves. "Give it here, you little bitch."

Her eyes blurred with tears and she leaned back, dropping the kale and planting a hand in the soil to support her as she shrank away. Her fingers touched something hard, and she dug them in, desperate.

She closed her hand around the rock, and with a mighty heave, brought it up and out of the earth, missing Uncle George's face, but striking him hard in the shoulder. From behind him, she heard the shrill whimper of the invisible beast.

George stood and staggered back, stunned. His eyes clouded in confusion, and he placed one hand on his knee as he struggled to catch his breath. "Sofia?"

She scrambled backward, and with one muddy hand, wiped at the tears on her cheeks, leaving a long, wet streak of dirt in their place. Behind George, Guillaume was racing down the row, and from the house, she could see Papa and Mama too. They were all running.

Guillaume reached her first and kneeled down beside her.

"Sofia," he panted, "are you alright?"

She hugged him tight and fought to speak between sobs. "It was horrible! Guillaume, he—there was something. A dog! There was—"

"Hush now," he said. "I know, Sofia, I know." Mama and Papa were in the row now, calling her name—nearly there. Guillaume leaned in close. "You and I may speak of it, but it must be our secret. Yes?" She nodded.

Papa was with George. "What happened?"

Shrill, unbelieving, Uncle George pointed his thick, meaty finger in her direction. "She hit me, Robert! Right here in the shoulder! Hit me with a rock! The girl is wild, out of control."

"Papa—" Sofia began to protest, but there was no need.

"And could you blame her?" Papa demanded. "You scared her half to death. What were you thinking, George? We saw you from the house, out the kitchen window. It looked like you were ready to attack. I think you'd better get out of here."

"Robert—"

Mama was beside her now, reaching a hand down, pulling her to her feet, and wrapping her up tight. She turned to Guillaume, fire in her eyes. "Thank you Mister Khoury, though I'd ask you not to touch my daughter."

"Mama," Sofia protested. "Guillaume helped me."

Guillaume raised his hands innocently, though Sofia could see the hurt on his face. "Sorry to offend, Margaret. I assure you—"

"I assure *you*, while I appreciate the gesture, you're

a stranger. We'll discuss this later."

Guillaume looked like he was going to speak—defend himself—but Mama continued to glare, so he lowered his hands and turned away.

A few steps away, George was mumbling. "...Absurd. Absolutely absurd. I'm not through with this, Robert. You'll see."

"I hope you're not threatening, George," Papa said.

"I'm coming back for that coin, one way or another."

"We'll see."

⩰

Guillaume lingered in the field as Margaret and Robert carried Sofia back to the house. He'd worried he waited too long, though, in the end, it had been long enough. He was proud of Sofia—of her bravery and ingenuity. Of course, in the old days, a single blow to the shoulder wouldn't have been enough to shake the bond between Destin's hounds and the poor men she held in her yoke. But she was weaker now—as weak as he was—and the little stun had been a sufficient interruption.

But that's all it was—an interruption. There was no time left to wait. He'd have to find her and convince her to release George Calisti, or he'd be back again. Of course, it would take some doing. He'd tried to reason with Destin before and to no avail.

Furthermore, Margaret's reaction to his help—her barely veiled accusations—provided a complication. He felt a shift in her and knew he'd have to tread lightly if he wanted to stay close to Sofia.

As he started his slow walk back to the house, he silently cursed his own struggles—cursed the rules of the game laid out by deities he was certain were long dead. Destin had the hounds at her disposal, and her diminishing-yet-invaluable ability to influence fate. She had a singular drive to reclaim the Chronicum and restore her goddess's place as arbiter of man's destiny. And what did he have? His apparent immortality? His ability to communicate with the Chronicum and guess at the meaning of its cryptic messages? A mandate to never interfere, upholding the ideas of free will and self-determination?

The odds had never been stacked in his favor, yet since the beginning, he'd endured. He'd kept Destin at bay. He'd chosen the keepers of the Chronicum carefully—weighed their possible futures insofar as he could see them—and stayed faithful to his cause. The Chronicum itself had nearly dissipated all its energy, and he felt certain this present situation was the coin's last gasp. 2019 would be the end of their struggle one way or another. He only had to fend her off a little longer.

And despite her superior gifts, he supposed he had one advantage he could use against her. He remembered their humanity—their history. There was a time when they'd been a man and woman. Priest and priestess. Their passion for one another had been as strong as their passion for the deities they served. And if he could appeal to that humanity, now in the gloaming hours of their struggle—

He walked up the steps to the house and stepped through the front door. In the kitchen, Margaret and Robert were talking, and he started down the hall to his bedroom, but Robert's voice stopped him.

"Mister Khoury—Guillaume?"

He turned. Smiled. "Yes, Robert?"

"Thank you for running out to help." He looked at his wife. "I'm not sure what's got into my brother. He's always been hot-headed, but this was extraordinary, even for him. My sincerest apologies. You must be quite disturbed."

Guillaume shook his head. "Nothing to worry about, I assure you. Sofia. She's alright?"

"Resting. I think we'll have her stay in bed the rest of the day."

He looked at Margaret, weighing the risk of his next question. "Ah. Would you mind if I visited her later?"

Robert nodded and looked at Margaret. "She seems to be fond of you. Let her nap a while, and I'm sure she'd be delighted with the company."

A knock on the door roused her from her sleep, and Sofia was grateful to realize she hadn't dreamed of Elliot. She hadn't dreamed at all. Sitting up, she regarded the light through the window, soft and warm. It was late afternoon. "Hello?" she called.

The door opened, and Guillaume stepped inside. "Did I wake you?" he asked. She shook her head. "May I sit with you?"

"Yes, please."

"Quite a day you had, no?"

Placing her lower lip between her teeth, she bit down lightly, considering which of the million questions she wanted to ask Guillaume first, and hoping he'd answer. "Mama and Papa. Could they see that dog? The one I saw?"

"No. It is not meant to be seen, but sometimes when it is angry, it gives itself away."

"Was it angry with me? Was Uncle George angry with me?"

"It seems to me that your Uncle George is an angry man, and that makes it easy for the hound to get in, you see." He shook his head. "But no, neither the hound nor your uncle are really angry with you. But the hound is a hunter, and it cannot fight its nature."

"Will it come back?"

He nodded, slowly, and she shivered beneath the covers. "Yes, and maybe more than once."

"Because it wants Nonno's coin?"

"Yes." She watched him breathing. Considering. At first glance, he looked no older than Papa, but as she watched him breathe in and out—watched the creases in his face in the soft, golden light—she realized how old he must really be. The skin was ageless but somehow ancient, and she wondered if she were to reach out and touch it if it would feel like stone. He smiled. "Do you think you can handle it when the hound returns?"

"Will it come back with Uncle George?"

"Probably, but maybe not. I'll tell you the truth. It could come with nearly anyone."

"With Mama or Papa?"

"Oh, yes. But I don't think it will. I need to know, though. Can you handle it?"

"What do you mean?"

"Because if you don't think you can, you may give the coin to me now and I'll take it far, far away from here. Then there'll be no more hounds. But it belongs to you, so you must choose, and I will respect whatever choice you make."

She continued to chew at her lip. She didn't want to see Uncle George under the spell of that horrible beast—didn't want to feel like she and Mama and Papa were in danger. But then she thought of the flood, and weren't they in danger anyway? She thought of Elliot too, who was in a different kind of danger he didn't know anything about. Reaching out her tiny hand, she lifted Nonno's coin off her nightstand and closed it tightly in her fist.

"Guillaume?" she asked. "My Nonno saw the hound too, didn't he? At least, he said he did, and the one I saw looked just like—"

A smile, wry and wide, crept across his face. "Yes. I think he did."

"And he was brave? He chased it away? He helped you?"

"Yes, he did."

She set her jaw. "Then I can be brave, too. For Mama and Papa. And for Elliot."

"I thought you might say so." He stood and touched her forehead. "Rest now, dear girl. Rest, and be strong."

Chapter Fifteen

August 20, 2019 - Tuesday

At the sound of Cameron's bike tires against the dirt path, Elliot leaped to his feet. Beneath him, the rotten wood of the farm house's derelict porch shifted and groaned. A moment later, Cam emerged from the saplings with the sun glinting off his black hair, and, unable to contain the rush of excitement and relief, Elliot jumped from the porch to meet him. Their arms twisted together, bodies tangled, and Elliot buried his face in the other boy's neck, breathing deeply of his light, clean scent.

Cam pulled him tighter—pressed into him until they were one being—and raked his lips lightly across the skin beneath Elliot's ear. "I'm alright," he said. "I'm alright."

Reluctant, Elliot disengaged and stepped away. "I was so worried. I could barely sleep. What if she'd come back?"

"She didn't. I'm okay, really." He reached into his pocket and removed Sofia's coin. "I think I'd better give this back to you, though."

Pressing his eyes closed, Elliot took the coin and felt a warm rush at the reunion. Holding it felt right. Necessary. "Just a few more days," he said, opening his eyes. "Once Sofia and her parents are safe, we're going to take this out on a ferry and drop it in the ocean. That's what the detective said we should do."

"What *is* it?" Cameron asked. "Destin said she was a priestess. Something about it being stolen from an old goddess. Honestly, I would have thought this was all totally insane, but after seeing Sofia—"

"I don't know, but the detective was terrified when I asked him about the case. He says the boarder wasn't the murderer, but whoever was—wasn't human?"

Cam shivered. "It sounds like dropping it in the ocean is a great idea. Do you think the killer could have been Destin? She's *definitely* not human."

"No. The detective clearly said *he*. The killer was male."

"And anything about Sofia?"

Elliot shook his head. "I'm nervous about seeing her. I wanted to have more, but—"

"But we have to ask her about Destin."

From behind them on the porch, Sofia's voice cut through the thick morning air. "Elliot! Elliot!"

He turned, smiling as she ran down the steps and straight for him. He opened his arms to embrace her, and she opened hers in turn, but the absurdity of the gesture was laid plain as her body passed through him clear to the other side, coming to rest among the saplings.

Sofia's shoulders slumped as she turned around, stomping her foot. "I don't like being in a different time from you, Elliot. I really wanted a hug."

He laughed, and it was rich and full and light. Extending his hand, he interlaced his fingers with Cameron's. "I wanted that too," he said. "Cam is here with me. Can you see him?"

Sofia nodded. "Hi."

"Hi," Cam replied.

"Did you find out anything about the flood, Elliot? Think of a way for Mama and Papa to believe me? They want to take me to a special mind doctor."

He shook his head. "No, Sofia, but—" he looked at Cam and sighed. "Has anyone tried to take your coin away from you? Is there a woman there? Destin?"

"No, but Uncle George—"

Cam stiffened. "Uncle George? What about him?"

"He wanted the coin. Yesterday he came to the farm, and he came after me. I thought he was a dragon, but actually, he was a mean old dog! Guillaume says it's the dog that's after it—that it got into him easy because he's an angry man anyways. But he pulled out a knife, and he called me something really terrible, and then I hit him with a rock, and it scared out the dog for a little while, but Guillaume says—"

"Woah." Elliot held up a hand. "Slow down, Sofia. Slow down. Guillaume? The boarder?"

"How did you know—"

"It doesn't matter. How much do you know about this Guillaume? You talk to him?"

"Oh yes. He's my friend. He's the one who gave the coin to my Nonno in the first place, all the way back in

Italy."

Cam swallowed hard. "Elliot," he said, voice above a whisper. "When we saw Destin together, and then when she was at my house there was this horrible animal smell, and it was like—"

"Like a dog." He sighed, pushing all the air from his lungs, tempted to give in to the overwhelming urge toward self-pity. It was too much, suddenly. Given the choice between laughter or tears, he chose laughter. How could he do anything else given the absurdity? He was twenty years old, struggling with his sexuality, an alcoholic mother, and her emotionally abusive boyfriend. Furthermore, there was a little girl sixty years in the past depending on him to solve the imminent murder of her parents—and possibly herself—and at the center of it all? A goddamned magic coin was being hunted in two separate timelines by an evil priestess with the aid of some kind of hell hound.

Cameron scowled. "What's so funny?"

"Nothing," he said. "Nothing is funny." Quieter, "I don't know if I can do this Cam. It's too much, it's too—"

"Well, we're in it too far now, aren't we?" He looked at Sofia. "This Guillaume. Has he told you anything about the coin itself? There are people here trying to get it too, and we don't know why."

Sofia shook her head. "No. But Guillaume says the dog will come back, with Uncle George or someone else. I told him I could be brave, because Nonno was brave, and Elliot was brave. And you're brave too, aren't you Cameron?"

"Yes." He nodded at Elliot. "We *are* brave. Elliot, I think we need to tell her the rest of it."

"Cam," Elliot whimpered. "I don't think she's ready."

Sofia raised her chin. "I'm ready. Tell me."

Cam sighed. Swallowed. "It's not just the flood. Your parents—"

Elliot squeezed his hand, hard. "Please, don't."

He closed his eyes. "Someone is going to try to hurt them, and maybe you too."

Sofia's legs folded beneath her, and she sat heavy on the ground. "Because of Nonno's coin?"

"Maybe. We don't know."

She looked at Elliot, tears in her eyes. "You didn't want to tell me?"

"Sofia," he said, "I did want to tell you. I was going to, but we wanted to find out who it was first. We thought maybe Guillaume, but—"

"Uncle George," she said. "He's going to come back, and this time he's going to hurt us." She leaped to her feet. "But he can't!"

"What?"

"Guillaume says I have to give the coin away. He can't take it from me. I have to give it to him. That's the way it works!" She crossed her arms, defiant and proud.

Elliot looked at Cam. She was an eight-year-old girl. Of course, it didn't cross her mind that her uncle might attack her parents to *compel* her to give the coin over. "Sofia, I think it's more complicated than that. I think you need to find a way to get away and stay away. It's going to happen on the day of the flood—two days from now."

Chapter Sixteen

August 20, 1959 - Thursday

Sofia began to pace, thinking as hard as she could. Two days from today was Saturday. She and Mama would be going into town for the market, and maybe she could persuade Papa to come too. And then maybe—but there was nowhere for them to go. And if Uncle George was going to try to hurt them, he'd wait until they got back. She looked at Elliot and Cameron holding hands and remembered the idea she'd had last time she saw him.

"Maybe you can tell Mama. I'll hold her hand, and she'll see you. She'll believe you, and she'll believe me too. Then she'll know you're not pretend. She'll know!"

Elliot's eyes widened, and he looked at Cam, who shrugged. "Okay. We could try it."

"Wait right there," she said. Mama was in the washhouse with Papa—had gone out a little before Sofia heard Elliot talking to Cam. Turning, Sofia sprinted across the gravel drive and down the short dirt road to where the washhouse stood at the edge of the field.

Inside, Papa was putting crates of zucchini on the scale, and Mama was writing down the weight of each on a pad of paper. Sofia jumped up and down and waved her arms until Mama looked over. “Come quick!” she said.

“Sofia,” Mama said, “We’re very busy. What is it, dear girl?”

“Elliot! Come quick. He’s here. I know how you can see him!”

Papa frowned. “*Mia bella*?”

“I’ve had quite enough of this, Sofia,” Mama said. “This whole business gets you very upset, and now I’m starting to get upset. You have too much time here alone. I’m going to call little Sue’s mother, and after lunch, I’ll take you over—”

“No!” Sofia stomped her foot. “Mama, hurry!”

“Margaret,” Papa said, “I’ll go. Let’s indulge her—”

“No,” Mama said. “I’m putting an end to this.” She dropped the pad of paper in a huff and marched forward. Sofia grabbed her hand and pulled her—half-running—toward where Elliot and Cameron waited back at the house.

They reached the drive, and Sofia looked at Elliot, expectant. “Can you see her?”

Elliot stared blankly, looking at the hand she used to grasp Mama’s. He shook his head. “No, I—is she right there?”

Mama scowled. “What am I supposed to be looking at?”

The tears came fast and hot—furious and ferocious little beads of acid burning down her cheeks. "Right there, Mama! He's standing right there with his friend Cameron. Mama! Why can't you see them?"

Cam spoke up. "Sofia, breathe. It's alright, breathe."

"No! It's supposed to work. She's supposed to see you. She's supposed to—"

"That's enough," Mama said, and her voice was mean and cold and impatient, but she lifted Sofia up and pulled her tight. "Stop, dear girl. Just stop." And then there was a quaver in Mama's voice, and it made Sofia cry all the harder, burying her face in her mother's shoulder. "You're sick, my love. That's all it is. You're sick and we're going to get you better. Now hush. Just—hush."

"Mama—" but Mama wouldn't listen, instead started to carry Sofia up the steps to the house. "No!" She wriggled and squirmed, but Mama held tight. "No! I have to talk to him more! Mama!"

"You need to rest, Sofia."

"Mama!" They were almost to the door now. Elliot had told her about the danger with Uncle George, but she hadn't had the chance to tell him yet about her dreams. Twisting her body, she locked eyes with him as Mama struggled to hold her while forcing the door open. "Elliot!" She screamed. "You're in danger too. There's a gun. Someone's going to shoot. Elliot! I saw it. I dreamed it. Elliot!"

She watched his face cloud with fear, but then she was inside, and the door was closing, and she couldn't see him anymore.

Guillaume appeared in the hall as Mama was taking

the first steps up the stairs to her bedroom. “Margaret,” he said. “Sofia. Is everything alright?”

Mama stopped. Turned. There was fire in her voice. “It would be quite alright if you’d mind your own business, Mister Khoury.”

“Pardon? Again, I assure you—”

“Guillaume!” Sofia shouted. “Elliot. He says Uncle George or somebody is going to hurt—says someone is trying to get the coin in his time too.”

She felt Mama stiffen. “What’s this? Have you been indulging her fantasies? I’m not sure what you’re after, but now I’m all but certain you’ve taken an unhealthy interest in my daughter. I’ve half a mind to ask you to go. If it were up to me—”

He raised his hands in innocence. “I *assure* you, it is not what it seems.”

“It had better not be, Mister Khoury.” She didn’t wait for a response, kept marching up the stairs, through the bedroom door, and didn’t stop until she’d put Sofia down on the bed. “Now, calm yourself, child. Breathe, won’t you?”

“Mama,” she sobbed. “Elliot says someone is going to hurt you and Papa. It’s Uncle George. I know it is. And the flood is coming. We have to get away!”

“Enough!” Mama stood and stomped her foot, which was enough to stop Sofia’s sobbing. “Your Uncle George isn’t going to hurt anybody. And there won’t be any flood. And *none of this* is real. Sofia, you must see that.”

“Please, won’t you believe me?”

“I won’t. This is madness.” She knelt down beside the bed and put her hand on Sofia’s forehead. Quietly, tenderly, she cooed. “I love you *so* much, dear girl. But you're sick, and you need to rest. We're going to take you to see someone soon—next week. He'll make you better. You'll be better. But for now, I need you to rest, alright?"

"Mama?"

"Now, lay here. I need you to lay here until you can calm down and see that this is all pretend. Just—lay here. I don't want to hear any more about Elliot or any of it, understand?"

She melted into the mattress and closed her eyes. "I understand."

Mama sighed, deep, then stood and left the room, closing the door behind her. Sofia heard her begin to sob in the hallway beyond.

Chapter Seventeen

August 20, 2019 – Tuesday

"A gun?" Elliot said under his breath. He walked slowly forward and placed his hand on the rotting rail of the porch–felt the rough, splintered wood, and stared down at the remnants of white paint that had sunk deep into the grain. He gripped it hard, needing to feel something solid and tangible. He hadn't heard her mother's words, but it was clear by the way Sofia's body levitated and twisted–the way she'd called his name as she struggled–that she'd been carried away. Her mother didn't believe her, and now maybe she was worse off than before. He didn't know why it didn't work–why when he held Cameron's hand, he could see her, but Sofia's mother hadn't been able to see them.

But at the present moment, it didn't matter. She'd said he was in danger too–that she'd dreamed of someone with a gun. He wasn't sure how much he could read into her premonitions, but it was enough to give him pause. It was only in the last day-and-a-half—since Destin had been waiting for him in the living room—that he'd even considered his personal safety. This was a further complication in an increasingly complicated scenario, and now the urge toward self-pity was almost overwhelming.

A little way off, Cameron stood by himself, staring at his feet. "What's wrong?" Elliot asked.

"Oh, I don't know." Cam shrugged. "I found out my grandfather is probably a murderer."

Elliot slapped his own forehead. Idiot. Of course, he hadn't even started to consider Cam in all of this. Slowly—penitent—he walked forward and put a hand on Cam's shoulder. "We don't know that."

"If it's not this Guillaume character, then who else?"

"Come on, though, George would've been so obvious. They would've caught him right away. That's like, police investigation 101. You always start with the people closest to the victims."

"Elliot. Think about it. You heard her talking about him being—I don't know—possessed? By a dog. Didn't the detective say *he wasn't even human*? And the detective knew, right? What if he knew it was my grandfather all along, but he was too scared? What if—"

Elliot wrapped him in his arms. "We're going to have to talk to him. We were going to do that anyways."

"And then what? How are we supposed to stop him? And what if we *do* stop him, and he goes to prison or something for, I don't know, assault? What if he never meets my grandmother, and then my dad is never born, and then I—"

Elliot pulled him tighter. "Listen. Shh. We don't know anything yet." He thought for a moment. "That's not going to happen. It *didn't* happen. You're here, right here with me. If we stopped your grandfather, and therefore prevented your father from being born, then you wouldn't be here helping me, would you?"

Cam stepped brusquely away and threw his hands in the air. "Then what are we doing here? Aren't we *trying* to change the past? I mean, what are you saying, Elliot?"

"I don't know. Yes, I guess we're trying to—" It struck him, suddenly. "I don't know. I'm not like, a quantum-physicist or anything. I didn't ask for any of this, and I know you didn't either, but, what if it's not about changing the past. What if it's about making sure certain things *come to pass*?"

"I don't follow. Like, we're supposed to warn Sofia about the flood? Just supposed to let her parents die? Can we change the past, or can't we?"

"Look, maybe it's not so black and white. We could save Sofia's parents and *not* necessarily jeopardize your existence, right? But that's not even worth thinking about right now—"

"Um, I beg to differ!"

"Okay, fine. Say we can't save them. Sofia remains the mystery. What if this is about her and *only* her, right? What if we have to make sure she gets out. Protects the coin. Passes it on to me. And what if what really matters is the present. Right now. You heard her say I was in danger. It has to do with the coin."

"We're not cut out for this, Elliot." Cam wrapped his arms around him. "I'm absolutely terrified."

Elliot pushed away and set his mouth. "You told

Sofia we were brave, right?"

"Yeah, but—"

"We have to go see your grandfather. We know her parents' fate, but hers? This started with her. I think it ends with her as well."

Chapter Eighteen

August 20, 1959 - Thursday

Quietly, Guillaume sat at the desk in his room. He was relieved to learn Elliot and his friend still held the coin in 2019 but was concerned as ever knowing he could do nothing in the present to help them protect it. Surely, he existed in their timeline, also. Surely, he was still in the game. That they knew nothing of him simply meant the version of himself sixty years in the future was keeping a low profile.

Because, of course, the alternative—

It wasn't worth considering; he needed to think about Sofia now, and Destin. He pushed back a little in the chair, allowing the front legs to lift off the floor, and balanced himself there. It was also curious that the Chronicum hadn't allowed Margaret to see the boys in the same way it allowed Cameron to see Sofia—when in direct physical contact with the keeper. Throughout its history, the coin had always allowed the keepers to share its visions through physical contact, so Margaret's exclusion was significant—unique.

Though really, wasn't this whole situation unique?

It was further evidence the coin had an agenda—whether its own, or Destin's in the future, he couldn't say, though the latter now seemed less likely.

She didn't have it yet.

Slowly, he lowered the front legs of the chair back to the floor and prepared to open his journal on the desk, when a noise from the hall stopped him. Ringing. Percussive and loud. The telephone. He could hear Margaret's footsteps pattering out from the kitchen, and then she answered.

A moment later there was a knock on his door. "Mister Khoury. You have a phone call. Out here in the hall." He felt the hairs raise on the back of his neck, and though the air in the bedroom was stuffy and warm, a little chill radiated down from the base of his skull, through his shoulder and arms all the way to his fingertips. He opened the door, and Margaret stood, glaring. "I trust you'll keep it short."

"Yes, ma'am." He nodded and followed her down to where the phone hung on the wall by the stairs. She gave him one final disapproving look before disappearing into the kitchen. He raised the speaker to his ear and said "Hello?"

"Mon cher," lilted the sickly-sweet voice at the other end of the line. It was cool and crisp, lush and honeyed. A French sunset. A chilled glass of Lillet against the tongue of the ear. "You seem to have installed yourself well. Close to the source. Imagine my surprise when I heard."

"Destin, you must let this go. There are things happening even I don't understand."

She laughed. "Let it go? You speak as though you don't know me at all. You know that I won't—can't."

"Please. If ever there was a time to listen to me—can I see you?"

"Would you dare?"

"I must. Now more than ever."

Through the speaker, the crackle of dead air punctuated her silence. Finally, he heard her sharp intake of breath. "Tonight then. The bar of the Hotel Haverford. Shall we say eight?"

"Eight then." He hung up the phone and crumpled against the wall.

Chapter Nineteen

August 20, 2019 - Tuesday

Elliot did his best to smile, despite the retching feeling in his stomach. The little light flashed, and the attendant at the front desk of Haverford Elms Retirement Community nodded, absently. A printer whizzed and whirred, and she handed him an enormous sticker with his face plastered across the upper two-thirds, and the word *VISITOR* printed in bold black letters taking up the remainder. "Enjoy your visit," she said.

"Uh, thanks."

A little off to the left, standing near the stairs leading to the lower level, Cam waited. Seeing Elliot's pale face—perhaps also the sweat on his brow—he raised his eyebrows. "Elliot, are you alright?"

"It's the smell," he said. "That sterile, antiseptic smell. It reminds me of hospitals—makes me a little sick."

"Really?"

It was his father, of course. He'd never minded until the night of the hit and run. They'd gotten the call when his dad was already in the ambulance and spent hours in the waiting room while he was in surgery, breathing the stale, sterile air, then hours more in the ICU, while he was still listed as critical. And then, when he'd taken the sudden turn—left them—and he and his mother had sobbed into each other, every soggy breath was a gulp of antiseptic. The taste of death. The scent of misery. He'd thought he was going to drown in it.

"Yeah. I'll um—be okay. Let's be quick, yeah?"

"Alright." Cameron led him down the stairs and to the right, past the cafeteria and the chapel, down to the end of the corridor and around a corner. Room 142. George Calisti. He knocked first, and then opened the door and started inside. "Grandpa?" he called. "It's Cameron."

The room was more than a room—a suite with separate living and sleeping areas, a little kitchenette, and a large bathroom. Two wide windows looked out onto the wooded slope of a hill. "Wow," Elliot said. "This is—"

"It's too much. That's what my dad says. The dementia is so far gone, he's probably not going to remember me—only does once in a while. But Aunt Kathy insists, like, maybe he's going to suddenly have a good day and want to fry up an omelet."

They continued to the back of the suite, where George Calisti—shriveled and slight—took up less room than he ought to in an overstuffed armchair. A television on the wall played an old game show at a low volume, and the elder Calisti watched blankly as an excited middle-aged woman hit a buzzer.

Cameron knelt down beside him and folded George's withered hand in his. "Grandpa?"

The old man turned his head, and Elliot registered the alarm in his eyes. "The hell are you?" he demanded, voice raspy and full of air.

"Cam. Cameron. Your grandson. You remember?"

George furrowed his brow, turning the skin into a complex, spotted topography of mountains and valleys. "Robert? What's going on?"

Elliot sucked in his breath. "He thinks you're his brother."

Cam nodded. "It happens sometimes. Apparently, the Calisti genes are strong. I'll go with it." He gave his grandfather a wan smile. "Yeah, George. You remember Sofia, don't you?"

"Oh, yeah!" He laughed. "Your daughter. Hey, Robert, you're too young to have a daughter." The creases in his forehead became impossibly deeper, and the corners of his mouth began to twitch in distress.

Cameron cooed. "Shh. It's alright. Grandpa—uh—George. Do you know what happened to her? What happened to Sofia?"

He blinked. Shook his head. "Robert? What are you doing here?"

Turning his face, Cameron sighed. "I think this is too much. He's ninety-five years old for god's sake. I'm sorry Elliot, he's too far gone."

"Wait," Elliot implored. He pulled Sofia's coin from his pocket and handed it over. "Don't give it to him, of course, but show him. Maybe it'll spark something."

Cautiously, Cam considered the coin. "Elliot, I don't know if—"

"What is that?" George demanded with a strength in his voice that was absent a moment before.

Cam held up the coin. "It's... father's coin."

George's eyes lit up—almost youthful. Hungry. He sat forward in the chair and reached out a hand, but Cam pulled the coin away. "You give that over now, Robert! Where'd you get that? From your little bitch of a girl?" He laughed, and it was cold and cruel. "Give it over now. What are you doing here, Robert? I thought I killed you!"

Cam recoiled in terror, but Elliot leaned down and put a hand on his shoulder. "Cam, we *have* to. Ask him. Keep going."

"Elliot, I can't. This is my *grandfather*. I can't—"

Elliot lifted his chin and looked at George, locking eyes. "How'd you kill him? Robert."

"Kitchen knife. Easiest thing. Right there on the counter." He cackled and looked at Cam. "Now you give that here or I'll do it again!"

Louder, Elliot continued. "What'd you do with it? The knife."

"I rinsed it off and put it back in the block. The hell else would I do with it?"

"And Sofia? Did you kill her too?"

"The little bitch. She ran."

"George, did you kill her?"

"She had my coin. *My* coin. It was supposed to be for *me*! That's what she said."

"Who said? Sofia?"

"No! Not Sofia."

"Did you *kill* her?"

"I'd do it again. I'd—"

Beside him, Cameron twisted, shoving the coin back into Elliot's hand. "Take it," he said. "I can't do this." Then he stood, wiping furiously at the tears in his eyes and fled out into the hall.

Elliot looked at George, and then toward the open door. He knew he should go after Cam—shouldn't wait a moment—but he was so close. "George, did you kill Sofia? Did you kill your niece?"

Blinking, George collapsed back into his chair. The corners of his mouth twisted. "The hell are you?" he asked.

≈

Outside, Cam was waiting on a stone bench beneath a sprawling crab apple tree, branches heavy and laden with fruit. When Elliot approached, the ice in Cameron's puffy red eyes cut through the August heat and froze him in his tracks. "Happy now?" he asked.

"Cameron, I—"

"You what? You *what*?!"

"I'm sorry. I had to know. We had to find out for sure."

Cam threw his hands in the air and started to cry. "For what? Why? What can we do? I'm so stupid."

"You're not stupid."

"Yes. I am. I'm stupid for trusting you. For falling for you. For forgiving and forgetting and carrying this fucking torch for you."

Elliot felt his face twist in anger, and regretted the sharp edge to his tone, even as the words fell from his mouth. "What the hell does that have to do with anything?"

"Oh, I don't know. The present situation? Our history? It's all intertwined, isn't it? Here I am patiently waiting, holding your hand. Being understanding because you can't say it. You can't say you're gay, and I don't know why. But I respected that it was too much for you. I held back. I didn't push. And then, we're in there and I tell you I'm not ready to hear that my grandfather savagely murdered at least two people with a fucking kitchen knife, and you don't have the decency to *let that go*?"

"There isn't *time* to let it go. It's going to happen in *two days*!"

"It happened *sixty years ago*! But I should've expected this."

"What the hell does that mean?"

"You know very well. You've been using me again, that's all."

"When did I ever *use* you?"

"Do I really have to spell it out?"

"Yes!"

Cameron wiped his eyes and crossed his arms. "How about that whole year after your dad died? How about that? You were my best friend before that. I told you I thought I was gay, and you said you'd keep it secret. And then what you did next? What *we* did? You were the only one I wanted to tell, Elliot. The only one who deserved to know. And then your dad died, and you changed. I tried to justify your actions—to justify the betrayal of my confidence with your grief. But you sold me out. You told anyone you could. You ostracized me in the name of making all your new friends. And I just took it. I knew someday you'd wake up and you'd come back to me. But you didn't. You used me to get what you wanted. Some shiny new life."

"Shiny new life?" Elliot sighed, deflated, and sat heavy on the bench beside Cam. "It was anything but shiny. And that's not an excuse. I'm sorry, Cam. You're right about all of it, of course. And I—but I *did* come back to you." He reached out and took Cameron's hands in his.

"Don't touch me!" Cam tried to pull away, but Elliot held tight.

"Please." He let go. "I'm sorry Cam. You're right. You've been patient and—" he took a deep breath, maybe the deepest of his entire life. "And I'm gay. And I love you. I'm *in* love with you, and I don't remember a time anymore when I wasn't. I regret every day what I did to you. I regret what I *just* did to you. I didn't listen, and I didn't—"

"I don't know if that fixes it, Elliot. I really don't."

"What?" His voice cracked. "You're going to tell me that you waited all this time, and forgave me for so long, and now that I finally said it—"

"I don't know. This business with Sofia, and my grandfather. I don't know."

"Please, Cam. Don't do this to me now."

He smiled, sad. "See, there it is. *Me*, you say. It's all about you, again. You don't get it. What do you want to do, Elliot? Go to the police? He's ninety-five years old. His mind is gone. He can't exactly stand trial."

"Cameron—"

"This could *ruin* my family."

"And what about Robert and Margaret? What about Sofia? Don't they deserve justice?"

Cam stood. "What about what I deserve?" Without waiting for a response, he started to walk away.

"Cameron!" Elliot called, but it was too late. Without looking back, Cam climbed onto his bicycle and started to ride away.

≈

Destin leaned against the wall of the corridor and struggled to catch her breath. She told herself it was from rushing down the stairs—ducking out of the way in time to avoid Cameron as he stormed away with his ugly tears—but not far beneath the surface, she knew that wasn't it at all. The fatigue came from the effort it took to compel the attendant at the desk to abandon her post for a minute, to suggest the feeling of a full bladder, and a need for immediate relief. A week ago, she'd been able to influence the mayor's former assistant from the other side of the continent. Today, she could barely influence a bathroom break from fifteen feet away.

She needed the Chronicum, and she needed it now.

From around the corner, the door to George Calisti's suite closed, and she heard Elliot's feet—muted thuds on the carpeted floor of the corridor—and leaned deeper into the textured wallpaper, feeling its grooved canyons and plateaus against her fingers. She focused on breathing. In. Out. In again. Finally, her heartbeat slowed, and she stood straight. This visit to George Calisti was perplexing. These boys had an agenda, and she feared it had something to do with her own loose ends; it was time to find out and assess the damage.

Checking twice to be certain the coast was clear, she waltzed quickly down the corridor and into George's suite, locking the door behind her.

The sight of him—shriveled in his chair—evoked dueling emotions of compassion and amusement. Time was a cruel beast. Last time she saw him, he was red-faced, fiery, fat and full of life. This withered shell that remained was nothing like the George Calisti she'd known so briefly sixty years ago.

He stared past the television mounted to the wall, but as she approached, he turned his head and there was a spark. A glint of recognition, and then a trembling, quaking aura of fear.

"Y-you!" he said, weak and airy. "What are you doing here?"

"Shh." She placed one hand squarely on each arm of his chair and leaned close—closer—until their noses were inches apart. "I see you remember me, George. Ge—orge, how could you forget? Oh, *mon cher*. You were one of my *greatest* disappointments."

"D-demon! Go!" he rasped.

She clucked her tongue and stood straight. "Demon? No. Ge—orge, please. Demons are not real. I could almost say I'm hurt. Almost. But I'll tell you what. I'll go soon. Right after you tell me what those boys wanted."

His face clouded in confusion. "Boys?"

"Ugh." The twisting of his face told her he'd already forgotten. His mind was rotten. Leaning forward, she placed one finger from each hand against his temples, and, though still hopelessly exhausted, mustered the energy to compel him. She evoked the devotion—the overwhelming need to please—and felt the shredded landscape of his mind fighting her influence. But she'd been here before, and though scorched earth now stood where verdant fields of thought and intellect once thrived, she could remember the terrain—the way through. "Ge—orge." she lilted. "Tell me. The boys were here. What did they want?"

Like a string wound too tightly, finally the tension overwhelmed, and his mind snapped in a beautiful release. Musical. Clean. She stepped back and watched as his eyes glazed over. Nodding slowly, he spoke. "They asked what happened to Sofia."

"Sofia? And why should they care about that?"

"I don't know. Wanted to know if I killed her. And Robert. And Margaret."

This was curious. Of course, Kathryn had mentioned Elliot's interest in the family history, but this utter fixation on the girl was baffling. She wondered for a moment if it had anything to do with the Chronicum, but dismissed the idea at once. The Chronicum concerned itself with events to come—allowed its keepers the foresight and ability to influence their own fates. It had been sixty years since Sofia's story was in any way relevant, and Destin would know.

The house then, perhaps. The murder scene. She surmised that's where Elliot had found the coin—where it had been these last six decades while she wasted her time in California. He must've learned it once belonged to a little girl that disappeared and gotten caught up in the allure of the mystery. They were bored post-adolescents at the end of a long summer vacation, playing detective. At the surface, it was harmless enough, and still—

"What did you tell them, George?"

"The truth," he droned. "With the kitchen knife."

A little shiver passed through her. What a mess he'd made—only half under her influence, because she'd been growing weaker even then. The urge to please her had driven him as much as his own rage. But in the brackish water where his dueling motivations eddied, he'd been careless. Cocky. He'd rinsed the knife in the sink and shoved it back in the knife block.

"And you told them what you did with it?"

"I put it back."

"Oh, Ge—orge," she sighed. "What an idiot you are." She cursed herself for interceding on his behalf all those years ago. She should've let him hang. But she'd thought there was a chance—infinitesimal—that after the coin went cold, it might become active again; a chance she might need him still. "Still making a mess of everything."

What were the chances the knife was still there? The house had been closed off as a crime scene after the flood, and when the case went cold, it was sealed up in the interest of preserving evidence. But that was sixty years ago. Was it realistic to think no one had entered since then—no teenagers looking for a place to drink stolen beer, or vagrants seeking shelter against a winter chill?

She wasn't sure she could afford to chance it. Not now when things were already so tenuous. She cared nothing for George, but if an investigation was reopened because of those horrible boys, or if Kathryn Locke was caught up in a scandal because of the sins of her father, then the distractions and pressures could cause everything to unravel.

In his chair, the glaze over George Calisti's eyes began

to dissipate. Rasping, quiet, barely above a whisper, he croaked. “You made a mess of me.”

She laughed and leaned forward, kissing him on the forehead. “Oh no, George. You didn’t need me for that.” Then she stood and headed for the door.

Chapter Twenty

August 20, 1959 - Thursday

Guillaume stood on the sidewalk outside the Hotel Haverford and soaked in the color of the evening sky. The sun had set twenty minutes ago, and now its remaining light diffused into the atmosphere in shades of plum and cobalt–streaked across high, thin clouds that reached out toward the ocean beyond like ghostly fingers. The warm light of the lobby beyond the glass doors of the hotel beckoned him forward, promising comfort and luxury and safety. But it was all an illusion because she was here. She was waiting.

He checked his watch. Two minutes to eight. The time for their reunion had arrived. Taking one last look at the beauty of the evening, he turned and entered the hotel, preparing for darker things.

The atmosphere of the bar stood in stark contrast to the lobby. The lights were low, and the walls clad with black wainscoting beneath lush crimson wallpaper. A few businessmen in their suit jackets and fedoras sat at the bar, fresh off the last train from Boston, sipping their highballs and keeping their own counsel. An older couple occupied a bistro table—laughing, touching hands. And there, in the deepest, darkest corner, in a round booth with a tall, plush, beaded back, she waited. Red dress. Hair pinned up—a streak or two of gray showing through the jet black. On the table, a Negroni, up, and a bubbling glass of something amber.

He approached, slow and cautious, and when she saw him, she smiled bright and wide—white teeth gleaming in the dim light. She stood and placed her hands on his shoulders. Kissed cheeks. "I ordered for you. Whiskey and soda?"

He swallowed. "Yes. That's fine," and took his seat. "It's—good to see you," he said, closing his eyes. Ashamed he meant it. Even after millennia, she was still the most beautiful woman he'd ever known. "Destin, there are things—"

"Shh," she said and took a sip of her cocktail. "It's always business with you, Guillaume. Why don't we sit a while? It is as though you willfully forget. You and I? We have nothing but time. In all this wide world, it is only you and I that matter."

He laughed under his breath. "It is you and I that matter the least. In this twentieth century, we are more irrelevant than we've ever been, and I think you know it."

"*Puh*, if you choose to think so, then I suppose it is true—for you."

"You must face the reality, Destin. Science marches

forward. How long can it be before man has no use for gods of any form? Ours are long forgotten—have been usurped by this new monotheism and its various iterations. But even this new god cannot expect to survive the next couple of centuries."

She sighed. "And yet we persist, and that means nothing to you. The Chronicum is real. Our gods *are real.*"

"They once were, but no longer."

"They *will be* again. This girl, Guillaume. This Sofia. Why don't you get the coin from her and give it to me? Then humanity will believe."

"Will be *enslaved.* They deserve more than to be at the whims of fate they are powerless to control." He considered how much of it to tell her. She shouldn't know about 2019. Of that, he was certain.

"Fate exists with or without me—without *Her*. It always will, Guillaume. You battle fate as I battle time. Both exist. Both are invincible."

"You mistake fate with chance, *cherie*. The fate you wish for man is one of your own design. But listen, we've had this argument before a hundred times. I know you won't be swayed, and you know I won't either. I've come because—"

"Because?"

"Because I believe it is coming to an end."

She blinked. Sat straighter, then narrowed her eyes in suspicion. "I don't believe it. How could you know this?"

He took a large swallow of his drink and shuddered as it burned its way down to his gut. "We have always known the energy of the Chronicum was finite. It is behaving oddly. It is different. And you are weak—weaker than you've ever been. I saw it yesterday when the girl struck George Calisti with a rock. She is eight years old, Destin—not strong at all. And yet it was enough to shake off your hound for a little while?"

"It means nothing."

"It means everything! Destin—" he reached out and grasped her hands in his. "Do you remember? Do you recall our humanity all those centuries ago? Those sunsets on the eastern edge of the Mediterranean? We worshipped our gods, but maybe more than that, we worshipped each other. How could we know they'd quarrel? How could we know their little game would lead to this existence—these millennia spent at odds with one another? I tell you, not as an immortal servant to Time, but as that *man* who loved you—*loves* you. It is ending. And I implore you, not as an immortal servant to Fate, but as the *woman* who loved me too. Let's forget it. When it's truly over, we will age. We'll grow old. Destin, we will *die*. Do you really want to waste another moment, apart?"

Slowly, carefully, she withdrew her hands from his and took a sip of her Negroni. "As usual, Guillaume, you neglect to consider the alternative. With the Chronicum in my hands, I could fill it up again. We could live forever, together. You ask me to defy my nature, my entire reason for existing as long as I have. Who is to say if I give it up I won't die immediately? Right here. In this moment? If the game is over, if I forfeit, what reason is there for me to continue?"

"Couldn't I be your reason?"

In one long, terrible draw, she downed the rest of her

drink and stood. "You were right all along, Guillaume. Down to business is best. There's no point in the two of us sitting here. I'll get the coin, and then perhaps you'll reconsider."

"So, that's it then?"

"That's it."

"I only hope you'll see reason...before it's too late for us."

She laughed and turned on her heel. "Goodnight, Guillaume. May we meet again on...different terms. Enjoy your drink."

There was more he wanted to say. He wanted to implore her to stay, but before he could form the words, she was already gone.

Chapter Twenty-One

August 20, 2019 - Tuesday

Still feeling weak from her encounter with the attendant at the retirement home and the effort it had taken to compel George Calisti to speak, Destin turned the key in the ignition and extinguished the engine. Hours had passed, and still, she felt heavy and slightly out of breath. Even a mere sixty years ago, she had the strength to recover. Now, she felt like anchors were tied to her legs, and as though life was seeping out of her pores.

Through the windshield, she looked at the sky—deep cobalt now, almost black—and closed her eyes. She was fading, faster than the light in the sky. And what of Guillaume? The coin had been in play for a week now, and still, there was no sign of him.

She recalled their last meeting, sixty years ago in the bar of the Hotel Haverford. He'd warned her of this, and she hadn't listened—thought it was a ploy. A strategy. And now? Had he already succumbed? Was he dead?

She couldn't think of it now. Her own survival was what mattered, and everything depended on getting ahold of the Chronicum once and for all. Opening her eyes, she sat forward and mustered the strength. She pushed open the car door—heavier than it ought to be—and stepped out into the surprisingly cool air of the evening.

The walk up the path to Kathryn Locke's house felt like miles. Rest was what she needed. A good sleep. After this, she could have it. But Kathryn had to know; she needed to act. Destin pressed the bell and waited, panting under her breath.

The door opened, and Kathryn regarded her with surprise. "Oh! Destin. I wouldn't have expected you this late. Do you have those polling numbers I asked for?"

Feebly, Destin reached forward and grabbed the mayor's arm—pulled her in close. "Forget the numbers. There is a different problem requiring immediate attention." The bond was weak—almost non-existent—but Destin pushed into Kathryn's mind with everything she had left. "Now, you must listen very carefully, because I may only be able to say this to you once."

Chapter Twenty-Two

August 21, 2019 – Wednesday

"Is there a chill in the air?" Farmer Melissa asked as she hoisted a black plastic crate of tomatoes up onto the scale.

"I don't think so," Cam said. Cold. His hands moved rapidly, separating fruit from last week's harvest that was ready for distribution from that which needed a little longer to ripen in the washhouse. He raised his eyes to Elliot and tilted his head toward a full crate. "Those are ready for the farm stand."

"Nope," Melissa said. "I think there definitely is." She put her hands on her hips. "I don't know what's going on with the two of you, but you'd better figure it out."

"Sorry?" Elliot said, lifting the crate Cam had indicated.

"Give that to me," Melissa replied, taking the tomatoes. "I'll take these out and um, spruce up the farm stand a little. You barely spoke at all and then last week you were thick as thieves, and now I don't think I could cut through the tension with a machete. Vegetables are sensitive, you know." She blinked her eyes rapid-fire and donned her most ridiculous frown. "You're *hurting their feelings*!"

In spite of themselves, the boys laughed. "Sorry, Melissa," Elliot said.

"Don't apologize to *me*. But when I get back, you'd better have resolved whatever this is." She turned on a heel and headed out toward the farm stand.

Elliot sighed. "Is it that obvious?"

Pressing his lips together, Cameron exhaled hard through his nose. "Who can say what's obvious to you, and what isn't?"

"Cam, I said I was sorry. And I meant it. So, what can I do to fix it?"

He shrugged. "Honestly, Elliot? You can't. You already did your part. It's up to me now."

"What do you mean?"

"Don't you think I've got a lot to unpack right now? I mean, my grandfather is a murderer. Do you know what that *feels* like? And I—right now when I look at you, I feel all that pain from when we were twelve. Thirteen. I thought it was behind me, but when you kept *pushing* yesterday—kept going until you got what you wanted—it was like being back in that time all over again. I can't shrug that off."

"Okay, well, first of all, I don't know if we can really blame your grandfather. You heard Sofia. If he was under the influence of some otherworldly beast—"

"They were still his hands. He still picked up the

knife—still used it."

"Look, I won't say anything except to Sofia. You're right. Because what's the point in dragging your family—"

Cameron threw his hands in the air. "What's the point of *any* of it, Elliot? It's not going to work. Her parents don't believe her. What's going to happen already *happened*. You can't change it."

"Then why do I see her?"

Quiet, Cameron put a hand on his forehead and leaned forward. There were tears in the corners of his eyes, and it took Elliot's full force of will not to rush forward, fold him in his arms, and kiss them away. "You said you weren't a quantum-physicist. Neither am I. I don't know why you see her."

Elliot couldn't handle it anymore. Moving swiftly, he grasped Cam's shoulders, found no resistance, and pulled him in. Their bodies together lacked the usual spark—Cam's rigid, and his own melting—and in the physical nearness, Elliot felt for the first time the true breadth of the distance between them. "Can't you see this through with me? It's Wednesday. Just today and tomorrow. Can't you wait to be angry on Friday?"

Cam twisted and pushed lightly, extricating himself from Elliot's arms. "I don't want to be angry with you on Friday. I don't want to be angry with you *ever*, but this is where we're at right now. Take that stupid coin and throw it into the ocean like you said you were going to. Do it today. This afternoon."

"But, Sofia."

"Elliot, you've already done all you can."

It wasn't true. There was still time. The flood was tomorrow, and so were the murders. There had to be something.

It occurred to him suddenly. A bolt of lightning. A deluge of inspiration. Maybe he could pull the trick with the newspaper again—he could read it, and Sofia could recite it to her parents. Tomorrow's edition. He'd go to the library today and get the headlines—all of them. He'd visit this afternoon, and if she could make them listen when they got the paper first thing in the morning, they'd know all of it was true. They could get out of town. It could all be avoided. There'd be no consequences for George—no prison, or chance of Cameron's father never being born. The plan was so perfect, he was frustrated he hadn't thought of it earlier.

He lifted his chin, and his voice was strong. Hopeful. "That's not true."

"What are you—"

Melissa came back into the washhouse. "Did you two work it out?" she asked.

There was no time to waste. He wanted to do it now. "What time is it?" he asked.

"Eleven forty-two," she said. "Why?"

"I know it's early, but do you mind if I take off? I can stay longer on Friday."

"Um," she looked around. Considered. "Alright, I guess. Is everything okay?"

"Yeah, fine." He smiled at Cam. "I've got this," he said and started toward the door to the washhouse.

"Elliot!" Cam called. "What are you doing?"

"I'll call you later," he said from the door, then headed into the bright sunlight and hopped on his bike.

⩰

The ride to the Haverford Free Library was an eternity in twelve minutes. Elliot pumped his legs as fast as they could go, spinning the thick tires of his too-small mountain bike hard against the asphalt. With every breath, he drank in the thick, sweet August air, and expelled it, thirsty for more. The mid-day sun burned against his skin, and together with the wind, stole away the sweat the moment it pushed up from his pores.

Already winded, he parked and fumbled with the combination lock on his chain. The urgency was real—thrilling—and he had to close his eyes for a moment to summon the concentration required to properly align the numbers. This was it. It was going to work. Sloppily, he looped the chain through the front tire and around the frame, secured the lock, and ran for the doors.

Inside, the shock of cold air conditioning highlighted the burning in his lungs, but he pushed forward, taking the stairs to the second floor three at a time. This was a sprint—the last half mile of a long and arduous race. Once he had these headlines, once he read them to Sofia and she relayed them to her parents, his part would be over. It would be in her hands. Their hands. He'd be free to do what Cameron asked. He could take an afternoon train to Boston and board the ferry to Salem—drop the coin into deep water halfway there. He'd call Lindsey, and she could borrow her mother's car to pick him up and bring him home. No more Destin. No more 1959. And maybe all this tension with Cameron could start to evaporate.

He kept going—running, sprinting. He passed the Reference Desk, planning to smile at his old friend, the attendant, but her chair was empty. Almost there now, he rounded a corner and spied the ancient computer console with the archives, but—

There she was—the attendant—bending over and rubbing at her temple as a man sat in front of the screen. He turned, pushed his glasses higher on his nose, and ran a hand through his hair—short and curling, jet black with touches of gray. The medium brown skin of his forehead wrinkled into a maze of hills and valleys, and he shrugged at the attendant.

"What's going on here?" Elliot demanded, coming to a stop and fighting to catch his breath. "Is everything alright?"

The attendant frowned. "I hope you got most of what you needed for your paper."

"What?"

"The disk is corrupted."

Elliot folded forward, feeling a crushing pain in the center of him, and steadied himself with his hands on his knees. He shook his head, wild and distraught. "No, that can't be. I—" he panted. "I *need* these archives. What about the microfiche? Do you still have those? You have to—"

The attendant put a hand on his shoulder. "Are you alright? It'll be okay. Mister Edwards here thinks it can be fixed. It might take a couple of days, but school isn't starting until after Labor Day. You've got time."

Time? Time was slipping away. He had hours—a little over a day—until it was too late.

Elliot lifted his face and looked at the man in front of the monitor. He could feel the heat in his cheeks, and the smoldering intensity of his eyes—burning into the man—accusatory and enraged. "What happened?"

The man—Mister Edwards—shrugged. "It's an old computer—should've been switched out years ago." He turned back to the attendant. "I'll take this with me if that's alright."

"But, the microfiche?" Elliot demanded.

Frowning, the attendant shook her head. "If you want to leave me a phone number, I can call you when it's all up and running again."

"No point," he said, then turned and started his slow slog away from the console, to the stairs, down, and out into the too-bright light of the day.

≈

All the energy he'd used to propel himself from the community farm to the library was spent, so the ride back home was slow and hot. He turned the pedals beneath his feet in resigned apathy, barely moving the bike fast enough to maintain his balance. A traffic light ahead turned red, and only the violent bleating of a car horn prevented him from coasting into oncoming traffic. He placed his feet solidly on the ground, waited for green, and closed his eyes for a long moment.

The archives had been his last, best idea, but it seemed fate had intervened. Maybe he couldn't change the past—shouldn't even try. What had it got him? A crazed, stalking immortal priestess? A rift between himself and Cameron? A dredging up of the toxic silt of their early adolescence? And the anxiety. The stress.

The light turned, and he continued on, wishing suddenly for Friday—for it all to be over one way or another.

When he finally turned his bike off Pentucket Road, down the drive to the New Colony Apartments, he was unsurprised to see both his mother's car and Tony's parked out front. Too exhausted to bother locking his bike, he leaned it against the rail on the patio and moped through the doors into the kitchen.

On the table, knitted hats of various colors formed an untidy pile. A lamp brought from the living room—connected to the wall by way of a dirty white extension cord—washed the tabletop in soft, yellow light. And his mother stood, moving a pink hat beneath the lamp's glow, arranging it just so. A scattering of rose petals and a pretty teal-and-yellow rattle completed the staging. She looked at Elliot and smiled, then lifted a phone—shiny, new, the latest model—and snapped a shot.

"Hey, El," she said. "You're home a little early, aren't you?"

"What is *that*?" he asked.

"What?"

"That phone. Is that the *new* iPhone?"

She chuckled, innocent. "Oh, yeah. Tony got it for me. We were trying to get good pictures of my hats on social media, but the camera in my old phone wasn't doing the trick. You know how it goes."

"Mom?" The warm, twisting, sick-making feeling of betrayal gripped him—closed its fingers around all the soft bits inside of him and squeezed. He fought to stand straight and look her in the eyes. "The *new* iPhone? The *thousand-dollar* iPhone?"

"Yeah, El? Are you alright?"

From the hall, Tony sauntered into the kitchen. "What's going on, here?"

Something in him started to smolder—to combust. In a matter of moments, the fire took, growing into an all-out conflagration. He fixed his gaze on Tony and stood straighter than he imagined possible. The fatigue was gone, and he was brimming with the white-hot energy of his ire. "You two couldn't spring for a hundred-dollar pair of running shoes that I *need*, but she's got a new fucking iPhone?"

"Woah there." Tony laughed, and it was mean. Cruel. His lips turned up into a hideous smile, and Elliot knew exactly how much he was enjoying this. "Maybe if you hadn't lost the mayor-lady's coin, I'd have bought you a pair of sneakers and a *new fucking iPhone* too, you little shit."

"Oh," his mother whimpered. "Tony is that absolutely—"

"Shut the fuck up, Larissa." She looked at the ground. "So, what are you going to do about it? Nothing? What happened to those balls you grew the other day?"

Elliot looked at his mother. Looked at Tony. He wanted to defend her, defend himself, but now, he couldn't. Wouldn't. He hated the way Tony talked to her—to both of them—but wondered if she didn't deserve it. "Fuck this," he said under his breath, then turned and headed out, back to his bike, and to where else, he didn't yet know.

At the top of the drive, he stopped and caught his breath. He wanted Cam most of all but knew better than to call yet, especially after his theatrical exit from the farm. He thought of Lindsey next and dialed her number. No answer. This was too much—all of it. He looked at Pentucket Road, and the river beyond—looked left, north, toward town, then right, south, toward—

Of course, the old Calisti farmhouse would be his solace. And Sofia would be there, for sure. He could talk to her. Sit with her. Maybe he didn't have a solution, and maybe Cam was right to see this endeavor's futility—*it already happened*—but she didn't have to face her fate alone. He breathed in deeply, feeling the air fill him all the way to his toes, then turned and started to pedal away.

Chapter Twenty-Three

August 21, 1959 – Friday

Sofia stood and pushed her chair back into the table, grimacing at the *shree-eek* of the legs across the kitchen's worn tile floor. The sound punctured the silence, and Mama looked up from the sink, Papa from the newspaper. She took her plate and glass—sides still coated with a film of milk from the last gulp—and set them on the counter.

"Mama," she asked. "Please, can I go out and play?"

Mama sighed and pulled her water-logged hands from the suds, turned and knelt down. Her fingers grazed along the sides of Sofia's face and tucked a few rogue curls behind her ears. "Sweet girl, I think it's just too wet. And I think—"

"Mama, it's barely a drizzle. I'll wear my boots and raincoat. I won't get too dirty."

"No, Sofia, I think—"

"You think I'm going to see Elliot." She began to pout. "You want to keep me locked up in here!"

"Sofia—"

Papa cleared his throat. "Speaking of locked up, I see the cinema is giving *Sleeping Beauty* another try this weekend."

Mama blinked. "Didn't that go out in the springtime?"

"Oh, yes. Well, this article says they were cleaning up the projection room and found the reels. They were supposed to be sent back months ago, but someone misplaced them. Anyways, tomorrow and Sunday only, they're going to have a couple of showings. Maybe we could go see it? *Mia bella*, would you like that?"

Sofia perked up. Little Sue's Mama had taken them to see it in January, and it had been scary, but good, especially the part where the mean fairy turned into a dragon. Since she'd already seen it, she didn't particularly care about the movie. But the opportunity? The chance at salvation? "Yes! Papa, please, can we?" She pleaded. Perhaps if they could be out of the house, they'd miss the flood.

"Oh," Mama said. "Robert, I don't know. Certainly not tomorrow. We have the market."

"That's what's perfect! The paper says they're showing it at five-forty. You two will be done at the market by four. Have an early dinner at the cafe, and I'll come meet you."

"Do you think such a fantastical film is really appropriate at the moment?"

Papa sighed. "Margaret, don't you think we could all use a little break from reality?"

Sofia clapped. "Mama, *please*? I promise I'll stay

inside. I won't complain at all. I'll be such a good girl. Please. *Please.*"

"Oh, alright."

Papa clapped his hands, and so did Sofia. Smiling ear to ear, he stood and brought his own plate over to the sink, planting a fat kiss on Mama's cheek. "Perfect. It'll be just what we need." He gazed out the window at the slow, steady rain. "And now, I'd better get back out there and see what I can get done this afternoon. The forecast is calling for a pretty hard rain tomorrow."

Sofia bristled. "Papa. The flood."

He laughed. "No flood, *mia bella.* The tomatoes especially are hurting, though. I'm not sure they're going to make it."

"Robert—"

He kissed Mama again. "It'll be alright. We've got Mister Khoury now. That'll help with the finances. And I'll bring in as many as I can."

"That's another thing we're going to need to talk about. You know I don't trust him, Robert. I don't."

"Nonsense. He's a fine man."

"Robert, we don't even—"

He shook his head and kissed Mama one last time. "Alright, alright. We'll talk about it tonight." He turned to Sofia and gave her a wink. "You be good now; I'll be back in as soon as I can."

"Alright, Papa." She smiled, hopeful, and scurried up to her bedroom where some clean paper and a few crayons waited to help her pass the afternoon.

At the little table by the window, she began to draw. First, a picture of Elliot. Then, Uncle George and the horrible hound.

She was halfway through a portrait of Franklin when she heard him—a scream of anguish. She leaped up onto the chair and kneeled on the table to better see out the window. There, below, he knelt on the ground with his face in his hands.

She fought from crying out—swallowed the wail building within her. Instead, she exhaled slow, letting the word slip from her lips, too quiet for Mama to hear downstairs.

"Elliot."

Chapter Twenty-Four

August 21, 2019 - Wednesday

Elliot knew from the moment he turned off Pentucket Road that something was wrong. Fresh tire tracks scarred the wide dirt path that led through the woods of the preservation land to the Wright-Calisti Farm, and overhead, the lowest branches of the maple and elm and beech seemed withdrawn—recoiled as if in fear. He reduced his speed and continued forward, feeling a near-crippling unease begin to further twist organs that had been tied in knots all day. Up ahead, the forest was too bright, somehow—too open.

He rounded the corner, prepared to hop off his bike and lean it against the usual sapling, but the emptiness that awaited forced him to squeeze his breaks too hard. He was skidding, falling, and righted himself just in time. With his feet on the ground, he began to pant. The tire tracks led off to the right, through where the saplings had been, straight to—

Nothing.

He let the bike fall out from beneath him and stumbled forward in disbelief. In the thick, August haze, the dust still hovered in the air above the wreckage. The farmhouse, if he could even call it that now, was nothing but a pile of rubble. A twisted, sorry mass of brick and wood and plaster and metal, eight feet tall. He blinked his eyes and shook his head, imploring himself to *wake up*. Perhaps this entire day had been a horrible dream. But no; this was too vivid. He could smell the mildew and the damp wood, taste the plaster in the air. His legs moved, pulling him forward of their own volition until he stood in front of the rubble.

How could this be? He closed his eyes and wondered if he could hear the universe laughing. Was this a sign? Another proclamation that he was powerless to influence the past? So what was the point of all of it? He felt the coin in his pocket—closed his fist around it and pressed hard, appreciating the pain of the metal digging into his flesh. Why show him? Why involve him when there was nothing he could do? And of course, the loss of this house had no bearing on Sofia's fate, but it was symbolic. This place was the one piece of her that clung to this world. Except for—

He had a sudden urge to yank the coin from his pocket and hurl it into the rubble. He'd watched his father die. Sometimes, he thought his mother wasn't far behind. Wasn't that enough for a twenty-year-old? He considered his bravado in coming here; he was foolish to think he could see Sofia, sit with her happily, and wait for her to disappear tomorrow. Or die. Or both. His knees began to give. Trembling. He landed in the soft dirt and crumpled forward, burying his face in his hands as he let out an agonized wail.

Chapter Twenty-Five

August 21, 1959 – Friday

In an effort to avoid detection, Sofia imagined herself as a cat. She turned and silently pressed her bedroom door closed, then perked her ears back and began to slink down the steps. Skip the fourth one down, she thought. It creaks. Reaching the bottom, she twitched her bottom and continued to creep down the hall. When she reached Guillaume's door, she stood up and rapped quietly against the wood.

From the other side, there was a rustling, and then the door swung inward on its squeaking hinges. Guillaume opened his mouth to speak, but she pressed a finger to her lips. *Quiet.* He blinked, nodded, and stepped aside. She crept through the room to the door that led out onto the veranda. Then she was through it, and outside, and bounding down to the ground and around the corner of the house—nearly to the front. She poked her head around the side and whispered, harsh: "Elliot!"

He looked up, and his puffy red eyes widened in surprise. "Sofia!"

She raised her hand and flicked her wrist. *Follow*. When he stood, she turned and bounded off behind the house and into the woods. She kept going, trampling the ferns and the low, wild blueberry bushes with their hard, tiny fruits, as she weaved between the trees. She stopped in a stand of beech and leaned her back against a wide trunk with smooth, light bark, then panted as she waited for Elliot to catch up.

He fell to his knees in front of her. "Oh, Sofia. I'm so glad to see you."

"Elliot. I had to sneak out. Mama doesn't want me talking to you anymore. She's taking me to see the mind doctor next week. Well, at least she will, if—if nothing bad happens tomorrow." She regarded him for a moment—looked at his puffy red eyes and thought of the wail that had caught her attention in the first place. "Elliot, what's wrong?"

He shook his head. "No. It's nothing, really."

With her hands on her hips, she gave him her most serious glare—the kind Mama might've used. "I don't believe it. I heard you. Please?"

"It's your house." He sighed. "Someone—it's been demolished."

"What?"

"This morning, before I got here. Someone brought a truck or—some machinery. I think it's because—I don't know. It's either because I was getting too close to figuring out what's going to happen to you, or because the universe decided I needed a kick in the gut. It doesn't matter. Oh, Sofia. What are we going to do?"

She smiled, and she meant it. "What time tomorrow?"

"Huh?"

"What time is the flood?"

"Um," she watched as he considered. "I think around—six-twenty?"

She clapped her hands, jumping up and down. "Mama and Papa and I are going to see *Sleeping Beauty*. At five-forty! At the cinema in town. We'll be okay, won't we?"

Elliot wiped his eyes, and he smiled too. A real, honest, broad smile, and she knew he was pleased. "Oh. Sofia. That's—how did you convince them?"

"It was Papa. He read it in the newspaper. They're not supposed to have it—the movie I mean—but they forgot to send it away in the springtime and they're going to show it a couple more times before they have to send it away for real."

He collapsed onto his back and extended his arms over his head, breathing deep and laughing a little under his breath. Sofia crept closer and wanted to lay down beside him, but Mama would ask why her clothes were so dirty; they were already wet from the ferns and the rain. "Oh, Sofia. You don't know how much I needed to hear some good news like that today."

As she watched him, his face clouded with sadness. "Is Cameron here, too?" she asked.

"No. I don't know if Cameron is coming again."

"Did you have a fight?"

"Sort of."

"Did you say you're sorry?"

"I did, but—sometimes that isn't enough."

She chuckled a little. "He's my family, isn't he?"

Elliot scowled. "What's so funny? And yeah, he is. How did you know?"

"He looks kind of like my Papa. Or maybe Uncle George. But mostly, Mama says Calistis are *a real stubborn lot*. So if Cameron is a Calisti, he's probably being stubborn."

Elliot laughed too. "Well, I'm not sure that's what it is, but thanks for letting me know."

"No problem." She looked through the woods back toward the house. "I probably better get going before Mama notices I'm missing."

"Okay." He sat up. "You said five-forty?"

She nodded.

"Alright, and it's at the old cinema on Main Street?"

"It's not very old."

He laughed. "No, I suppose not for you. But yeah, the one on Main Street, right?"

"Yes."

"Okay. I'll be waiting for you there. I'll get there at five and look for you, to know you're really safe, okay? And you'll see me too."

"Yeah," she said. "Okay, Elliot. I'll see you tomorrow." She turned to go but paused and looked back at him one more time. "And Elliot?"

"Yes, Sofia?"

"Thank you for trying to save me."

There were tears in his eyes that made her blush. He nodded his head. "Of course, Sofia. Of course."

≈

She made it back to the house in time. Guillaume was

waiting for her on the veranda, and he ushered her quickly into his room. Silently, he held up a hand for her to wait, and retrieved a hand-towel from his little bathroom. He wiped at her rain-streaked face, and the damp curls that hung heavy down her forehead and ears, scrubbing, squeezing, crimping. When it was done, he smiled and winked, then nodded toward the door. She crept forward and out into the hall. Fast, she zipped up the steps, not daring to breathe until she was safe behind her bedroom door.

From downstairs, Mama called out, and Sofia heard her footsteps leaving the kitchen. She looked down at her wet clothes and started to panic. Then, quickly—nimble, really—she tore them off and pushed them under the bed, donning her pajamas instead. With a mighty leap, she bounded into bed and pulled the blankets up, tight around her neck.

Mama knocked lightly and opened the door. "Sweet girl?" Her eyebrows pushed together in confusion. "What are you doing? Are you wearing your pajamas?"

"Yes, Mama. I didn't feel well all of a sudden. You were right, I shouldn't go outside."

Mama rubbed the skin above her eyebrows and considered. "Alright, well, can I get anything for you? A little broth?"

"No thank you, Mama."

"Okay then, you rest, I suppose. If you feel better, come on down. I could use some help."

"Alright, Mama." She closed her eyes, and Mama closed the door but didn't pull it all the way shut. Once she could hear Mama's footsteps safely at the bottom of the stairs, she leaned over the side of the bed and fished

Nonno's coin out from her wet clothing and closed it in her fist. Maybe she really was a little tired—under the weather. She'd take a brief nap. Tomorrow was a big day, and she figured she could use the rest.

As though channeling her own thoughts, Franklin pushed his head through the bedroom door and leaped up beside her. With a mighty stretch, he yawned and curled his long orange body onto the blankets beside her.

"Good kitty," she said as she ran her hand along the length of his back. "We're going to be alright, Franklin. Everything is going to be alright."

Chapter Twenty-Six

August 21, 2019 – Wednesday

The high, whining buzz of a mosquito hovering around Elliot's ear brought him back. He swatted and slapped, and in the exertion found more were coming–thirsting, hungry and incessant. He took one last look at the stand of mature beech, the carpet of ferns and wild blueberries, and turned back toward the rubble of the farmhouse some meters away. For the past few minutes, he'd been somewhere else–caught up in the sublime peace of this little grove. He'd put his hands in the dirt, digging through the detritus of fallen leaves and peeled bark to feel it–root down into the timeless majesty of the space. He'd realized suddenly it was the closest he'd ever come to her–Sofia. They'd shared this grove. Of course, he'd been in the same physical place as her before, plenty of times at the old farmhouse, but the knowledge that she'd stood here–right here–

felt different somehow. How had it looked to her? The trees were younger then, but how much does the forest change? How much does it remain the same?

He was relieved about the movie—content to know that when the flood hit, she and her parents would be in town. Of course, it was still possible for things to go awry. George Calisti would try to murder them before the flood. But when? It could be any time, really. Any time tomorrow. What if the movie had always been part of the plan, and they couldn't get out in time? What if George stopped them?

As he started his walk back to the rubble, he felt his spirits falling. But no, he reasoned. The window was too small for George. Tomorrow was Saturday for Sofia, which meant she and her mother would be selling at the market in town. If it went until four or five, they'd barely have time to go home before needing to turn around for the film at five-forty. Perhaps they'd stay in town. Of course, that might leave Robert Calisti exposed, and that would be a tragedy, but it would still be a change in the pattern of history. Perhaps George Calisti would have only one victim. Perhaps, alone, Robert might overpower him.

He came back out of the trees to where the rubble sat, still sending its dust up into the heavy, humid air. Cam needed to know about this. Cam needed to—

His phone began to ring. Lindsey. "Hello?" he answered.

"Hey, sorry I missed your call."

"It's alright. Are you—free?"

"Um, no. Sorry. Jared got some free concert tickets, so I'm in Cambridge today. But he wants your email address. I guess he learned something about your coin? He won't shut up about it."

"Really?" Elliot rattled off his address. "That's huge. When is he going to send what he's got?"

"Um, tonight?" She was quiet for a moment. "Elliot?"

"Yeah?"

"Is all of this—real?"

He laughed a little but felt the sadness behind the gesture. "Yeah, Lindsey."

"Okay, well, be careful, alright?"

As if he had to be told. "Is there anything I need to know, right now?"

"Jared'll be in touch, okay?"

"Okay." He hung up the phone. Looking toward the rubble one last time, he dialed Cameron and was unsurprised when the call went to voicemail. After the beep, he inhaled—filled his lungs all the way and held it for a moment. "Hey Cam, it's um—it's Elliot, but I guess you probably knew that already. Um, I'm sorry. *So* sorry. I wanted you to know that, and also something's happened. I'm okay, but your family's farmhouse is gone. I don't know how. I don't know if it was your aunt or Destin, or—but it's gone. I, um—I know it's always *all about me*, and you're right about that, like everything. But, if you could see a way to forgive me—" he began to cry and did nothing to wipe away the tears that wet his cheeks. "I could really use you right now. Um, love you. Okay. Bye."

He pulled his bike up off the ground, climbed on, and started the long ride back home.

Destin knocked lightly on the door to Kathryn Locke's office and waited. Even through the cardboard sleeve, the heat of the coffee in the paper cup she held was starting to burn her hand. How degrading—fetching coffee for a hack small-town politician all in the name of maintaining some semblance of normalcy and protecting her identity. She was weak, and she was angry. One way or another, she needed the Chronicum. This farce was not befitting of a priestess—a priestess soon to be a goddess in all reality. From the other side, Kathryn called her in, so she wrestled open the heavy door and stepped inside.

Kathryn's eyes were empty. Dead. The bond between them was so weak, Destin wasn't sure it existed any more at all. The mayor blinked absently as Destin handed over the piping hot cup. She took a sip, and if it burned her mouth, she didn't seem to notice.

Destin gave her best impression of a concerned smile. "Is everything alright, Madame Mayor?"

Kathryn nodded. "Oh yes. Yeah, I suppose." She fixed Destin in her gaze. "Thank you again for your—information. It's not the kind of thing you take in stride—that your father is a murderer, and the murder weapon is probably right there at the scene. Of course, they probably wouldn't be able to do anything about it now. What good is the weapon when all the rest of the evidence is decayed or missing or—" she shook her head— "Anyways, I'm going to need you to sign a nondisclosure agreement." She pushed a paper across her desk.

"Oh, yes, of course." Destin perused it quickly, then

picked up a pen and signed.

"And also, sorry, this is a bit awkward. It occurred to me I never got a chance to check up on your references. I wouldn't have thought of it, but those polling reports you gave me are a little sub-par. Your resumé suggests you have a lot of experience with this kind of thing, so I thought I'd reach out and see if you were having a bit of an off week, having just moved here and all. Um, I can't seem to get ahold of anyone. Perhaps your information is a little out of date?"

She swallowed hard. "Oh, yes. Probably. I'll see if I can track them down and give you some updated contact information."

"Okay." Kathryn's gaze was stern, cold, and suspicious. "Because unfortunately, if you can't, I think we might have to reconsider your employment here."

"Mayor, is that really—"

"Necessary? Oh, yes, I think so. Mind you, on your advice, I ordered the demolition of a community treasure—a hundred-and-fifty-year-old piece of architecture with significant historic value to this town *as well as* my family. That your...intelligence...on this matter was sound, I have no doubt. I always suspected there was more to the story than my father let on, but how or why you came to this information I don't know. I don't know much about you at all, Destin. This is an election year, and I worry that you might be a bigger scandal than my father. So yes. Why don't you get me those references? That'll be all."

Destin nodded. "Understood." She turned and closed the office door behind her, then sank back against the wall. She might've tried to re-forge the bond with the mayor—might've put her dwindling energy into smoothing all this over—but the reality was clear: Kathryn Locke wasn't the answer. Not when there was a better option—one that hit closer to the source.

Tony was angry. Tony was greedy. Tony, like George before him, would act of his own volition when pushed just so. Destin checked her watch. Four-eighteen. Maybe it was time for a drink at Tony's favorite place.

Chapter Twenty-Seven

August 21, 1959 – Friday

Ever since waking from her nap, Sofia hadn't been able to put Guillaume out of her mind. She'd fallen asleep next to Franklin with Nonno's coin still in her hand, and she supposed maybe that was it. The dreams of Elliot came from the coin. It spoke to her in images and moving pictures and words that weren't quite words. And now it told her Guillaume was the answer—that it needed him, somehow. She remembered the first time she'd seen him hold it—the way he'd looked at it like it was an old friend and the joy that colored his face when he held it.

"More peas?" Mama asked as she and Papa sat at the dinner table.

Sofia looked at her empty plate. She wasn't hungry; she'd only forced down the ham and peas and summer squash because she knew otherwise Mama would be cross. "No thank you, Mama. Papa?"

"Yes?"

"May I go sit with Guillaume for a while?"

Mama bristled. "Sofia, I don't think so. Robert, I told you I don't like the man. I think he needs to go."

Papa chuckled. "Nonsense. I've told *you*—you worry too much Margaret."

"That man has an unhealthy interest in our daughter. How is it you don't see that?"

Sofia sat straighter in her chair. "He doesn't, Mama. He's my friend. Oh, please, Papa."

Papa considered. "He may not be done with his dinner yet, *mia bella*. Why don't you wait a while?"

"I'll bring his dishes back from his room. *Please,* Papa."

He smiled. "Alright, but if he doesn't want to be disturbed, you come right back."

Mama scowled. "Robert. This is ridiculous!"

"What's going to happen? I think you're overreacting. Anyways, they're both right here. We'll discuss this—"

Sofia didn't wait, instead leaped out of her chair and bounded down the hall. She knocked furiously at the door until it swung inward, and Guillaume stared down at her, startled. She hugged his legs and looked up at him. "Mama doesn't want me to talk to you."

"I know," he cooed. "I know."

"But I had a dream," she pulled Nonno's coin from her pocket and placed it in Guillaume's hand. "It needed to talk to you."

His body seemed to quake at the contact, and he closed his eyes, smiling. Tilting his head back, the smile grew broader and broader until suddenly he was laughing, first soft, then louder and louder. He opened his eyes, and there were tears at the corners. Slowly, he handed the coin back to Sofia with the smile still plastered across his face. "I understand now," he said. "All of it." He touched her head as Mama rounded the corner from the kitchen.

"What's going on here?" she demanded.

"A joke," Guillaume lied. "Your daughter is quite the comedian."

"That's enough. Sofia, come over here. And goodnight, Mister Khoury."

Still chuckling, he nodded. "Goodnight Margaret. Goodnight Sofia." Then he closed the door.

Chapter Twenty-Eight

August 21, 2019 – Wednesday

Flat on his back, Elliot gazed out the window from the bed, drinking in the inky black of the night. It was minutes to midnight, and he ought to be asleep—tomorrow everything happened or didn't happen. Tomorrow at this time, it would all be over, one way or another. He pulled down on the inbox of his phone, watched it rubber-band back and return no new messages. How long was this concert? Clearly, Jared couldn't have found out anything truly pressing, or he'd have sent it over by now. But the memory of Lindsey's apprehension on the phone earlier stuck with him. She'd been worried, so—was it something, or wasn't it?

It was about time to give it up. Out in the living room, he could hear Tony singing along drunkenly to the radio—turned up too high. He wondered why the upstairs neighbors hadn't complained yet. He and his mother had been out there all day—hadn't left for anything—drinking and laughing and hollering. She'd sold her first hat, as if she needed an excuse for a bender. *See El*, she'd told him. *All because of the camera on that new phone.*

He hadn't wanted to think about it—couldn't find it in him to be happy for her. He'd retired to his room, took a sandwich on stale bread for dinner, and waited for the email from Jared, or a call or text from Cameron. Now it was late—too late.

He set his phone on the nightstand and picked up Sofia's coin, turning it over and over in his fingers. Tomorrow, one way or another he'd be rid of it.

His phone bleated, and he shot up in bed, reaching—fumbling in the dark. The blueish light of the screen lit the room, and he sighed with relief. Cameron.

"Let's meet tomorrow?"

He unlocked the phone and started to type, thumbs suddenly clumsy and too fat for the cracked little screen. He considered, deleted, typed again. There were so many things to say: *I'm sorry*, *I love you*, *have you forgiven me*, *what are we going to do*, *how can I make it up to you*. In the end, he kept it simple.

"Breakfast?"

The response came quickly.

"Sure. Little cafe by the station? Eight-thirty?"

He smiled. It was perfect.

"Deal. Love you. Sorry."

Beneath his last message, three little gray dots bounced happily. Typing. They stopped. Started. Elliot sighed, watching them stop and start, stop and start. The three dots of death. He felt himself begin to sweat, closed his eyes, and focused on breathing. Maybe he shouldn't have said it—typed it—but it was how he felt, and he'd spent too long denying it. Now that he'd said it once, twice, he was powerless to stop. He wanted to say it again and again, over and over, wanted to take Cameron's face in his hands and repeat it until he believed it—felt it—knew that no words had ever been truer.

The *dots of death* disappeared entirely, stubbornly refusing to return, and Elliot collapsed into his pillow. He should've known it was too much, and could he really blame Cam after everything he put him through?

He thought back to the moment everything started to change: twelve years old, almost thirteen. He and Cameron on the edge of the mattress shut away in the attic bedroom at Cam's house. Late July with no air conditioning all the way up there. Thin cotton shirts still too thick for the stagnant air.

Do you promise it doesn't change anything? Hands touching. Fingers that intertwine.

No, Elliot says. *I think maybe I'm...*

Really? Cameron asks.

And then the unforgivable thing happens, though it's innocent—even sincere—in the moment. It's only a kiss, and it's Elliot's idea, and it's so clean and pure and right.

Elliot lingers—holds onto the moment longer than Cam does. He likes it—this feeling—but he doesn't consider what it means to Cam. How *much* it means.

Now, in retrospect, Elliot realized, that kiss must have become the twisting of the knife. The ultimate betrayal. It was bad enough that later after he lost his father, he sold Cameron out—did the one thing he knew would well and truly push Cam away, as he'd done with everyone else through his grief. But to have done all that after sharing such an intimate moment—after admitting something at twelve years old he still had trouble embracing at twenty? The hypocrisy was staggering.

He closed his eyes, defeated, and then, finally, another bleat.

"Love you too. Goodnight."

It was short—terse—but it was enough. With a great sigh of relief, Elliot set the phone on his nightstand. No matter what tomorrow held, it would hold Cameron. In the rest of it, he might be powerless, but in the moment, only Cameron mattered.

Chapter Twenty-Nine

August 22, 2019 – Thursday

Hey Elliot,

Sorry, this took so long. Crazy busy day and all. The concert was good, and Ernesto says hi. Lindsey said you were anxious, and truthfully, so am I, so I'll get right to it.

I suppose there are certain opportunities afforded a lover of French literature by working in the library of a prestigious university; I've stuck my nose in a lot of old, rare, obscure books. When you showed me the coin you found, I knew I'd seen it before, and as I thought and thought, I kept coming back to this book I'd seen. It took a while to remember the title, but sure enough, I found it. It's called Le Chronicum du Sort Futur by G.E. Khoury. I've been unable to find any information or other works by the author, and the copy we have here might be the only one that still exists. It was published in France in the 1760s—very likely a vanity deal, which is to say the author financed the production.

What is most odd about the book—well—there are a lot of things that are odd. The title is a mix of Latin and French, and translates to 'Chronicle of Future Fate,' or maybe 'Chronicle of the Future of Fate," or perhaps even "Chronicle of the Fate of the Future,' but these latter two are more interpretive, and having read through parts of the book again, I stand by my first translation. The thing is, Le Sort Futur is referenced within the text as an object rather than a concept. Specifically, your coin. But then it gets even stranger. The author seems to reference Le Sort Futur and Le Chronicum Posterum interchangeably. This caused me a lot of confusion. Chronicum Posterum ought to mean something like 'Chronicle of the Future,' but it seems to be referring to your coin.

Of course, when I really sat down with a dictionary, I saw that Chronicum can also mean 'pertaining to time,' and taken in the context of an object...

Linguistically, it doesn't seem to add up. But I won't bore you, because the story is the interesting part.

The book describes an ancient tribe that lived in relative obscurity under the nose of Hellenistic rule in the eastern Mediterranean (in what is now Lebanon). They worshipped two principle deities—a god of time, and a goddess of fate. While some other minor deities are described, it is these two that we're concerned with. Time wielded a scythe, which is not unusual, as this is fairly typical imagery for "Father Time." Fate carried a dagger, and together they lorded over their worshippers, spreading prosperity and longevity when they were well served, famine and death when they weren't.

The story goes on to say that Fate grew ambitious watching the spread of the Roman Empire. Rome's General Pompey was storming through the area, and when it looked like the whole living-in-obscurity thing was going to go out the window, Fate thought the best idea would be for the tribe to assert its independence and maybe establish an empire of its own. As if that would be an easy or simple thing to do, right? Time, on the other hand, saw a future where His people were conquered—forced to abandon their gods and assimilate into Roman culture. While He regretted the inevitability of this outcome, He wished for his people to exercise a freedom of will—to fight if they chose, or assimilate. The gist of it is that Time didn't like the odds of an all-out war against the Romans (as if a relatively tiny tribe could wage war on the Roman Empire), and Fate was motivated to compel Her people to defend their land, their ways, and Her.

Eventually, the Romans set their sights on our little tribe, and one night, as they advanced, Time crept into Fate's chambers and stole Her dagger, which was the source of most of Her power. Along with His own scythe, He melted them down, mixed the metals and minted Le Sort Futur, or the Chronicum Posterum, or whatever you'd like to call it. More than one actually. It seems there were six originally. Within the coins, the abilities of Time and Fate eddied around, slowly dispelling the gifts of the deities out into the world of man.

The priests that served Time were given the coins and instructed to deliver them to the men of the tribe, that with the power of the coins, they might gain some insight into their possible futures and thereby control their own destinies. Of course, when She learned what He'd done, Fate was furious, believing Time had betrayed their people. Time, for His part, argued that their people were better served by free will, and the existence of the Chronicums (this eventually becomes the author's preferred terminology for the coins) would prove it.

Fate, because so many deities of antiquity are a little twisted, proposed Le Jeu (the game) in which Time's idea would be put to the test. Was man better off creating his own destiny? Could mankind stand against the forces of a fate that sought to control it, and still triumph? Using maybe the last of Her innate power, She charged Her priestesses with the task of retrieving the coins and restoring them to Her (against man's own interests). Time, proud and also a little twisted, granted the priests and priestesses alike a measure of immortality so they could play it out. And, according to the author, so it has been ever since.

What happened to the other Chronicums, I couldn't say, but the rest of the book follows one coin as it moves around Europe through the centuries and the struggle of a particular priest and priestess. There are some dark, horrible things—references to terrifying hell-hounds, abuses of power, etc. And then it gets really philosophical, talking all about the virtues of free will, and how once the Chronicums expend all their energy, mankind will really be free—that kind of stuff.

Then it gets even worse. The author imparts these dire warnings. Kind of apocalyptic stuff. He muses on how dangerous it could be if one of these priestesses got her hands on a coin—really fantastical writing about the complete enslavement of mankind. Personally, I don't see it. I mean, supposing any of this were true, I'm not sure how a relic from a goddess that served a tiny tribe of people could enslave a planet of seven billion.

Regardless...

Sorry, I'm writing a novel here. The point is, there is an illustration of the Chronicum in the book, and I compared it to the photo I took when we were at lunch, and I can't see any possible scenario where your coin isn't one of the ones described in the book. Unless, of course, it was manufactured by someone who read the book...

I'm a rational human being. I don't believe in gods or goddesses or obscure old mythologies, but I told Lindsey and she freaked a little. She said you've been seeing this ghost, and you really believe it. I'm also rational enough to acknowledge that there are things we don't know, and there is nothing in this weird little book to suggest the Chronicum could make you see ghosts, but...

It's got me feeling uneasy, and I wanted to pass on what I know. You should probably bring the coin back and sit down with some scholars at the very least. And if somehow we're living in some alternate universe where gods and goddesses and immortal servants are a real thing? Well, be careful I guess.

I hope you can do something with all of this. Looking forward to seeing you soon.

Jared

Across the table, Elliot watched Cameron's face as he read Jared's email—observed the way his eyebrows lifted, scrunched, lifted again. When he was done, Cameron handed the phone back, and Elliot exhaled. "Sure you don't want to see it through with me?"

"It doesn't make any sense," Cam said. "You haven't seen the future at all. This has been all about Sofia—all about the *past*. I mean, Destin said she was a priestess. That part lines up, but the rest of it?"

"Did you see the author's name? G.E. Khoury. It's Guillaume—Sofia's boarder."

Absently, Cam cut at the over-easy eggs growing cold on his plate. "I don't know, Elliot. This is like—Lord of the Rings or something. What are we supposed to do—take the coin to Mordor and throw it in a volcano?"

He laughed and was thankful for it. He'd barely slept at all, and his stomach was in knots. Looking down at the lukewarm pancakes on his own plate, he wished he could eat, but worry spoiled his appetite. It was after nine in the morning—only about nine hours now until the flood. "I don't know," he said. "I think we have to get through today."

Cameron tore a piece of toast, dabbed it in the yolk, and took a bite. He chewed, thoughtful. "What are you going to do all day? How are you going to make it through?"

"I don't know. Pace nonstop? All day? I want to be outside the theater at four-thirty. I need to see her—

know that she's there, and safe." He turned his eyes to Cameron—held the gaze and refused to flinch at the little glimmer of hurt that still lingered there. "Maybe you'd want to keep me company?"

Cameron broke the stare. "I would love that, but, I don't know, Elliot. I'm taking this thing with my grandfather really hard. I don't think I can be that close to it. I mean, I guess if you really need—"

Cam's face said more than his words, and Elliot was paying close attention. Yes, he did need Cameron, now more than ever. But he understood from the little things—the downturn at the side of Cam's mouth, the set of his eyes and the gentle creases of his forehead—that Cam couldn't be involved. Not today. This was Elliot's chance to prove it wasn't all about him. That he loved and cared and wasn't selfish after all. He forced a smile, and after a moment, felt it become genuine. "No Cam," he said. "You're right."

"I am?"

"Yes. I can make it through today—promise you'll see me tomorrow?"

"Of course. And—I've been thinking."

"Oh?"

"If somehow tomorrow everything is the same? If my grandfather is still a murderer?"

"Oh, Cam, let's not—"

"If he still is, I'm going to talk to my dad first, but, I think I'll go to the police."

"You really don't—"

"I do, though. You came on a little harsh, but you're right. Robert and Margaret—and Sofia—deserve justice, even after all these years. I hope it doesn't come to that, but, they do."

"But your family, Cam. It must've been your aunt that ordered the demolition of the house. If she gets caught up in all this—"

"Then that was her choice. And don't start about Destin. If Jared's right, that's the point of all of this, isn't it? Free will?"

"But if somehow she didn't *have* her free will—I mean, come on, she has to be under Destin's influence, doesn't she? Why else would Destin be there? The same with your grandfather."

"I told Destin when she was in my house—and I meant it—I don't believe in her. I won't live in a world where my actions aren't my own."

"You seem very sure."

"I am."

"Tomorrow then," Elliot said. "And Cam, about what I said yesterday in my voicemail? Then what I texted? You know it's true, don't you?"

Cameron smiled. "I love you too, Elliot."

***

Across town, Destin stepped out of the little gun shop, tucked the box with the pistol under her arm, and rubbed at her head. She couldn't go on like this—not another day. She'd waited for Tony in the bar for hours, and to no avail—drunk far too many Negronis, and now her head was throbbing. Was this her mortality returning? This hangover? She'd never had a hangover before. And curse this modern world. When the clerk told her she'd need to pass a background check to buy the pistol, she'd panicked—used the tiny bit of influence she could muster to compel him to give the gun to her without it. It wasn't a criminal record she was worried about, it was all the holes in her identity that might've flubbed her up. Living an immortal life in the twenty-first century was a logistical nightmare; one couldn't just adopt a new identity without a lot of tricky paperwork, and on paper, *Destin Duprée* was eighty-nine years old, though she looked as she always had, in her mid-forties. Her driver's license spelled it out—the youthful face with the impossible age, renewed perilously through yet more tricks of influence every decade. A background check would've raised too many questions—could've landed her in handcuffs.

But as she walked slowly back to her car, she exhaled, realizing that soon it might not matter. She didn't have the strength anymore to compel Tony to retrieve the coin when she finally saw him—not after her tussles with George Calisti, the mayor, and the gun shop clerk—but she was sure she wouldn't need to. She'd seen the greed in his eyes after their last meeting. She'd have to make an offer—something he couldn't refuse. She'd write him a check for half in advance, because what did it really matter as long as the boy gave it to him? She'd have to emphasize that part in particular. If he just killed him or took it, the Chronicum's power would remain locked against her.

Damn the rules of the game. It had to be given. Always given.

Safe inside her little sedan, she closed her eyes for a moment. Tired. So tired. She'd return to the bar this afternoon, and try to drink less as she waited. And if Tony didn't come today, she'd seek him out—find him at work. One way or another, she'd see him, he'd agree to her terms, and then finally—

It could be over.

Chapter Thirty

August 22, 1959 – Saturday

Traffic at the market was slow, and by lunchtime, Mama was cross. Sofia watched the lines in her face grow deeper as the morning stretched on—observed the rain on her cheeks, running down the little ravines from nostrils to the corners of her lips. Even under her hat, Mama's hair hung wet and heavy. The normal Saturday customers were feeling the weather, it seemed, and deciding to stay in. All the merchants around them grumbled and groaned as well, knocking away the rain that pooled at the corners of the white tents they'd erected over their tables and goods.

Sofia might not have minded the rain—might have enjoyed splashing in the puddles with her big rubber boots—but today she was solemn. Mama seemed to know it, too, and that made things even worse. "There's not going to be a flood," Mama said, over and over, and

"Why don't you go visit Mister Crane? He always has a new joke for you." It was true; Sofia loved Mister Crane, the fishmonger, but today her heart wasn't in it. She wasn't sure she could stand a joke—not today on the brink of such an extraordinary tragedy. She wanted to run up and down the rows of the market, shouting for everyone to go home and get inside—to stay as far away from the Pentucket as they could. There was a flood coming.

Instead, she stayed by Mama's side—kicked at the little puddles beneath their own tent and watched the rain that blew in bead off the tomatoes and fennel and eggplant. A few customers stopped by and picked at the tomatoes. They were small and under-ripe, and Sofia could read the disappointment sketched in their eyebrows and the downturn of their lips. Mama assured visitor after visitor that a few days on the kitchen counter and they'd ripen right up, but there were few takers. *Such a shame, Margaret, the Calisti tomatoes are always the best...Bad year for it...Maybe the late season crop, a little sun'll turn it around...*

Shortly after noon, Mrs. Parker, the baker's wife, leaned over from the stand adjacent and looked at Mama. "No sandwiches today. Are the two of you hungry? I'll watch your produce for a few minutes if you want to get something from the deli—dry off a little."

Mama nodded, "Oh, Alice, thank you. And we'd be happy to do the same when we return." She looked at Sofia. "Does that sound nice?"

"Yes, Mama." It sounded very nice. Normally Mama packed lunch, but this morning the mud made it difficult for Papa to get the fennel out of the field and Mama had to help. They'd almost been late, and there hadn't been time. "Can I get bologna?"

"Yes, yes." She nodded at Mrs. Parker. "Thank you, Alice; we'll be right back."

Mama grabbed her hand and started to pull her out into the row between the vendors, walking so fast Sofia nearly had to run to keep up. "Slow down."

Scowling, Mama shook her head. "Mrs. Parker is doing something very nice for us. The least we could do is hurry."

"Why are you so cross? Are you cross with *me*?"

Mama stopped and squatted down, pushing Sofia's heavy curls back behind her ears. "Sweet girl, no. It's a difficult time, isn't it? We're going to have to bring most of this produce back home with us because of this godawful weather, and—"

"And?"

"And I suppose I wish it was already tomorrow. Then you'll be able to put all this business about floods out of your head. And next week I'll take you to the psychologist, and before you know it everything will be fine again." She kissed her forehead. "Now come on, I'll try to be less cross, but you'll have to hurry. We're getting soaked out here."

Mama took her hand, and they continued, out of the market square and down the street to the deli. They passed the cinema, where a man on a ladder was changing out the marquee. "Look, Mama." Sofia pointed. Mama followed her finger—*Sleeping Beauty - Sat - 540*—only, the man was taking down the *5* and putting a *6* in its place. "What is he doing?"

Mama stopped and turned her face up to the man.

"Excuse me?"

He wobbled a bit on the ladder. "Yes, ma'am?"

"The paper said *Sleeping Beauty* was at five-forty this afternoon."

"Our apologies. We got it wrong—six-forty now."

"I see—" she pulled Sofia onward. The deli was at the end of the block. "Well, I suppose we can still go, but we'll have to go home first—probably would've had to anyways."

"Mama. No! The flood, we can't—"

"Sofia, enough. I've told you a million times there'll be no flood. And anyway, you should be grateful they changed the time because I was thinking we wouldn't make it for five-forty. We can't leave our unsold produce in the back of the farm truck all evening. Come on now."

She swallowed hard. Maybe it would still be alright. Elliot said the flood would come through at six-twenty. If they left the market at four, they could have everything unloaded by five, and then Papa could come back into town with them with plenty of time to spare. They were nearly to the deli now. Sofia squeezed Mama's hand. "Promise we'll come back?"

"If you promise you won't talk anymore about this flood, then yes. I promise."

"Okay, Mama. Promise."

Chapter Thirty-One

August 22, 2019 – Thursday

At three minutes after four, Destin heard the door to the bar open. She swiveled on her stool, mimicking a grace she didn't feel and donned her most seductive smile. Tony's eyes widened in surprise as he sauntered forward and sat heavy on the stool next to hers. "You again," he grunted. "Sorry, if the kid's got it, I haven't seen it."

She pouted in that particularly French way she'd perfected over the centuries and swiveled back to the bar. "*Quel dommage.* He *does* have it, you know. Just needs to be persuaded to give it to you." Behind Tony, the air shimmered, and she detected the faintest growl. Good, she thought, turning her head to see the near-invisible outline of the beast she'd tagged him with.

The connection lingered.

"What do you want me to do? Toss his room when

he's not there? His mom's only got half a brain cell, but even *she* might take objection to that. Trouble I don't need—it's tough enough keeping her in line."

"*Puh*, no, no. I told you, he must *give* it to you. But that doesn't mean he can't be compelled." She tapped a foot on the box at her feet and used the toe of her shoe to lift the lid enough for Tony to see.

His eyes widened, and he laughed. "You're crazy, lady."

The bartender wandered over and gave Tony a nod. "The usual?"

"Better make it a double." He fixed Destin in his gaze. "You're out of your mind. I'm not getting mixed up with that."

"You don't have to use it," she lilted. "Not really. Of course, this is indelicate, but that coin is incredibly precious to me. I've told you it's valuable, but—shall we discuss a price?"

"Really?"

"Really. Name it."

Tony considered, and Destin shivered a little as the corners of his mouth turned up with evident malice. "Fine. Two million."

She laughed. Choked. She searched his eyes, looking for clues to whether it was a serious offer, or one designed to make her balk. Well, she wouldn't balk. "Alright. Two million."

Tony's jaw dropped. "You haven't got it."

She had him now. Grinning, she removed her phone from her purse, flicked over to the investment company's app, and logged in. "Would you like to see my account?"

As he gazed at the screen, she imagined his jaw

falling further. "I should've asked for more."

"So you'll do it?"

"For *that*? Yeah, I'll do it, but—not that I'm complaining—why not buy it off the kid?"

She pouted. "Tony. He doesn't want to part with it. The truth is, he believes it is as priceless as I do."

"I don't understand what makes it so—"

Enough of this. She looked back at the invisible hound, waiting patiently, and implored it. *Become one*! The hulking beast shimmered and lunged forward—melted into Tony's skin, igniting his greed and rage, clouding his judgment. She watched his eyes as his mind struggled against the invader. *Easy, you don't need total control.* His eyes settled, and she knew the connection was weak, but it was enough. The hound would feed the darker aspects of Tony's personality. It would be enough. She leaned close. "Never mind the details, *mon cher*. Just get the job done, understand?"

He nodded, and there was more gravel in his voice than usual. "How about a good-will payment?"

She laughed and pulled a checkbook from her purse—made it out to CASH in the amount of one million. "And speaking of good-will, I'll make it another one-point-five on delivery. I'm at the Hotel Haverford. Room 312." As she stood to go, Tony stared, and she was sure his mouth was watering. "Don't forget—*that*." She tapped the box on the floor with her foot. "See you later. Do it tonight."

⩯

Elliot checked the time on his watch; it was five-forty-three. In 1959 the movie would be starting. He'd waited since four-thirty—leaned uncomfortably against the too-hot brick facade of the theater, next to the doors. Twice, the attendant from the ticket booth had come around and told him to stop loitering. Twice, he'd told her he was waiting for someone. He'd kept his eyes open the entire time, afraid to blink in case he missed her. She'd be with her parents, unable to call out to him, or even wave. But she hadn't come—he was sure of it. Something was wrong. The clock on the cracked screen of his phone clicked forward to five-forty-four.

He couldn't wait here any longer, he realized. The house. The preserve. If what happened was *about* to happen, that's where he needed to be. Maybe he'd see something—some clue as to Sofia's fate. If he couldn't save her—he shuddered—at least, perhaps, he could bear witness.

The whole thing was horrible. Sickening. As he climbed on his bike, he realized with complete certainty that he couldn't stand living in a world where Sofia Calisti didn't exist—where her sharp, bright little light was snuffed out by the actions of an angry man and a mad priestess. But no, there was still time. If she was at the house, he could see her—talk to her, and lead her away, up from the river to higher ground. They could wait out the flood together. He pumped his legs and sped down the traffic-laden streets of town, cutting through yellow lights turning red. In four minutes, he reached Pentucket Road and turned south, watching the town fall away.

He was coming toward the drive down to the New Colony Apartments—wouldn't stop there—but then changed his mind. It was a few minutes to six now, and the old Wright-Calisti Farm was still a fifteen-minute ride away. If he took his mother's car, he could be there in less than ten. That would give enough time to find Sofia and lead her away. He sped down the steep descent and flew around to the back of the building, dropping his bike on the patio. He shoved the sliding door hard and bolted through the kitchen down the hall into the living room.

"Mom!" he called. "I need the—"

A glint of metal. A flash of dirty teeth. Tony stood by the front door, laughing under his breath as he pointed the pistol. "Nice of you to join us."

"Where'd you get that, Tony?" his mother asked as she backed against a wall in the corner. "What are you doing?"

"Shut up, Lari." He waved the gun, and she collapsed to the ground, hugging her knees. Turning his gaze to Elliot, his smile broadened. "Get over there with your mom."

Elliot swallowed hard. "Tony, what are you—"

"Shut the fuck up and *get over there*!"

He raised his hands above his head and crept slowly to his mother's side. "You're making a huge mistake."

"That remains to be seen. Phone, please." Elliot hesitated, and Tony stomped his foot. "Now, goddammit!"

Slowly, Elliot reached into his pocket and pulled out his iPhone, bent low and tossed it across the carpet to Tony's feet. "Let's talk about this Tony, let's—"

"Oh yes," Tony said. "Let's talk. This is going to be real easy. It'll all be over in a second. Promise. All I need you to do is give me that *fucking* coin."

Chapter Thirty-Two

August 22, 1959 – Saturday

Baby Kathryn's wailing was almost a reprieve—almost. For the briefest moment, as she screamed and thrashed in her mother's arms, her tantrum drowned out the howling in George's head. He stood brusquely from the table and shook his head in an effort to restore a glimmer of clarity.

"Where are you going?" Dorothy asked. "I could use a little help here, you know. Take her, won't you? Then maybe I can get this dinner done."

George looked at his wife and daughter. Shook his head. The pressure between his ears was nearly crippling now. His father's coin was the answer. The woman, Destin, had explained as much, but he hadn't listened. He'd tried before when the pressure got bad the last time, and as he'd gotten closer to it—nearly had it—he'd felt the most extraordinary relief. It was almost euphoric, but then, instead of giving it to him, his little bitch of a niece had hit him with that rock.

As angry as he'd been, and confused, that little blow had worked miracles for a time. He'd felt like waking from a deep, deep dream. The howling was gone, and he'd felt like himself again. But now it was back, louder than ever, and if he didn't do something about it, he was sure his head would explode, leaving pieces all over the walls and ceiling of the kitchen.

"I have to go out," he said.

Dorothy scowled. "I'll divorce you, George Calisti. Don't believe that I won't. You're a rotten man, anyways. The least you could do is take your daughter for a few minutes so I can finish dinner. Honestly, I don't know why you don't get me some help around here. You've got the money. I know you do. A nice domestic, that's what I need."

He waved her off. "Yes, yes. I'll be back soon."

"George! Don't you—" but he wasn't listening. He went to the front door and grabbed his coat. It was raining buckets, and he hated getting wet, but he was going to get his hands on that coin one way or another, and tonight.

The howling. The howling was incessant.

Cramming himself into the driver's seat of his Galaxie, he closed his eyes for a moment before turning on the engine. To think Dorothy thought she deserved a domestic. Didn't she know how hard he worked? He had money, sure, but he wasn't made of it. Maybe if his idiot brother would agree to sell that goddamned farm, he'd get Dorothy *two* domestics. Hell, maybe instead he'd be the one to get the divorce and find a woman who was a little more grateful.

He thought of his brother and felt a heat work its way up past his collar. Their father had always loved Robert more—the older brother, the gentler one. And he'd doted on that little bitch Sofia. When Kathryn was born, his father barely batted an eye. And that he'd given Sofia his coin? Their most precious family heirloom?

He started to drive, mostly out of instinct, not always able to see the road ahead through the pouring rain. Instead, he *felt* it, inherently understanding the curves. Maybe he'd kill them all. It would be the simplest thing. Robert, Margaret, Sofia. All three dead. He was smart enough, and anyway, he had half the town in his pocket. Who'd dare accuse him, or bring charges? The farm would pass to him in full. No need to split the profits of the sale to the developers. Really, he wondered why he hadn't thought of it sooner.

Of course, the boarder might be an issue. Or an opportunity. He'd think about it for a day or two, no need to be slapdash. But as he turned the idea over and over in his mind, the nature of the howling changed. It was less anguished and more—encouraging. Pleased. Happy.

Up ahead, he spied a phone booth and thought maybe he should call. He wasn't sure he could stand it if Robert wasn't at home—not now that he had this delicious idea tickling his brain. If he decided to do it, he wouldn't really wait a couple of days, would he? He was a glutton for instant gratification. And what if he lost his nerve in a day or two? *Yes*, the howling seemed to say. *Good idea, George. Better call ahead.*

He pulled over and forced his large body into the

small booth, inserted a few coins and dialed the number. Robert picked up on the other end of the line. "Hello?"

"Yes," George said, a little surprised by the gravel in his voice. "I'm coming over. I have to see you right away."

"I don't think that's going to work, George. Hey, have you got a cold?"

"What do you mean it isn't going to work? I said I have to see you, right away."

"We're heading out, I'm afraid. Tomorrow will be fine, won't it?"

"Afraid not, brother. It really is *that* urgent."

"Come off it, George. What's this all about?"

"I'll explain when I get there." He hung up the phone and headed back to his car.

He wound his way through town, reached Pentucket Road, and turned south toward the old farm as sheets of water swept across the road.

He was glad he'd called ahead, and the howling was almost soothing now. He thought he really might do it, and tonight. In one fell swoop, he'd get the coin *and* the farm, and finally, all the noise in his head could go silent.

Good idea George. Very good idea.

"Mama, no!" Sofia screamed. "We have to go. Right now. Mama, the flood!" She looked at the clock on the kitchen wall. It was five fifty-two. There was less than a half hour to go.

"Sofia. I've told you a hundred times. A million. There will be no flood. Now, your Uncle George needs to see Papa, and he says it's very urgent."

She ran to Papa, folding his big hand between her two tiny ones. She gripped. Pulled. "Papa, *please*, *please*."

He bent forward and kissed the top of her head. "*Mia bella*, everything is going to be fine."

"But look at how it's raining! Have you ever seen it rain so hard?"

The deep lines in Papa's face told her the truth. He *was* worried, even if Mama wasn't. Still, he lied, and she knew he was trying to make her feel better. "Yes, I've seen it rain this hard before. I promise you, everything will be alright. Maybe Uncle George won't be here long. We could still make it."

"He's going to hurt you, Papa. Elliot said. And—and Guillaume. He knows too!"

A sharp sting radiated from the center of her cheek outward, and she blinked, stunned, as she realized Mama had slapped her. "That's *enough*! You go upstairs right now young lady. You go upstairs and you don't come down until I say so, you understand?"

"Margaret!" Papa's voice was sharp.

"She won't listen, Robert. This is killing me, you know."

"Be that as it may, the Margaret Ward I married would never have struck—"

Sofia looked at Mama and Papa and felt a heavy stone in the very center of her rumble to life and weigh her down with an extraordinary sadness. It wasn't she who wouldn't listen. She wondered, what was the use in knowing everything Elliot had told her if she couldn't do anything about it? Mama had never struck her before. There was no level of tantrum she could throw that would sway Mama now. A line had been crossed. Trust destroyed. But despite all of it, she looked on for another minute, watching her parents argue, and felt such a swelling of love. But then she felt the stone again—felt it all eclipsed. Slowly she walked forward and wrapped her arms around Papa's legs, then Mama's. "I love you," she said.

Mama stared, confused. "I love you too, dear girl, and don't you ever think I don't. But you have to learn to mind. I'm sorry I struck you, but you need to go to your room now."

She looked at Papa. "I love you, Papa."

"Oh, *mia bella.*" He kissed her. "I love you."

Sofia wiped at her eyes and walked out of the kitchen into the hall. She looked at the stairs, and then at Guillaume's door at the far end. Maybe it was too late for Mama and Papa, but not for herself. Quietly, she lifted the keys to the farm truck from where they hung on a hook by the door and crept down the hall.

She was nearly there when Guillaume's door opened a crack. Peering through, he beckoned her inside, silent, closed the door behind and crouched down. Quiet, above a whisper, he said "Have you come to ask me for help? I can help you, but you must *ask*, and it must be *your* decision. You understand?"

Sofia reached into her pocket and felt the cool metal of Nonno's coin, where she expected it to be. She nodded. "Yes." Tears clouded her vision, and when she spoke, there was a quaver in her voice she did nothing to hide. "Can you—you take me to see—" she choked. "*Sleeping Beauty*?"

He smiled behind tears of his own, and she knew he understood; it wasn't about the film at all. "Yes, Sofia.

Let's go." He led her out the back door onto the veranda, took the keys, and they ran together through the driving rain to where the farm truck waited by the wash house. "Hurry," he said against the wind. "Before they see." He swung open the door and lifted her inside, then climbed in after her and closed it as quietly as he could manage. A clap of thunder provided sound cover as he jammed the key in the ignition and switched the truck on with a mighty rumble.

As Sofia watched, Guillaume winced in pain—gritted his teeth and began to hum under his breath. Impatiently—worried—she tugged at the sleeve of his shirt. "Guillaume. We have to go. What are you waiting for?"

He winced one last time and gave her a weak smile. Then they were off. If it had been dry, Mama and Papa might have heard the sound of the tires against the gravel of the drive, but as Guillaume guided the truck past the front of the house—headlights off despite the oppressive gloom of the storm—Sofia spied her parents' silhouettes through the kitchen window, still arguing and completely unaware. Guillaume turned onto Pentucket Road, and through the sheets of rain and fog on the window, she could see the river—swollen, churning, angry and high. The banks had all but disappeared and the water was dangerously close to the road.

Up ahead, headlights barreling toward them announced another vehicle, and Guillaume switched on the truck's lights in time. He began to hum again. Louder this time. The other car sped past—salmon colored and resembling a rocket ship. Sofia began to shake. "Guillaume, this is wrong, isn't it? I should have stayed. That was Uncle George. He's going to hurt them! Mama and Papa."

"Shh, child," Guillaume cooed with a shudder. "You've done what you could."

"But, we have to help them!"

"Dear, sweet Sofia." He reached a hand over and placed it on her knee. "I've spent my life in the pursuit of allowing man to choose his own destiny. You know what that means, don't you?"

"Yes, I think so."

"And your parents have chosen theirs. They had the option. You gave them the knowledge. Now it is done, and there are some things we cannot control even though we may wish to. It's like this storm. No amount of knowing will stop the rain. But you? You've chosen a different path."

"Guillaume—"

"My heart breaks for you, Sofia."

Out the driver's side window and up ahead, a warm yellow light caught Sofia's eye as it cut through the gloom. The truck plunged forward. "Slow down!" she shouted.

"What?" Guillaume asked, but he obeyed.

Out there, to the left, down a slight embankment in an open meadow, she saw him. Elliot, bathed in yellow light as though from a lamp. He was crouched—shaking. Terrified. She'd seen this before, in her dreams, only, now she wasn't dreaming. Now it was happening, sixty years in the future. Though she couldn't see them, she knew there were at least two other people with him—another figure crouched beside and a man with a ham of a fist. A man pointing a gun. A gun that was going to go off.

"Elliot!" she shrieked. Guillaume looked to the left and seemed to see him, just as she did.

"Sofia," he said. "There is nothing you can do for him at this moment."

She plunged her hand into her pocket and felt for her coin, even as she was sure Elliot was doing the same sixty years from now. His coin. Her coin. She realized suddenly this was the moment to give it to him—leave it for him. The coin had protected her, just like Nonno said. She was in the truck now with Guillaume, speeding away from Uncle George, and from the flood. That was proof, wasn't it? And Elliot needed it—needed its protection—but he'd never get it if she didn't leave it for him.

"Turn around."

"Sofia, there's no time. You can't help him."

"The coin. Guillaume. I'm not ever going to go back to my farm after today, am I?"

He slowed the truck and checked his watch. "No, I don't think so."

"Then we have to go back. I have to leave it under the steps. That's where he finds it. Guillaume, we have to go back."

He exhaled. Winced. "Then we must be fast. We have only fifteen minutes until—"

"Guillaume! Go!"

He didn't wait any longer—swung the truck wide and headed back, driving faster than before, pushing the pedal all the way to the floor.

Chapter Thirty-Three

August 22, 2019 – Thursday

On the carpet in front of Tony's feet, Elliot's phone began to ring, shattering the temporary silence in the room. "The fuck?" Tony said, looking down. "Cam Calisti? Must be your boyfriend, huh? Sounds like a fairy name if I ever heard one."

Elliot knew he should keep his mouth shut, but Tony was crossing a line with Cameron. "You don't know anything. You'd better let me answer it. He'll be worried if I don't."

Beside him, his mother stopped her quiet sobbing for a moment and gave him a look. Hopeful. "Cameron Calisti?" she asked. "You've been spending time with Cam?"

Tony scowled, raised his foot, and stomped down on Elliot's phone. It screamed through its final ring, before the sound cut off abruptly, replaced by the sharp grinding of glass and metal as Tony twisted his heel back and forth. "Why don't the two of you ever *shut the fuck up*? Now, I'm getting pretty tired here. Just give me the damned coin already, and neither of you will ever see me again. It's so fucking simple."

"Elliot," his mother implored. "Please, if you have it—"

But it wasn't that simple, was it? Surely this was all Destin's doing—she'd gotten to Tony. And if he gave the coin to Tony, and Tony gave it to her—

Through the apartment wall, up by the road, he swore he could hear a tiny voice calling his name. Sofia. But that was impossible because, at this moment in her time, she was likely at the farmhouse—likely in a scenario much like his own. George would be there now—had maybe already come and gone. Maybe they were already dead, the three of them. He plunged his hand into his pocket, and closed his fingers around the coin, taking little comfort in the feeling of the cold metal.

As though sensing the action, the presence of the coin, Tony's smile broadened, and he laughed with an unusual amount of gravel in his voice. Behind him, the air shimmered, and Elliot began to tremble as he observed the hulking shape of a terrible beast. It flickered into life—solid, black, growling—and then it was gone, back, gone, back again. Tony menaced—took a sharp step forward. "Yes, you've got it. Just hand it over, kid. Just hand it over." He waved the gun, and Elliot and his mother melted into the wall. "Give it here!"

There were rules to this game—Elliot knew. Tony couldn't take it from him. It had to be given. And what could the beast do to him, he wondered. Nothing. The hound was a scare tactic, or maybe a means of control. Either way, as long as the coin remained in his possession, he was safe. Emboldened, he raised his chin and focused on breathing to slow the trembles. He cleared his throat and willed the words to come out without a stutter. “Why don’t you take it from me?”

Tony laughed. Frowned. When he spoke, Elliot felt the hairs on his neck and arms stand at attention, realizing the words were less Tony’s and more the hound’s. “You know I can’t. You know the rules, don’t you? But there are other ways.”

“Wh—what do you mean?”

“I can hurt you. I can do that. Shoot you in the leg? Yes. Or better yet—” he turned and pointed the gun directly at Elliot’s mother. “I can just kill *her*. How about that, you little shit? Fair trade?”

“What?”

“The coin for your mother’s life. I’ll give you ten seconds.”

Chapter Thirty-Four

August 22, 1959 – Saturday

As Guillaume whipped the farm truck off Pentucket Road and onto the gravel drive, the tires sent sprays of water from a deep puddle into the air, only to be swallowed by the torrential rain and driven downward again. Sofia placed her hands on the dash and dug in her tiny fingers. The truck bounced and rumbled and finally came to a stop behind Uncle George's car. She looked over, gripping Nonno's coin, hard—feeling it dig into the flesh of her palm one last time. "How do I do it?" she asked.

"Easy," Guillaume said. "It's the easiest thing. Just give it to him. Say it out loud. Say it with your heart." He checked his watch. "But hurry. If Elliot is right—and I believe he is—the flood is only seven minutes away now. There's no time to waste."

Sofia closed her eyes and breathed in, out, in. She

began to imagine herself as Sofia the Cat, but then forced her eyes open—looked out at the rain. None of this was pretend. Not this time. There was no room for imagination. The flood was coming, and it was a *real* danger. Uncle George was here, and he was something worse than a dragon. She thought of her Nonno—of the story he'd told her a million times about being on the pier in Palermo, finding the courage to act. His blood was her blood. His courage was her courage. She set her chin, nodded her head, and forced open the door.

Then she was out in the rain—thick, solid, unrelenting. Looking at the house a handful of steps away was dreamlike—a vision seen through the waves and distortion of a wall of glass bricks. She pushed forward, defying the wind and disregarding the constant barrage of water against her face. Closer now, the house came into better focus. The lights in the kitchen were still on, and a silhouette passed back and forth in front of the window. Papa? Uncle George? She shivered, not knowing the answer—not sure she *wanted* to know.

She reached the steps to the porch and climbed onto the second tread, where there was a small gap between the boards. Water pooled, drained, pooled once more. This is where Elliot said he'd found it—beneath the steps. She looked at the coin in her hand and hesitated a moment. Without it, would she be safe? It was Nonno's, and it was hers, and she was losing so much today—everything. But if she didn't leave it, Elliot would never find it, and if Elliot never found it—

She raised the coin to her lips and kissed it gently. "I love you Nonno." Then, with a deep breath, "Elliot, this coin is for you." She said it out loud, and she said it with her heart. Then, before she could change her mind, she shoved it through the gap—let it fall down beneath. There was a slight pain—a sharp cut. A severing. And then—nothing.

Peace. It was done.

Something brushed up against the left side of her body, and she shrieked. Franklin looked up at her, soaked and surprised, a question in his bright yellow eyes. He mewed. "Good kitty," she said, brushing her hand across the rain-flattened orange hair on the top of his head. "I'm glad to see you. You can come in the truck with me and Guillaume." She wrapped her arms around him—began to lift him up—but then a flash of lightning lit the sky and the thunder that accompanied startled the cat. He clawed at her arms and leaped away, up and around to the left, past the kitchen window and toward the far side of the porch.

Sofia looked back at the truck, then toward Franklin. She wished she'd thought of him sooner—taken a moment to try and find him before she and Guillaume left the first time. But she couldn't leave him now—not after losing everything else. Guillaume was waiting, she knew, and there wasn't much time, but if she ran up the steps and across the porch—grabbed him—she could still make it back to the truck, and they'd have plenty of time to get away. Standing, she flew up the remaining couple steps, then slowed, and crept across the porch.

She was beneath the kitchen window when another clap of thunder startled the cat, and he bounded down, off into the fields. "Franklin!" she cried, but he was already gone.

Inside the house, something blocked the light of the

kitchen for an instant, and Sofia realized her mistake. She shouldn't have cried out—shouldn't have gone after the cat at all. Back down in the drive, the farm truck waited—safe and warm—a short sprint away. The light returned to the kitchen window, and she thought she could hear a sound—a groaning. She knew better than to look—knew she should run straight back to Guillaume—but the groaning sounded like Papa.

She turned toward the house—the window—and lifted herself on her toes to peer over the sill. On the other side, she saw them—Mama and Papa, laid out on the tile floor. Mama wasn't moving at all, but Papa—he was twitching. The slight kick of a leg. The slow opening and closing of a hand. And all around them, pooling on the tile, deep red blood. Almost black. Papa's face turned toward the window—fixed her with a glassy stare. His lips moved, and though there wasn't enough air coming out of his lungs for her to hear the words, she knew them—had seen his face form them a million times.

Mia bella.

She screamed, loud and full, expelling from her lungs the air her Mama and Papa would never taste again. "Papa! Papa!"

To her right, the front door of the house banged open. Hulking, more massive than she'd ever imagined, Uncle George stomped his way onto the porch. Even in the deep gray light, she could see the blood on his hands as he shoved one into his trousers and pulled out a pocket knife. He looked at her—smiled and laughed, waving the blade. "There you are, you little bitch. I was wondering when you were going to show up."

Chapter Thirty-Five

August 22, 2019 – Thursday

"Nine!" Tony boomed. "Eight! I'm not kidding here. Seven!"

Elliot gritted his teeth. The decision should've been easy. His mother's life—his *own* life—was more precious than any supernatural coin. In his pocket, he gripped it harder, knowing suddenly it was the last time he'd feel it pressing into the flesh of his palm. Or maybe not. Maybe he could get it back once this situation de-escalated. But at the moment, it was laughable. He knew Tony wasn't kidding—knew as certainly as he'd known anything that in another six seconds, the gun would go off if he didn't act.

"Six! Five!"

He began to pull the coin from his pocket. Now or never.

"Four!"

A sharp knocking on the door startled Tony, and Elliot shoved the coin back into his pocket.

"The fuck?" Tony mumbled.

From outside, a woman's voice boomed. "Haverford Police. Everything alright in there?"

Tony's face reddened—turned to purple. "How did you—"

"Sir," the muffled voice of the officer continued. "Sir, can you please open up?"

Beside him, Elliot's mother began to shake. "Help!" she screamed. "Please! Help us! He has a gun! Please!"

"Sir, is this true? Sir, I'm going to need you to open this door. Don't do anything hasty."

Turning, Tony closed his ham of a fist and slammed it against the door. "I'll kill them both! I will! Get out of here! Go away!"

"Sir, I can't do that. Why don't you open up—let whoever you've got in there go, and we'll talk about this."

"I can't. I won't."

"Sir, if you don't, I'm going to have to call in the negotiator. This'll all be easier for you if—I'm sure it's all a misunderstanding, right?"

Tony growled. "I won't ask you again."

"Sir—"

Blind and enraged, Tony faced the door and leveled the gun.

Like everything else in the shabby apartment, the front door was light—thin. Elliot watched in horror as Tony measured. "Watch out!" he screamed only a moment before Tony pulled the trigger.

The sound of the release was deafening, accompanied by something softer—the shattering of wood. For a moment, Tony looked down at his hand—regarded the gun as though he'd never seen it before. Destin's horrible hound whimpered and flickered out of view. Then there was another *pop pop* and more shards of wood spraying into the living room.

Tony was on the ground, flat on his back, and two large red blossoms expanded across his upper chest. Stunned, Elliot yelled, "He's down!" Then, with a staggering effort, he climbed onto his feet, moved forward and pulled open the front door.

On the other side, a young female officer bent forward, one hand on her knee, the other holding a radio close to her face. "Officer shooting," she panted. "The suspect is down, send an ambulance. The New Colony Apartments, off Pentucket Road." She looked up at Elliot and offered a compassionate smile through her heavy breathing. "Are you alright?"

"Yeah, just—"

From behind, her partner appeared—a man, middle-aged—and pushed through, gun drawn.

"Okay, step aside," she said as her partner swept the living room and continued further down the hall.

Elliot complied. The officer knelt down beside Tony, whose eyes were frozen in an expression of surprise. She took two fingers to the side of his neck and pressed hard—leaned over his horrible face to listen and feel for breath.

From the corner of the room, his mother's voice cracked. "Is he—is he *dead*?"

The officer nodded, solemn. "Yes, ma'am."

"Is there anyone else here with you?" she asked as she turned her face to Elliot.

From the kitchen, the partner called "All clear!"

Elliot shook his head. "No. Just us. How did you—who called?"

The officer crossed her legs and sat heavy on the floor—looked at her hands, then at Tony, then at her hands again, perhaps surprised to recognize them as her own. Haverford was a sleepy town, and Elliot thought she'd probably never had to fire her gun in the line of duty before. "Anonymous tip," she said. In the distance, sirens wailed, coming closer. The officer looked at him and gave a half smile. "Thanks."

"For what?"

"The warning."

≈

"Are you sure you don't want to at least get checked out?" The detective asked his mother.

She shook her head. "No, I could really use a drink though." She laughed, nervous. "Just um, kidding."

The detective gave her a stern look. "No one would blame you tonight, but, yes. I'd say it's probably best if you lay off. Seems like maybe you had a few already? I really think you should get looked at. A shock like this—"

Elliot watched from the side of the ambulance as his mother put on her best smile—there she was, the slightest glimmer of the radiant woman she'd once been—and patted the side of the detective's arm with her hand. She let it linger there for a moment, and the detective regarded her with surprise, and maybe even a little—

Of course, it was all too soon. Tony wasn't even cold, but he thought he could detect a spark. A little bit of smoke. The detective was probably about his mother's age, clean-cut and handsome. More importantly, he was kind. Intelligent. When this all blew over, and she had some time to heal, he might encourage her to call him up.

"Really," she said. "We'll be fine. How long do you think until we can—I mean, it's our home."

He laughed and put a hand on her shoulder. "And right now it's a crime scene. Like I said, the apartment manager has the show unit all set up for you two to stay there a few days. Though, really, I don't know if it'll take that long. This seems pretty cut-and-dry. And really miss—"

"Larissa, please."

"Really, Larissa, you might not want to go back. A lot of people, after something like this, want to move—"

In the distance, a car door slammed, and Elliot heard feet running toward him.

Cameron—beautiful with his blue eyes and black hair moving lightly in the wind—bounded forward, arms open. They fell into one another, and before there were words, there were lips—at once soft and firm, questing, seeking. Elliot's eyes closed and surrendered to the embrace, both rigid and melting, electrified and subdued. His inner conflict—what little remained—evaporated in an instant, and there was only goodness and light. This was right. It was everything that could be, and everything that always should have been. Tongues touched for an instant, and then Cam's face moved away—came back again, kissing madly up and down the nape of his neck, in short, frenzied pecks.

"Elliot," he panted. "Elliot! You're alright. Oh my

god. You're—"

He pulled Cam close and held a hand against the back of his head. "Yeah, I'm okay. How did you know? Were you the one that called the police? You can't know how glad I am to see you, Cam. I love you. I *love* you."

"I love you too, Elliot. I'm sorry I was angry. I should've been here."

"Shh, no. Don't. You didn't do anything wrong. But it *was* you, wasn't it? Who called?"

Cam extricated himself from Elliot's arms and wiped the tears from his eyes. His thin lips stretched into the brightest smile Elliot had ever seen. "No." Taking a quick look behind, he tilted his head. "*She* did."

"Who—"

Standing off a little distance, with her hands interlaced, a slight woman waited. The light of a street lamp at the entrance to the parking lot cut through the gloaming and lit her curly silver hair. She smiled, chewed her lip, and started to walk slowly forward.

He knew the moment he saw her eyes, shimmering blue—Cameron's eyes—that it was *her*. It could only be *her*. The tears came fast and furious as she stopped in front of them. He tried to speak, but his voice cracked once, twice. Finally, "Sofia?"

She smiled and sniffed hard against her own tears before folding him in a tight embrace. Warm. Familiar. "I waited sixty years to do this." She laughed. "Feels pretty good. Hello, Elliot. It's nice to meet you—in the flesh."

He sobbed into her shoulder. "I can't believe this. You're—alive! You're here! But how did you—"

"Hush," she said. "Hush now. Plenty of time for that.

Plenty of time."

Another man appeared beside them—oddly familiar with his medium brown skin and black hair flecked with gray. Cam brightened. "Oh, and Elliot this is—"

His eyes widened. "Mister Edwards? From the library? The tech guy?"

The man chuckled. "What's that expression?" he asked. "And if you'll believe that, there's a bridge I'd like to sell you." He extended his hand. "Very pleased to meet you, Elliot. My name is—"

"Guillaume," Elliot said. "You're Guillaume Khoury."

Chapter Thirty-Six

August 22, 1959 - Saturday

Guillaume felt the sharp pinch of the severing and sat back in the seat of the farm truck. She'd done it then, and for the next sixty years the Chronicum wouldn't—*couldn't*—be in play. Not until a young man who wouldn't even be born until the final months of this century found it, right where she'd left it for him. Through the wall of rain, he watched out the windshield, imploring her to hurry back—George was inside the house with one of Destin's hounds. The howling only he could hear was incessant, and as hard as he tried, he couldn't drown it out any longer. A bolt of lightning lit the sky, and then a crack of thunder. A flash of orange leaped from Sofia's arms, and he watched as she flew up the steps of the porch after it.

The cat, surely. "Sofia," he said under his breath as another sharp cry from the hound ripped through his skull. He doubled forward in the seat. "Leave it. Come back."

He forced himself up and gazed through the watery windshield. She was beneath the kitchen window standing on her tiptoes. He heard her shriek cut through the air and knew she'd made a grave mistake. Without hesitation, he forced open the door to the truck and barreled out into the rain. No time to waste.

The hound's voice changed—morphed from cries of agony to pleasure and excitement. The sound was deafening, and Guillaume felt his knees give. He was down. In the mud. Then George Calisti was there on the porch, marching toward her and waving a knife. Through the wind, Guillaume heard his words. "...I was wondering when you were going to show up."

Guillaume willed himself up, but his limbs refused to move. He was weaker now than he'd ever been, and wasn't there a terrible irony in that? The Chronicum was inactive. The game and all its rules were suspended. In this moment, when he was free to fight—*wanted* to fight for Sofia—it was Destin's hound and not the rules of *Le Jeu* that held him back. He'd spent millennia defending humankind's right to free will and now found himself with none of his own.

He laughed. Cursed. The blood rushed into his frozen legs as the realization hit him. Free will wasn't always easy—could never be taken for granted. But it could be *taken*. It was there for him too, if he only found the courage to seize it. He laughed once more—deciding to truly be his own man for the first time since the Chronicum was minted—and the wails of the hound no longer reached his ears. He leaped to his feet, closed the distance and wrapped his arms around Sofia's waist, pulling her down off the porch. She kicked and screamed, but he was running now—didn't stop until he reached the truck. "Calm, child! Calm down. It's me. Can you climb in? We have to go."

"Mama and Papa! Guillaume, they're—"

"I know."

Once she was in the seat, he slammed the door and ran to the driver's side. George was only a few steps behind now. He switched on the engine and backed up as fast as he could, leaving George to wave his knife in a blind rage. The truck whirled back toward Pentucket Road, and Guillaume cut the lights as he heard George's car door slam. Which way? Surely George would think they'd headed north—the direction of town—but to the south? He closed his eyes and weighed the possible futures. Yes, George would think they headed north.

The flood would come from the south. Guillaume checked his watch. Six-sixteen. Four minutes. He had to risk it. He turned right and slammed the gas pedal all the way to the floor, squinting to see the road through the torrential rain and absence of headlights.

"Guillaume!" Sofia screamed. "No! Wrong way, *wrong way*!"

"Trust me, child." He was certain it would work—that they'd make it in time. And for once, it was entirely his decision—his own destiny he was making. For the next four minutes—the next *sixty years*—his life was his own, and right now what he wanted more than anything was to save this remarkable, brave little girl. She'd grow up. She'd grow old. And in the end, she'd repay the kindness Elliot had shown her—*would* show her—because he'd understood, finally.

He'd known it the last time Sofia placed the Chronicum in his hand.

It was never about Sofia. It was Elliot. It had always been Elliot who needed saving. And of course, Guillaume knew he had no obligation to make sure she saved him—but he was determined to make sure she had the option. Because there was a promise there, too, in that last contact with the coin he'd served for two millennia. It wasn't a word, but a feeling the coin had communicated. *Finished. Done. The end.* If he could let it happen, he understood, that would be it. No more game. The end of *Le Jeu* for good.

At a safe distance now, Guillaume switched on the headlights. A pair of steep hills rose beside both banks of the swollen river, closing it in like a canyon. Up ahead, across the top, a bridge waited, offering a turn away from the river—salvation. The road climbed, and as the bridge neared, he could see the trouble. A couple massive trees had already washed out upstream and were jammed beneath, damming the rushing water, and forcing it up over the bridge surface. He stopped at the top—looked left and right, weighing whether or not to cross. The road to the right led downward, to land that would surely be flooded, but to the left, continued upward beyond the bridge.

"Hold on," he said and turned the wheel sharply left. He stomped the gas and felt the tires lift slightly from the bridge surface before touching down. The truck fishtailed, but he held the wheel firmly, slowed, accelerated again. Beneath them, the bridge strained.

"Guillaume. What's happening?" Sofia cried as rain

continued to thrash the windows of the truck.

"Almost there!" He pushed the pedal harder, and the truck shot forward, clearing the bridge onto solid ground. He continued up the hill twenty feet and hit the brakes, panting. "There. We made it, Sofia. We're going to be alright."

Sofia gripped his knee, and then a sound like thunder ripped through the air, only, it wasn't thunder. It was louder, and there was a groaning. A snapping, and a mighty roar. In the rearview mirror, Guillaume watched wide-eyed as the bridge gave way, crumbling, engulfed by a monumental surge of churning white water.

"Guillaume," Sofia sobbed. "Thank you, Guillaume."

He placed a hand on top of her wet curls. "*De rien, cherie*. Of course."

Chapter Thirty-Seven

August 22, 2019 - Thursday

Elliot sat so far forward on the edge of the sofa, he was certain he could fall off at any moment. "And *then* what happened?" he asked.

Sofia laughed, and it was warm and bright. "Sit back, you're making me nervous. Like it's happening right now, instead of sixty years ago."

"Isn't it? In a way?"

"Perhaps. I don't know. Are you sure you don't want to rest? I know today has been difficult for you, and—well, the last nine days, really."

Elliot looked at the clock on the wall—eight-forty—and knew he couldn't possibly lay down. He might not sleep at all tonight. Maybe not ever. And it wasn't the excitement of being with Sofia in the flesh—of knowing she was alive—it was the feeling of this moment. He passed his eyes over the living room of the show unit where they'd be staying until their own apartment was declassified as a crime scene. The layout was the same, of course, but it was brighter. Clean. There was no lingering scent of smoke or dirty film on the walls. The furniture was new and comfortable.

There was nothing to remind him of Tony's presence. The space was everything their home ought to have been—could become—but furthermore, it was filled with people he loved.

Next to him on the sofa, Cam placed a hand on his knee. "It might not be a bad idea, Elliot. Your mother might like the peace. We could all meet tomorrow."

"No," he shook his head. His mother was sleeping already, and he knew she'd be out until morning. When he'd brought Sofia and Guillaume to meet her, she'd simply accepted them as his friends—bought the story he'd met them at the community farm. They'd come along to help Elliot and his mother settle into the show unit and sat in relative silence as she mused about where the anonymous tip might've come from. When she'd decided to lay down a half hour ago, everyone agreed it was a good idea. Elliot knew she wouldn't mourn Tony—had never *really* loved him, because how could she love a man like Tony after the years she spent with his father—but he worried about her still. "My mom will be fine."

He meant it.

Sofia sighed and sat back in her armchair. "What happened next? Well, to be honest with you...Memory is a funny thing, isn't it? You know, there are certain things that get etched so deeply, you could never forget them if you tried, and others—" her voice cracked, and she pulled a tissue from her purse to dab at the wetness around her eyes. "I'm sorry. I'm not sure I can tonight. Maybe I'm the one who needs a rest. I'm so sorry, Elliot, would you mind horribly if we waited a day or two—for me to get my bearings and really—"

"No. No, of course not."

She sighed. "Guillaume, would you be so kind as to take me to the hotel?"

"Of course not, *cherie*," Guillaume said. Then he turned to Elliot. "And if she cannot remember, well—I'll tell you the rest of it. But for now, we'll let her rest."

Sofia stood, and Elliot met her at the door—embraced and held it. "I um, I don't have a phone at the moment, so—you'll call Cameron when you're ready?"

"Yes," she said and stood on tiptoes to kiss his cheek. "Yes, soon."

"Goodnight, Sofia."

She smiled. "Goodnight."

When they were gone, Elliot fell back onto the couch and laid down with his head in Cameron's lap. "Well, this has been—"

"Shh," Cam whispered, bending his face down and touching his lips to Elliot's. "Let's take a break from it also, right? Let's forget for a moment that any of it happened at all." He began to work his fingers through Elliot's hair—pressing, massaging. "Let's—be."

"Okay," Elliot said. "Let's be." He closed his eyes and felt the gentle warmth of Cameron's breath caress his face. Then there were lips again. Soft. Parting.

Peace.

He wanted to say it—*I love you*—but this moment between them spoke louder than his words ever could.

This was the culmination of it all. The attraction was finally realized, sure, but it was infinitely more than that. The years that divided them fell away. All the pain washed out like the bridge over the Pentucket had done sixty years ago. The detritus was cleared away now, and what remained were two souls. Bare. Resonating around one another. A promise of trust—of *enduring*. Something tested and proven unconditional.

Cameron withdrew his lips. Laughed happily under his breath. Brought them down once more, searching. With one last exhale, Elliot melted into the kiss, and then all else was forgotten.

Chapter Thirty-Eight

August 24, 1959 – Monday

Guillaume leaned against the farm truck and turned his face up to the sky, drinking in the full heat of the late August sun. What a miracle, after so much rain. In the meadow to either side of the dirt road, birds sang. Bees buzzed. The sweet scent of grass and wildflowers and damp earth eddied around in the humid air. The day was a gift—a salve against the enormity of Sofia's sadness. There was more to come for her, and as he held her tiny hand, he wished her a lifetime of sunshine to dispel the shadows that would follow her in some fashion to the end of her days.

Around a bend in the road, the rumble of tires against the dirt announced the police car a few moments before it came into view. It drove forward slowly and came to a stop behind the truck. White-faced and harried, the detective climbed out and approached, looking over his shoulder once, twice.

"Detective Mulvaney," Guillaume said, extending his hand. "A pleasure to meet you."

The detective crossed his arms and scowled. "I don't happen to see it that way, Mister Khoury. What exactly do you expect me to do here?" He looked behind him again.

Guillaume laughed. "There is nothing there, detective."

"Bullshit there's nothing there. I've been a devout Catholic all my days—*raised* on the fear of god, and marveling at all His creation and forgiveness—but I'll tell you *nothing* prepared me for this. I'll tell you. God has no hand in *this*."

"Of that, sir, you are correct. But if you're looking for more of—what you saw with the girl's uncle, I assure you, you are safe."

"Safe! If you'd seen what I saw—he wasn't even human. There was this *hound* and this *smell*, and he wasn't the least bit remorseful—going on and on about a magic coin. By god almighty, I'd have locked him up right then and there—thrown away the key if I didn't think he'd set that beast on me. But it's not that—not just me I'm worried about. George Calisti owns me now—knows a little too much about some business I got mixed up in back in Boston. I have to think of my wife, Mister Khoury. So I get a call saying you've got the girl, and what am I supposed to do here? This is a problem for me, don't you see?"

Guillaume nodded. "Yes, I do. She saw everything that happened. You can't bring her back to Haverford, because either her uncle will come after her, or she'll tell what she knows, and her uncle will ruin you. Quite a conundrum. Perhaps you shouldn't have told the newspaper you were looking for information as to her whereabouts."

"I thought she was dead. I really didn't expect—"

"Well, she isn't. But don't worry, I am of the opinion it isn't in anyone's interest to bring George Calisti to justice at this time. He was not acting entirely of his own volition, and the future has a certain vested interest in his continued freedom."

"What shit is this?"

Guillaume laughed. "You know, I've spent my life battling fate, and yet I am able to accept that sometimes there truly is a grander design. And you, devout Catholic you say? Yet with everything you've seen, you have a difficult time accepting this idea of a grander design yourself?"

"What the hell are you? Some kind of angel?"

"No, nothing like that."

"You still haven't told me what you expect me to do."

Guillaume shrugged. "Make her disappear. Find her a new life—a family. Somewhere far away." He closed his eyes and felt the sun. "Someplace warm. Bright. Perhaps California?"

"And how the hell am I supposed to do that?"

"I'm sure you'll find a way." He turned away from the detective and knelt down beside Sofia—wiped at the tears softly rolling down her cheeks. "And you, dear child. You've been surprisingly quiet."

Sofia shook her head. "I don't want to go with him. Why can't I stay with you?"

He kissed her forehead. "The safest place for you is

far away from me. That's what is important now, isn't it? What would Elliot think if you escaped the flood and your uncle, just to remain in danger by my side?"

"But I can be brave Guillaume. I can!"

"I know, Sofia. That's what I'm asking you to do now. Be brave for me. Brave and happy. *Thrive.* I will see you again someday, I promise. So, don't forget me. And don't forget Elliot."

"Guillaume. No! I lost Mama and Papa, and Nonno and—and everyone. Please."

"Shh. You haven't lost me, child."

"Guillaume."

He wiped at his eyes and stood, turning to the detective. "And should anything happen to her before she is safely away? Those hounds will be the least of your worries."

The detective swallowed. Frowned. "Understood," he said.

Sofia choked down her sobs as she watched Guillaume walking farther and farther into the distance. She believed him—believed she'd see him again someday—but watching him walk away from her felt worse even than knowing Mama and Papa were gone. She wanted to cry out to him, maybe run after and refuse to leave his side, but she knew it wouldn't matter. It was just her and the detective now.

"Well," he said, "I guess we'd better get going then."

Sofia crossed her arms. "I don't want to go with you."

"Well, join the club. I seem to be collecting angry orphans today."

She cocked her head. "What do you mean?"

"Why don't you come and see?" Her curiosity piqued, Sofia reluctantly walked to the detective's side and followed him to the police car. He pointed through the window of the back seat to a banker's box with holes cut in the top. "I found this mangey scoundrel out on the road earlier this morning—not far from your farm, actually. I'm thinking I'll call him Cheddar, at least until I find a proper home for him. You don't like cats, do you?"

Sofia shrieked with joy and pulled open the car door—ripped at the tape that held the lid closed.

From within, Franklin peered up and gave her a *mew* of relief before leaping into her arms. "Franklin!" she cried. "Oh, Detective Mulvaney. You found my Franklin!" She held the cat tight against her chest and kissed his orange face. "Thank you. Thank you!"

As she watched, the detective sighed, and his shoulders relaxed. "Well, at least I've done one thing right today. Alright then—mangey scoundrels the both of you. What do you say we go? The sooner I'm rid of you both, the better."

Sofia grinned mischievously as she climbed into the back seat. "Alright. I can be brave. Let's go."

Chapter Thirty-Nine

August 24, 2019 – Saturday

The whistle of Elliot's new hand-me-down iPhone roused him from contemplating the scrambled eggs congealing on his plate. They'd gone cold five minutes ago, and it wasn't for a lack of hunger. He was distracted. Still processing. He reached over and unlocked the screen to see a message from Cameron, and felt his blood begin to course, hot.

From across the table, his mother looked up from the magazine she'd been perusing, her own plate already cleared away and cleaned. "Cameron?" she asked, with a smile.

"Yes." he replied, pushing back hard from the table. "We're going to meet Sofia in town."

She laughed. "That's the most excitement I've seen out of you in the last day or so. Just hold on a minute. I liked Sofia—well, *think* I did. Everything was such a blur the other night. How did you become friends? The farm?"

He laughed as well. "You wouldn't believe me if I told you."

She crossed her arms. "You could give it a try sometime. I know things have been—I'm sorry about Tony, El. I really am. Ever since your father died, I've struggled. You know that. And sometimes someone walks into your life and tells you they've got all the answers, and even when it seems too good to be true, you want to believe it so badly."

"Mom—"

"No. Please, Elliot. Let me finish?"

"Okay—"

"I know I've been—ugh. I've been a terrible mother."

"Mom—"

"And there's not a lot of time before you're out of here. I know you're going to transfer away and never look back—though I hope you will—and I couldn't blame you but, well...I love you, Elliot. You're the most important thing in my life and you always have been, even when I didn't show that in the right ways. Even with Tony, I thought maybe it was better to have the stability for you—for us—and to suffer his...I know now that was wrong. I'm going to go back to work, and I'm going to go to alcohol meetings and—"

"Mom, stop. Please. You don't have to say—"

"And I was thinking."

"Thinking?"

"This online business. That was my idea, you know. I've only sold five hats so far, but this is something I think I could be good at. It's something new, and it's something I can call my own, and sure, it's not going to make us a living right now, but I'm proud of it. And I think I realized the only thing in my life I've been proud of in a long time is—well, you. And I'm *very* proud of *you*."

In spite of himself, Elliot felt wetness at the corners of his eyes. "I love you, Mom. You're not going to give it up, are you?"

"Well, it's going to be tough to balance with me going back to work. I was thinking, maybe it's something you and I could do. We could build it together and it could be—ours?"

He laughed. "I'd love that, Mom."

"Okay." She dabbed at her own eyes now. "Alright. You'd better not let Cameron wait too long."

≈

Elliot took a sip of his coffee and waited as Sofia chewed her words. The little cafe was quiet—just the four of them. Beneath the table, Cameron reached out and grabbed his hand, and Guillaume nodded patiently.

She exhaled. "After Guillaume gave us over to the detective, it's a blur. Like I said the other night, some things get etched so deeply, while others fade away. Franklin and I spent a couple of days with some people in Boston, and then we were on a train all the way to San Francisco. We bounced around a couple of homes until I ended up with a really nice couple. They didn't know my whole story—just that I was an orphan who'd gone through some trauma—but they took me in, and Franklin too. Adopted me. From that point on, I was Sofia Robertson. And you have to understand—eight years old is still so young. They took me to see several psychologists to deal with my trauma. I can't really say if it worked or if it didn't, but after a while I—I kind of forgot my former life."

"Really?" Elliot asked. "All of it?"

She considered. "Well, no, not all of it. It was always there, but by the time I was a teenager, it was more like—a dream. Something that happened to someone else. And you, Elliot? I *never* forgot you. But I did wonder more than once if you were real, or—"

"Just—"

She laughed. "Well, that's the problem with psychology, isn't it? Everything was always rational. And by the time I was in my twenties, I was as convinced as my doctors that you were something my mind invented to cope with all of it. But anyways—I went to school, settled down and got married. I have two amazing children, and five grandchildren now. I've lived a good life. I have. And I never came back here. I stopped thinking about it, really, but every once in a while, I'd dream of you. And then this year, ever since New Year's Day, when I put up the 2019 calendar on the wall—I haven't been able to get you out of my head. I sat down one day and googled Haverford High School running—I remembered your running clothes, and of course the picture was a few years old, but—"

"And there I was."

She nodded. "And there you were, and I thought, oh my god. He's real! And then I remembered what I saw that night and those dreams I had, and, well—it was crazy. All of it was absolutely insane. But if you'd never come into my life, I'd probably have been washed away in that flood. Or worse. So, I thought, I have to pay him back. It was difficult for me coming back here, because, like I said, it felt like something that happened to someone else. But I got on that plane out of San Francisco two days ago, landed in Boston, and drove straight up here. I'd barely checked into the hotel, and I thought it was about time, so I called the police and then—"

Cameron smiled. "And then we were there. Guillaume came to my house and explained all of it. We met Sofia at the hotel, and by the time we got to the parking lot of your apartment—"

Elliot whistled. "Wow. Well, thank you. All three of you." He reached into his pocket and felt the Chronicum, right where he always kept it. He closed his fingers around the coin and brought it out—set it on the table. "But there's still this. What happens to it now?"

Guillaume chuckled. "That old thing? Throw it away if you like. It's worthless."

"What?"

"It *wasn't* worthless, of course. But now it is nothing but a relic of a little Mediterranean culture no one even remembers existed. It has expended its energy. It is *inert.*"

"Okay, okay, but—how did it come to be in the first place? That's the part I'm having a tough time wrapping my head around. I mean—fate, time, free will. How does science explain it?"

"The short answer is: it doesn't."

"Alright. And, the long answer?"

Guillaume sighed. "People underestimate the power of belief. The deities that Destin and I served existed because our people *willed them* into existence. You see? It is the same with this modern god. They were real because we made them, and in turn, they made the Chronicums. But the Chronicums were physical objects—they persisted even after our deities and culture perished, and so did the consequences of their existence. It is, however, not a unique story. The tale of Adam and Eve in the garden of Eden. Isn't it the same?"

"I don't see how."

Cam spoke up. "The apple from the tree of knowledge. Right? Free will. That's what all this is about?"

Guillaume nodded. "Very good."

"So, this one is done," Elliot said. "Its energy has been dispelled, but—what about the others? In your book, you wrote that there were six."

"Yes. There were. And perhaps they still exist, and perhaps they don't. Each priest and priestess was bound to a single coin. I have no way of knowing the fate of the others."

Elliot looked at Sofia. "So, what will you do now?"

"I may stay a few more days, but my life is in California." She reached across the table and rested her hand on top of Cameron's. "Of course, I'm delighted to get to know some new family members, and I'd love to see my cousin Kathryn, but—"

"Yeah," Cameron frowned. "I'm still not sure what to do about that."

Sofia shook her head. "Nothing. I came to peace long ago. My uncle's mind is rotten, and maybe that's justice enough for my parents, who never had to suffer the ailments of old age. There's no sense in ruining your aunt's life over it."

Elliot looked down. "Will you keep in touch?"

"Of course." She laughed. "I've been carrying you around with me for sixty years. Do you think I'm going to stop now when it's getting good?"

He smiled. "Alright. I'd like that."

"So would I."

"And you, Guillaume?"

He flashed a wry smile. "I have a little business to take care of yet."

⩰

Hand in hand, Elliot, and Cameron stood at the edge of the meadow, watching the deep orange disc of the sun as it slid beneath the trees on the western edge. The air was heavy and sweet, and off in the distance, a chorus of crickets accompanied the evening songs of the birds. Elliot looked at Cameron and smiled. "Do you want to do the honors?"

"Nah. It's yours, after all."

"Alright." With his free hand, he pulled the Chronicum from his pocket and looked at it one last time. "Thanks for all the trouble. And thanks for Sofia." With a mighty heave, he launched it into the air, spinning, catching the last of the sun's rays as it came to rest in the meadow where once Robert Calisti had tilled the earth, and Stefano before him.

It was done. Over.

He turned to Cameron and held his gaze. Their faces drew closer, lips parted. They were about to touch—to engage in a delicate dance of tongues when Elliot drew back. Held his breath. "I love you, Cameron Calisti."

Cam smiled and moved in—completed the kiss. It lingered, swirled, and all the old electricity was there, where they'd left it. Just where it would always be. He didn't say it back, because he didn't have to, and as they held each other, Elliot didn't need the words. Cameron understood all of it.

He always had.

Chapter Forty

Marseille, France - September 6, 2019

Destin gazed past the balcony—down to the lavender-colored water beyond—as she felt strong fingers run the length of her scalp. They gathered her silver hair into threads and began to weave—braid—even as they caressed. She tilted her head back and felt Guillaume's warm lips against her forehead—a little bit of heat against the cool of the evening.

He held her gaze from above and frowned. "What troubles you, my love?" There were lines in his face that weren't there a week ago, and his hair—like her own—was moving swiftly from black to gray.

"How long do you think we have, *mon cher*?"

He paused a moment, then shook his head and continued to braid. "It doesn't matter how long we have. It matters that we have right now."

"How can you say that, when I've been such a fool? I

should've listened to you sixty years ago. All this wasted time—"

"*Puh*, it is nothing. I knew even then you wouldn't listen to me. You said it yourself—how could I ask you to defy your nature? How could a servant to Fate ever truly have the freedom to decide her own destiny? But it doesn't matter." For a few minutes, they remained in silence as the sky took on shades of violet. He finished the braid and stepped away to observe his work. "Ah! Still, the most beautiful woman I have ever seen."

She stood. Kissed him. "And you, the most handsome man. And most benevolent. That you could forgive me our entire history—"

"Our history?" He laughed. "Our history ended when *Le Jeu* began, and as far as I am concerned, it has only now resumed."

"But you never forgot what we were. A man and a woman who loved each other even more than the deities we served. That's how you like to say it, isn't it?"

"Well, we are that man and that woman again, are we not? But now we serve no one but each other."

"But for how long? Guillaume, we are aging so quickly. Now that the Chronicum has lost its power, at this rate—"

"Shh," he whispered. "Look out at the sky. Do you know why I wanted us to come here?"

"No—"

"Because whether we have hours, days, years—I want to spend them with you. Eclipsed by you."

"And Marseille?"

"Makes me think of you. Every time you speak. Hold on." He slipped away from her into the villa and returned a minute later with two glasses of pink liquid—the color the sky had been a quarter hour ago.

She took one and raised her eyebrows. "Lillet?"

"Oui. Lillet Rosé. Chilled. A sunset on the French Riviera. These are the things I hear—everyone hears—when you speak, my love."

She drew back, horrified. "When I *compelled*, you mean. When I *invaded*. You would choose to associate me with that, even now?"

With an arm around her shoulders, he drew her in. "No. Perhaps your intent was not always pure, but your voice? It has always been yours. Since before you were Destin Duprée, since the time when we were a man and a woman who loved each other—a man and a woman whose real names we haven't uttered since."

"Can you even remember mine? Can you really remember *her*?" He leaned forward. Whispered it in her ear, and she melted against him. "Then it is she I will be, for the rest of our days."

"And I shall be him. And there will be nothing else. Nothing but you and I."

"And our love?"

He nodded. Kissed her. "And our love."

Acknowledgments

The creation of a work of fiction requires more than the author's time at a keyboard. In my case—in the case of *this* work—it required years of ideas and experiences, and a small village of friends and allies to breathe this story to life.

First and foremost, thanks go to my extraordinary husband Brian, whose unwavering support allows me to charge headlong toward achieving my creative dreams. I once said "...With you, all things are possible." Today, I know that to be as true as it's ever been.

Heather Griffith, thanks for taking me to see *that house* all those years ago. Who could have known a couple of seventeen-year-olds exploring a derelict bungalow outside town would, some seventeen years later, be the seed from which this story sprouted.

Thanks also to all my friends at the Lexington Community Farm. Tim Hines, the invitation to get involved changed everything for me. Elena Colman, I learned so much from you. Your passion and knowledge have made an indelible impact on my life. Allison Ostrowski and Emmy Smela, thanks for your friendship, and for continuing to make my time at the farm one of the most enjoyable parts of my week.

And of course, without @DVPit and Beth Phelan, I might never have connected with my outstanding editor, Patrick Munnelly. Thank you, Pat, for taking a chance on me, believing in this story, and pushing it to become the best it could be. And thanks as well to Susan Brooks, who also pushed me to dig deeper, and everyone at Literary Wanderlust for being the vessel to bring this story to the world.

I'm fortunate to be unconditionally supported in life and art by an incredible mother and father, brother, sister, grandparents, aunts, uncles, cousins, and in-laws. It is upon your indestructible foundation of love that I build this dream of writing. Speaking of...

This story would not have taken its current shape without invaluable insight from my mother Kelly and sister Hayley, and my sister-in-law Stef. Other early readers who made important contributions include friends Chris Lancaster, Morgan Anderson, and Linda Greene. And fellow author S. M. Holland, your encouragement and friendship continue to inspire me. Thanks for reading.

And Erin Kress, who, alongside my husband, I will always choose as my earliest reader. Thank you!

Last, but far from least, I'd like to thank *you*, dear reader. Whether you've been with me since before my first novel, or are only getting to know me and my work: Thank you! A writer cannot survive in a vacuum.

His words are meant to spread and grow. Thanks for spending your valuable time with me. Let's keep in touch. Until next time...

Gregory

About The Author

Gregory Josephs is an author of speculative and LGBT fiction who spends a lot of time indulging his insatiable curiosity—about everything. He believes in self-love, authentic food, and that procrastination is the product of an intensely creative mind.

Though he was raised in Colorado, Gregory spent many of his summers in Wisconsin, where he fell in love with the idea of everything North.

Growing up in the west, at some point there was more hot sauce than blood running through his veins, and thanks to his foodie parents it's a rare day that he doesn't down a jalapeño. He's a foodie too, now (with a serious addiction to cooking magazines). When he isn't writing he's likely in the kitchen fermenting something—bread dough, cheese, sauerkraut, and of course, peppers!

Unable to resist the allure of a northern climate, Gregory relocated to Massachusetts in his early twenties, where he's lived ever since. He is passionate about the local food movement and has been volunteering one day a week at an organic community farm since 2016.

Alongside his photographer husband, Gregory regularly collects Fiestaware and sips whiskey while entertaining his two rambunctious cats, and a dog. He can't imagine a better life.

www.gregoryjosephs.com
Twitter: @gjosephs
Facebook: /gjosephsauthor

CPSIA information can be obtained
at www.ICGtesting.com
Printed in the USA
BVHW030207010720
582718BV00001B/98